Once upon a time in the Black Country

Thomas J.R. Dearn

Once upon a time in the Black Country

A 1950s Gangster Novel

Paperback Edition First Published in the United Kingdom in 2020 Amazon KDP Publishing

eBook Edition First Published in the United Kingdom in 2020 Amazon KDP Publishing

Disclaimer
This is a work of fiction. All characters and incidents are products of the author's imagination and any resemblance to actual people or events is coincidental or fictionalised.

Note from the author

This is a story based very loosely around historic events that happened in the mid-1950s. The rest of the story is entirely fiction and is a product of my imagination. The places in the story are historically accurate and reflect the Black Country region as it was in the 1950s. The music, cars, pubs and other places mentioned here are also historically accurate as are the historical anecdotes included in various parts of the novel. Parts of the dialogue are written in 'Black Country Spake' and portray the accents and spoken grammar of the Black Country characters in the story.

I was born in the Black Country and come from a Black Country family background which has helped me when writing this book. I would like to thank Steve Edwards and his book 'Black Country Dictionary and Phrase Book' which has been a really useful companion when writing some of the dialogue. I would also like to thank Andy Frazier for his help and advice, my brother Giles Dearn for the cover artwork and my wife Leah Dearn for her support and help with the editing process.

January 1954

Mucklow sat in the back seat and admired the countryside at dusk. The remnants of snow on the trees and the miles and miles of vast white fields looked somewhat spectacular in the clearness of the night sky. There was not a single cloud visible and Mucklow thought that it would be a long cold night.

***

Mucklow slammed the cup down on the table and gave Tanner a back handed slap with such force that the chair flew onto its side. He turned to the briefcase and took out a pair of pliers which he held high so that Tanner could see them clearly.

"Danks took things too far Billy!" Tanner pleaded again as he lay tied to the chair on the floor. The swinging lightbulb cast a ray of light straight onto Mucklow's face and Tanner could see a man haunted by his past, haunted by the horrors of the Second World War and livid with the actions of a man who had threatened his family! Brian Tanner felt afraid.

***

The two men walked deeper and deeper into the woods until they came to a remote spot that would haunt Harry Scriven for the rest of his life. He dug deep within himself to find the strength to cut through the icy ground with his shovel, with each stroke he pushed himself further as if the physical activity of what he was doing could dissolve the recent memories from his mind.

Scriven wished that he could accept the magnitude of all that had happened and he wished that he did not fear the burning guilt and responsibility that would haunt his future dreams.

***

Chapter 1

A few weeks earlier…

It had snowed heavily in mid-January 1954 and Harry Scriven could not quite understand why he was taking a car out in such treacherous weather. *He did as he was told.*

As he drove through the snow-covered streets, he followed in the not-too-distant tracks of a previous vehicle. He could not help but wonder who else had tried to drive in these conditions. *Would they be waiting for him when he reached his destination?*

As he travelled through the affluent Halesowen suburb of Lapal he glanced at the grand 1920s detached houses that stood decorated in crystalline white snow. They looked like a scene from a dreamlike Christmas card and he wondered if a man in his position should appreciate such romantic sentiments. *What would Dickie Hickman and the lads down at the pub think? But he was not like them.*

He allowed his mind to wander off to the past winters of his national service in the RAF. In the great winter of 47, he had been stationed at an RAF barracks not far from Wolverhampton. He remembered the time he had been forced to spend the entire night inside a Lancaster bomber that he had been servicing and repairing. Overnight, the temperature had dropped to almost minus 20 degrees! Scriven shuddered at the memory and how in the cold of the night he had not minded huddling together with his pungent RAF comrades for warmth.

Then there had been previous winters when during the War he had been stationed in Cornwall at RAF Perranporth. He fondly remembered drinking heavily with good friends and laughed aloud at the memory of falling off his bicycle, pissed out of his skull.

Harry Scriven was not a fantastically wealthy man, but his dubious and unethical employment enabled him to own a relatively new car. The Second World War was not a distant memory and many young families were getting there first motorised transport in the way of motor bike and side car or an ageing motorcar from the 20s or 30s. Scriven drove a jet black 48 Ford Prefect with a red vinyl interior and a three-speed column shift gear box. Its 1172cc side valve engine was hardly brisk, but today on this uncertain snow covered track it was doing a more than adequate job of propelling him through the slush. It was not as glamorous as his cousin's new Riley RM, but it did the job.

As he drew closer to his destination, Scriven began to feel slightly uneasy as he neared enemy 'territory'. The Royal Oak pub was right on the borders between Scriven's hometown of Halesowen in the Black Country and Bartley Green in Birmingham. It was a hotly contested establishment in a long running turf war between rival gangs from both areas and Scriven knew that in going there today he was running the risk of becoming the next victim of the conflict.

Two nights previously a young colleague had been savagely beaten and had suffered the misfortune of having both of his legs broken by 'The Brummie Boys.'

Wilf Dugmore was just a 22-year-old lad with a young family and a promising future as a footballer. Scriven thought about how much of a callous act it had been for his rivals to do such a thing to a young family man. Sure Wilf could get 'mouthy' when he had had a drink, but he didn't deserve what had happened to him. Now it was Scriven's job to find out who had carried out the attack and report back to his vengeful family.

Alf Spencer was unaware of Scriven's approach. He had been the Landlord at The Royal Oak since the early 40s and he polished his bar with pride. He had gotten a little pre-occupied with 'protection' lately and was beginning to wonder why he had to pay money to either side.

The brewery had told him that it was "Necessary to protect everyone from union problems." *But what did the brewery know? What did he get in return? A half-cut gangster sat about the place drinking away the profits in return for 'security?' What fuckin' security had that young lad from the football club offered when Northfield Ronnie Hall and his mates came in the other night? And now Ronnie wants me to pay him instead?* Alf didn't know what to do for the best. If he switched allegiance he would be putting himself in danger and everybody knew that the Police were on the pay roll so what could he do?

Just then a jet-black Ford Prefect parked up outside. Out got a well-built man in his mid-thirties who was dressed in a long black Crombie coat that covered a smart black suit. He wore a dark trilby hat that slanted slightly casting a shadow over his wide face and a reputation for violence preceded him.

Harry Scriven locked the car and strolled casually towards the pub, his footsteps crunching in the soft powder like snow. Alf Spencer knew who this man was and he knew exactly why he had come. Suddenly he had less questions and was not feeling quite so brave.

As Scriven entered the pub and neared the counter, he pulled out a silver-plated cigarette case and placed it meticulously on the bar in line with his silver plated lighter. He opened the case, pulled out a Players Medium cigarette and lit up.

"Pint of mild please," he said exhaling smoke across the bar. As he spoke, the volume level within the room suddenly dropped and Scriven could feel eyes around the bar gazing at him.

The young bar maid poured the drink and before she could ask for payment Alf Spencer stopped her.

"There's no charge for Mr Scriven Betty, it's on the house."

Scriven nodded his thanks and looked at Spencer. "Is there somewhere we can talk Alfie?"

"Are you gunna' hurt me Mr Scriven?" the Landlord asked.

"Dow be saft Alfie, ar just wanna' find aaht what happened th'utha night."

Alf Spencer looked up at him nervously and pleaded. "You don't need me to tell you who did it surely?"

4

"Look kidda, ar've drove over here in the fuckin' snow to find aaht who done our boy the other night." Scriven took a long drag of his cigarette. "Ar bay gooin noweya til yow tell me whar happened."

Alf paused for a moment then beckoned towards a small snug at the back of the pub.

The Royal Oak was a large pub that served its local community of mainly affluent detached and semi-detached homes. Many of the locals had found the recent events rather distasteful, others had found it somewhat entertaining to watch the 'ruffian scallywags' banter with each other in the bar.

The two men sat down in a quiet corner at the back of the snug. They sat at a small circular, wooden table with an ornate metal stand. In the middle stood a white ashtray with two Hanson's beer mats placed either side. Scriven placed his cigarette case and lighter on the table in front of him and took a long gulp of his beer.

"It's a nice place yow got here Alfie."

"Thanks." Spencer stammered as he glanced nervously around the room.

"Yeah, it's alright ay it. Bet ya dow get much trouble raahnd here?" Scriven asked as he took out another cigarette.

Alf Spencer looked at the big man, his eyes pleading for him to leave well alone. "Look, I didn't really see what happened that night, I was out the back changing a barrel."

Scriven lit his cigarette, breathed in deeply then exhaled with a subtle, patronising sigh. He could feel the Landlord's fear and he desperately hoped that violence would not be required. After a long and deliberate pause Sciven finally replied.

"Yes, it's a very nice place yow have here mate." He looked deeply into the Landlord's eyes and slowly raised the cigarette from his lips.

"Yow need to meck sure yow look after what you have Alfie." Scriven spoke in a slow, forbidding tone. "You really should think about," Scriven paused again and shot Spencer a cold threatening stare. "Your family." He stared hard at Spencer and calmly savoured the tobacco smoke from his lungs.

Scriven really hated making such threats. Never in a million years would he ever dream of hurting innocent families, but his cousin had always taught him to make use of the fear that stemmed from others and use it to his own advantage.

Spencer looked at him with pure terror in his eyes.

"Dow worry Alfie." Scriven suddenly became more reassuring in his manner. "Look… Yow pay us to look after yower business for yer dow ya? And if yow tell me where ar can find the people responsible for the other night's attack, ar would be incredibly grateful" Scriven's cheery Black Country accent returned to his speech and the gangster produced a wad of notes from his pocket. Alfie Spencer had no choice. He might as well profit from the situation.

Three miles away, between Halesowen and Old Hill in The Black Country, Harry Scriven's cousin Bill Mucklow sat in a private room inside The Haden Cross pub.

The pub was situated in the relatively affluent area of Haden Hill which straddled the borders of Halesowen and Cradley Heath. The area's most famous landmarks were the Haden Hill Park and the historic Haden Hill house which were both constructed during the 19th century.

Another prominent feature of the area was the River Stour which flowed through Haden Hill and formed the ancient county border of Staffordshire on the Cradley Heath side and Worcestershire on the Halesowen side.

The small but well-appointed room at the side of the pub was reserved almost exclusively for Mr Mucklow and his associates. It was his office, meeting room and personal drinking spot. Much to the annoyance of his wife it was his natural comfort zone and he liked it.

In a corner of the room stood a wireless and, on this day, Mucklow sat listening to the smooth tones of one of his most favourite singers: Frank Sinatra.

The song currently playing had been a hit for Sinatra in the previous year and it reminded Billy of his own current situation. 'I've got the world on a string' was relevant to Mucklow because of at this time in his life, Billy very much did feel like he too 'had the world on a string.'

Mucklow also remembered far, far darker times, but he did not like to think about those. *He could not think about those times.* It was true that after a few drinks he would often bring into conversation, desolate and morbid memories from his past, but here on this snowy day in 1954, Billy Mucklow most definitely did have 'The world on a string'.

Mucklow sat in a cosy and dimly lit room with an old-fashioned fireplace at the centre. To the right of it was a rectangular shaped table which had an elegant art deco lamp perched in one corner casting a ray of colour into its dark, shadowy surroundings.

Upon the fireplace stood a 1940s mantel clock that indicated that it was 5 o clock in the afternoon and the window at the near side of the room revealed to Billy that it was already dark outside.

Bill Mucklow liked the window as he could see who was walking or driving past the pub. On this evening he did not expect to see many cars on account of the snow. He drained his beer glass and glanced from the window to the adjacent door where he was pleased to see Dickie Hickman appear with a tray of ale.

"Where the fuck yow bin?" Mucklow joked as he grabbed another jug of beer from the tray.

"Get it yer fuckin' self next time" Dick retorted, taking his place lent upright against the fireplace. Beer in one hand, his other elbow supporting his suited left arm on the fireplace.

Hickman wore a smart brown suit, so dark that from a distance it looked black. A red tie was held to his immaculate white shirt by a gold-plated tie pin.

"It's 5 o clock, no sign of Scriv?" Dick glanced at the window. "I gor him a pint."

"Yow paid for it did ya Dick?" Mucklow laughed.

Bill Mucklow was the sort of man who could fit in anywhere. He was equally at home sat in the officer's mess (back in his army days) drinking sherry with the Toffs or sat in the pubs with Chain makers in Netherton and Cradley Heath.

He had had a very mixed upbringing and as a result was able to drift between social classes. He was a leader of men, gang boss, loving father, war veteran and a man capable of extreme violence.

"We should have all gone daahn theyur" Hickman suggested.

Their associate Harry Scriven had been sent to carry out an errand alone and Dick Hickman had been fretting.

"Dow worry Dick. Scriv'll be fine." Bill Mucklow reassured his employee.

"We should have all gone daahn The Wellington in Colmore row an smashed the whole fuckin' place up. Glassed every bastard in the pub!" Hickman searched his pocket for a cigarette.

Billy Mucklow looked at him with a mocking smile.

"Look at me Ma! I'm on top of the world Ma" Billy joked doing his best James Cagney impression. "Yow bin watchin' too many cowboy pictures mate"

"Ok fine, he'll probably come home kaylied anyway." Dick Hickman was a slim man in his mid- twenties of slightly less than average height. He was hot headed, a ladies' man and an amateur boxing champion with very realistic ambitions of making it as a pro fighter.

Hickman usually spent his time hanging around his employer Bill Mucklow. He was his right-hand man, bodyguard and general nuisance.

He secretly envied Harry Scriven for his close family ties to the boss, but it was Dickie Hickman who was usually at Bill Mucklow's side. Standing by as Bill laid down the law or beat the shit out of anyone who crossed him. Hickman may have been the boxer, but Billy Mucklow was the most vicious, toughest 'mother fucker' Dick Hickman had met in his entire life.

"Yow gor a fake?" Hickman's search for a cigarette in his pocket had proven unsuccessful.

"Fuckin' hell Dick, do yow wanna' come raahnd mar house an sleep with mar wench tew? Ar buy yower ale, gid yow mar fakes, what next?" Mucklow tossed a cigarette at his friend and pulled one out for himself.

Where was Harry? Mucklow thought to himself as he lit his cigarette. *Maybe he shouldn't have sent him there alone?* His thoughts drifted for a moment as he imagined the brutal consequences he would deal to anyone who dared harm his family. Then he remembered that his cousin was every inch as tough as he was and was more than capable of looking after himself.

His mind wandered back to when they were both young kids with their old grandfather. How they would take turns hitting the heavy bag and the encouraging words the 'ode mon' would say to them. How he would count double on every second as the boys held themselves in a press up position whilst the other lad sat on their back.

Mucklow started to feel slightly melancholy at the thought of his long deceased relative, but it was short lived as he noticed a jet-black Ford Prefect come slowly down the road from the direction of Old Hill.

"I already got yow a beer!" Dick Hickman blurted out as Harry Scriven appeared in the doorway with a recently purchased pint.

"It's alright mate, ar'll have that one in a bit." A gentle piano tinkled in the background as the wireless played Ella Fitzgerald's version of 'Autumn in New York.' "It's fuckin' freezin' aaht theyur!"

"Do yow want a drop of whisky mate?" Mucklow asked.

"Maybe later… Ta"

"So what happened'?" Hickman asked impatiently.

Let me sit daahn mate!" Scriven sat down next to Bill Mucklow and took a large gulp of his beer.

"I went over theyur and had a chat with the gaffa. Apparently, it was Ronnie Hall and a couple of his crew who did Wilfie over." Scriven explained as he opened his silver-plated cigarette case.

9

"You know this for a fact?" Mucklow asked taking on a more serious tone.

"Ar believe so" Scriven replied. "Ar know he guz in the Oak sometimes and he is well connected within The Brummie Boys... Looks like they'm trying to move in on our patch." Scriven held his hands up to the fire and felt the heat start to warm his bones.

"What's this Ronnie Hall like?" Mucklow asked as he extinguished his used cigarette.

"Loud, mouthy, thinks a lot of himself. Like ar said, he's well connected. One of their top blokes." Scriven drew his hands back from the fire slightly as they started to burn.

"Right, its Friday night and that bastard is gonna be out on the beer. He woe goo far in this weather. Where does he drink?" Mucklow looked at both of the other men.

"Dow ask me, ar dow know." Dick Hickman said looking at Scriven.

"I think he guz in the Black Oss on the Bristol Road." Scriven looked at his cousin awaiting his next set of orders.

"In Longbridge?" Hickman asked.

"Nah, its more Northfield." Scriven explained.

Bill Mucklow thought for a minute then looked at his cousin. The two relatives looked very similar, more like brothers than cousins. Harry Scriven was a few weeks older than Bill, but Bill had had the more privileged up-bringing.

Both men were broad shouldered, just below six feet tall and both had been bald and without hair since their mid-twenties. Now they were in their mid-thirties and their waistlines were starting to reveal their over fondness for beer and fried breakfasts!

"I want to send them a message tonight" Mucklow finally announced.

Scriven groaned inwardly. He had hoped to be going over to Tipton that night to catch up with his latest love interest. A nice blonde lady who was a little older than himself and Landlady of a half decent boozer. "What am yer thinkin' Bill?"

"Go to the Black Oss, pick up Ronnie Hall, teck him somewhere discreet and break his fuckin' legs." Billy Mucklow looked at Scriven and raised his finger to make his point. "Then dump him outside The Wellington off Colmore row. Show them fuckers that we mean business. We woe back daahn an we ay afraid of them big time city boys!" Giving orders was second nature to Mucklow.

Scriven finished his pint and stood up. "Right, yow might as well have that then." He said pointing to the extra beer Dick Hickman had fetched earlier.

"Teck Barry O'Leary with yer." Mucklow suggested. "He's thick as pig shit but he's a ruthless, big bastard."

Scriven nodded, placed his trilby back onto his hairless head and left the room.

"Can I have that then?" Dickie Hickman smirked pointing at Harry Scriven's untouched second pint.

Chapter 2

The journey from The Haden Cross to Barry O'Leary's parent's house in Old Hill was a relatively short drive, even in the snow.

Barry O'Leary had been something of a juvenile delinquent. At the age of 15 he had tried to stab a Police officer and after getting out of Borstal on his 18th birthday, he had immediately set out on a crime wave throughout the local area.

Billy Mucklow, as leader of the local underworld had been obliged to intervene. The Police were getting tired of giving O'Leary a good hiding and then hoping that he would see the error of his ways! Of course, he probably should have been sent back to prison. But the local Police enjoyed a special, mutually beneficial relationship with Billy Mucklow.

He paid them to look the other way and in return he would do the odd thing to help them out too. But mainly he sent them illicit payments. With regards to Barry O'Leary the Police actually felt a 'talking to' from Billy Mucklow would help him to see the error of his ways.

There was only so far that the Police officers could go and they felt that Mucklow could be much more convincing.

However, it was much easier for Mucklow to simply buy Barry a suit and put him on the payroll. This gave O'Leary an elevated sense of status and he actually came to respect and listen to his elders within the gang. He was never going to win any prizes for his brains and intellect, but Barry O'Leary had his uses. He was a big lad and was good in a fight.

Finnbarr Seamus O'Leary (Barry) had come from a poverty stricken and deprived background. His parents had migrated from

Ireland 5 years before his birth and his father had often struggled to find work.

O'Leary senior had been a violent and abusive father and husband. Both him and later his wife were terrible alcoholics and had neglected and beaten their son throughout his life. It was no surprise that Barry would grow up to be completely out of control and violent himself. It was almost fortunate that Harry Scriven had very much taken Barry under his wing and the young 21-year-old was slowly learning some manners and self-control.

The O'Leary family lived in a dreary little Victorian house in Pear-tree Street, Old Hill. Locally, the street was known as 'Bug Street' due to the vast amount of bugs that were reputed to live in the houses there. Harry Scriven had no doubt that there were probably many bugs of different shapes and sizes within the O'Leary household.

The windows were black with dust and dirt and the paint was all but worn away from the rotting front door. Scriven hoped that he would not have to go inside. On a previous occasion Barry had invited him inside to wait for a couple of moments. The smell inside the house had been unbearable and the filth was worse on the inside than it had appeared from the outside.

Scriven knocked the door loudly and stood back to wait for his accomplice. For a moment he thought he would have to face the usual angry comments from O'Leary senior, but at this time of day the old Irishman would be drunk and supping ale in The Spring Meadow House pub.

He knocked again but there was still no answer. *I cor dew this on me bloody own.* He thought to himself. *Billy and Dick will have to get their hands dirty and come with me.*

Just then Barry appeared at the door in his suit and tie. He was about six foot two and of above average weight. This was somewhat surprising due to his upbringing, however in recent years O'Leary had spent much of his newfound finances in cafes and pubs widening his waistline! He had jet black hair and wide, staring, unintellectual eyes.

"Sorry Scriv, ar saw it was yow and thought ar better smarten' meself' up."

"Hurry up, we gor a job ter dew" Scriven beckoned with his head for Barry to get in the car. "Ar'll explain on the way."

They both got into the Ford Prefect and just as Scriven was about to pull the starter he stopped and looked at Barry...... "Yow gor a shoota' aer kid?"

"Dow be saft Scriv! Do yow really think Mr Mucklow ud' trust me wid a gun?"

Scriven agreed. He had a pistol tucked away at his own house but that meant going back to Colley Gate. *At least the roads had thawed a little.* He started the car and headed back through Old Hill and up Barrs Road where Bill Mucklow lived.

Harry Scriven lived alone in a two bedroomed terraced house in Talbot Street, Colley Gate. He had grown up in that house and it had originally belonged to his parents. They were both still alive but had moved out of the area five years previously when Scriven's father had reached the age of retirement.

His mother was the sister of William Mucklow senior. A wealthy man on account of him being the previous leader of the lucrative Mucklow crime family.

The senior Mucklow had passed control of his empire to his son before going to live a more peaceful existence in the nearby village of Clent. Being a man of wealth, he also purchased a nearby cottage for his sister (Harry Scriven's mother) and her husband Horace.

The terraced house in Talbot Street now belonged to Harry Scriven and for a while his neighbours had looked upon him in disgust as he had been 'living in sin' with a women whom he was not married to.

To make matters worse, the woman, from Dudley, was still married to a man who was serving in the Royal Navy! She also had two young children who had been brought to live with them.

The relationship had not lasted long and Scriven had felt quite relieved when she had moved out to go back to her husband in Dudley when he returned from over seas. It appeared that he was making quite a habit of getting involved with married women!

Sometimes Scriven felt alone, but he passed the time mainly with his pals at The Haden Cross or with the various other female acquaintances he met along the way. He was also member of a local boxing club in Halesowen and had developed quite a reputation as an aggressive and accomplished fighter.

Scriven parked his car at the bottom of the street and walked up the hill leaving O'Leary to finish his cigarette on the passenger's seat. He lived on a steep incline and knew there was no chance of him getting the Prefect up it with snow on the ground.

He climbed three quarters of the way up the hill and then turned right into the narrow-cobbled entry that led to his house. He fumbled in his pocket for the key and opened the door. The house had been left all day in the cold and Scriven noted that it was hardly any warmer inside than it was out.

He went through the living room, up the stairs and then pulled out an old shoe box from under his bed. He gently opened it and pulled out a black and grey Webley revolver. Scriven held the gun in his right hand and slowly raised it to his face to feel the cold steel against his cheek. He had never fired a gun in anger before and for this he was very grateful.

During the war he had served in the RAF as an aircraft technician working mainly on Hawker Hurricane fighter planes at an air base in Cornwall. Bill Mucklow had been an Army officer in the 1st Battalion Worcestershire Regiment and had been stationed in India at the start of the Second World War. The Battalion later transferred to the 214th Infantry Brigade and landed in Normandy as part of Operation Overlord on 24th of June 1944.

Bill Mucklow had eventually reached the rank of Captain and had been directly and brutally involved in some of the roughest fighting on the Normandy beaches and then across Europe and into Germany.

Bill was a decent man, so Scriven believed, but his wartime experiences had made him cold and had given him the ability to detach himself emotionally from situations where violence was required.

Harry Scriven was rather different to his cousin. Of course, he enjoyed a good scrap and he was bloody good at it. He had boxed at a relatively high standard and was more than capable of looking after himself. But in his mind there was a big difference between "slappin' somebody abaaht a bit" and actually pulling the trigger. He always told himself that *when you pull that trigger, you take away everything that a person has ever had and everything that they ever will have.*

There was also the ever-present fear of 'Ong' Mon's noose!' Harry Scriven was well aware that murder was a crime punishable by death and he certainly did not want to be sent to the gallows!

Between 1900 and 1949, 621 men and 11 women were executed by hanging in England and Wales. In 1949 the Home Secretary James Chuter-Ede set up the Royal Commission on Capital Punishment which lasted until 1953 with the intent of determining whether capital punishments should be abolished.

Alternatives to hangings were discussed including electric chair, gas inhalation, lethal injection, shooting and even the guillotine. It was also suggested that Capital Punishment should be abolished completely, however, popular opinion maintained that the death penalty acted as a deterrent to many would-be criminals.

It suddenly occurred to Scriven that if something should go wrong that night and Ronnie Hall was to end up dead, then he himself could be dangling on the end of 'Ong' Mon's noose!' *What if Barry O'Leary got carried away and went too far? What if the gun went off by mistake? What if they dumped Hall outside the Wellington and his own people slit Ronnie's throat and told the law that he and Barry had done it?*

He reached into the pocket of his Crombie over coat and took out a small hip flask. He raised it to his lips and took a sip, the hot, sweet flavour of the Johnnie Walker blended whisky instantly warming his throat and slightly easing his worried state. He put the flask and the gun back into his pocket and went back down the stairs.

As he left the house, he felt grateful that Carol and her two children had left him a few months previously. This way there was no chance of them being caught up in the repercussions of the night's activities. This was the life that he had chosen, it was no place for women and children.

On the journey over to Northfield, O'Leary and Scriven smoked as the older man explained what had to be done.

"Is he hard?" O'Leary asked as he wandered about what the night would have in store for him.

"Ar reckon so yes" Scriven answered calmly and coolly.

"Ow many will there be?"

"We will wait till he comes aaht the booza'. He will be kaylied and hopefully on his own." The thought hadn't occurred to Scriven that Ronnie Hall may leave the pub with friends. "Just keep yower cairk'ole shut and do nothing till ar say."

O'Leary nodded and sat back in the seat. "Gonna' get me a motor soon Scriv."

"Yow gorra' license?" Scriven asked curiously.

"Nah."

"How the fuck am yow gunna' get a car then?" Scriven laughed shaking his head.

"Ar can drive! Ar used to nick um' all the time!"

Scriven sighed. "If yow ever nick mar car ar'll fuckin' knock yow aaht!"

"Dow worry Scriv, we dow shit on our own."

The car park to the left of the Black horse was all but empty when they arrived at the pub. Harry Scriven figured it was due to the snow, though he had found the roads relatively passable. Even more so in Birmingham than back home in Halesowen.

Alfie Spencer at the Royal Oak had informed him earlier that Ronnie Hall drove a light grey Morris eight, though at this time Scriven could not see such a car on the car park.

"We gonna' wait around eeya all night for a Morris to turn up?" O'Leary asked impatiently.

"No. He may av walked in this weather." Scriven did not entirely trust Alfie Spencer's description of Ronnie Hall's car. The Landlord was nervous and anxious not to get caught up in things. *Maybe he thought that in giving wrong information, Hall would not be found?*

"Right. Let's pop in the pub an av a look abaaht. He woe know yow but he might recognise me." Scriven pulled up the collar on his dark Crombie and pulled the rim of his hat down.

The two men got out of the car and walked across the path towards the pub. The Black Horse was a huge pub that stood at the side of the Bristol Road in the Birmingham suburb of Northfield. The current building had been constructed in the late 1920s and was currently owned by the Davenports brewing company. A pub had stood on the site for many years and it was popular with local residents and weary travellers who were travelling into Birmingham on one of the major routes into the city.

Harry Scriven knew of the pub but had never ventured inside before. It was nearly 9 miles from his hometown and he had never had cause to go there until now.

Just as they were about to enter the pub, a light-coloured Morris eight pulled onto the car park. Scriven ducked into the shadows and pulled O'Leary with him hoping that the occupants of the car had not seen them.

He was relieved to see that only one person had got out of the car. It was an exceptionally tall man in a long black coat.

"That him Scriv?" O'Leary asked.

"Shut the fuck up!" Scriven snapped as he moved slowly behind a near wall where he knew he could not be seen. The figure appeared to stop and look in their direction. Scriven's heart sank as he hoped he had not been spotted. That would jeopardise the whole job and he would have to go back to Billy and Hickman and tell them that the night had been a failure.

The figure continued to move towards them and he slowly emerged into the light emitted from the windows of the pub.

It's him! Scriven thought to himself with a mixture of relief and disappointment. *There was no going back now! Gone was any chance of him getting over to Tipton that night!*

The figure passed their hiding position and went into the pub.

"Well where is he then?" O'Leary asked in frustration. Falsely thinking that the figure had not been Hall.

"That was him!" Scriven started to walk back towards the car.

"Ay we doing it then?" Barry O'Leary was confused.

"Ar said before day I! Let him sup ale, we will tek him when he's arf' cut!" Scriven explained as he opened the Ford Prefect's door and settled back into the driver's seat.

"He might be in there till kickin aaht time! It's fuckin' freezin' an ar bay got no fakes left!" O'Leary protested.

It was bitterly cold and the two men shivered inside the car as the temperature plummeted. Harry Scriven sipped on the scotch from his hip flask and chain smoked whilst O'Leary moaned and constantly asked for a sip of whiskey.

"Fuck off! Ar dow know where yower maarfs bin." Scriven grunted as he watched the entrance to the pub intently. They were so close to getting their man. The last thing he wanted was to miss this opportunity or for Hall to come out of the pub with company.

Scriven slumped back in the car seat with his left arm draped over the huge steering wheel. His right arm periodically raised to lift the ever-present cigarette from his mouth. As he watched the pub his mind wandered off again to memories from long ago.

He remembered playing in the snow with his cousin Billy at Haden Hill Park. It would have been in the mid-1920s. They would use whatever rubbish they could find to make sledges and ride down the 'bonk' and then fall off at the bottom.

The Park had always seemed such a peaceful place to play until one day some older boys had set about them and threatened to hurt them. Scriven smiled as he remembered how Billy had ran and picked up a couple of big sticks. Then the two boys had charged the older kids and started hitting them wildly!.Life hadn't changed too much he thought.

At about half past eleven a slightly drunk Ronnie Hall emerged from the front of the pub. He wasn't exactly falling over but he stumbled slightly as he neared his light grey Morris.

Hall had left the car at the front of the car park facing towards the Bristol Road. As he walked he could see the dark outline of the art deco building that housed Northfield swimming baths to the left of him.

He paused when he reached his car and searched his pockets for his keys. He could tell that he had been drinking but considering he had drunk eight large scotches and two half pints of bitter, he probably wasn't doing too badly. *I'm a big lad, I can handle my booze* he thought proudly to himself.

Life was good for Ronnie Hall. He was respected by the other members of The Brummie Boys gang and he was having lunch the next day with Isiah Boswell himself! *The main boss, an original Peaky Blinder from back in the day, the legend!*

Now he was going to have a slow drive home (it needed to be slow after the amount of alcohol he had drank.). The next morning, he would have a lie in and then put on his best suit ready for the meeting with the boss.

In his head he imagined himself sat with Isiah Boswell, lapping up the praise for his recent beating of that 'Yam Yam' kid.

"Dow mek a sound or ar'll blow yower fuckin' brains all over the floor!" A gun was suddenly thrust into the back of Ronnie Hall's head.

"Do you speak English mate?" Hall said, raising his hands in the air.

"Ar'll spake whatever fuckin' language ar want too!" Harry Scriven thrust the gun harder into the back of Hall's head.

"What d'ya want?" Hall asked in an angry snarl.

"Get in the fuckin' car." Scriven opened the rear door of the Prefect and used his free hand to push Hall onto the back seat.

At first Ronnie Hall was reluctant to get in. "Get in the car, we just wanna' talk." Scriven lied.

Hall moved onto the back seat and Scriven got in himself, the gun pointing firmly at Ronnie Hall the whole time.

Barry O'Leary was already in the driver's seat and started the engine. Scriven hoped that O'Leary could drive as well as he had made out earlier!

"Turn right off the car park and keep gooin." Scriven knew exactly the right spot just a few miles down the road.

"So what the fuck is all this about?" Ronnie Hall did not have time for any of this. He had to get some sleep ahead of his special meeting the next day.

"Yow tell me?" Scriven asked.

"You will regret this you pathetic fool. Do you know who I am?" Hall was losing his patience.

"Ar know exactly who yow am. Do yow know who Wilfie Dugmore is?"

Hall gave Scriven a knowing look. He knew exactly what all of this was about but doubted Harry Scriven's courage to pull the trigger.

"You don't have the balls to use that gun kid." Ronnie Hall was a good ten years older than Harry Scriven and was soon to reach his half century.

Hall started to laugh mockingly. "You're a fuckin' joke. Go on then shoot me! I'm fuckin' getting out. Stop the car."

Just then, the car hit a skid on the snow and O'Leary lost control. Ronnie Hall saw his opportunity and lunged at Harry Scriven, knocking the gun hard into Scriven's throat and in the struggle the gun went off inside his mouth!

Scriven instantly felt relieved that he had never loaded the weapon but flinched with the pain of the metal barrel smashing his tooth.

He tasted the metallic flavour of his own blood and in that instant the huge man opposite lunged at him with his free hand to grab his throat!

In the darkness of the car Hall missed Scriven's throat and thrust is hand into the younger man's already bloody mouth. Scriven winced again with the pain and then bit down as hard as he could…

He held onto the bite and could now taste Hall's irony blood mixing with his own. Hall let out an almighty scream and Scriven hit him hard in the face with a straight right-hand punch, one, two, three times.

As the car skidded to a halt in the middle of the road, Hall flew backwards out of the door through the force of the third punch.

Scriven immediately dived out of the car, grabbed Hall by the scruff of the neck and continued to pummel straight right-hand punches into the big man's face.

Hall's nose burst open and blood suddenly exploded into the clean white snow making a disturbing pattern that protruded from Hall's head like a crimson spider creeping across the gleaming white floor.

As Hall lay semi-conscious in the snow, Scriven ventured to the rear of the car and pulled out some rope from the boot. He tied Hall's hands together then instructed him to get back into the car.

"Fuck you!" Hall snarled, blood dripping from his broken face. He looked up at Scriven. He had misjudged the man and started to laugh as he coughed on his own blood.

How could he get Hall back into the car quickly? Scriven thought to himself. Then he remembered something he had heard about from his cousin.

Scriven grabbed Hall's hair with his left hand and lifted him to his knees. He then pulled a small flick knife from his pocket and held it to the side of Hall's mouth, applying just enough pressure to make a small cut. "Get back in the car or ar'll meck yow smile for the rest of yower fuckin' life!"

Hall had heard of London gangsters who had had their faces cut from one side of their mouth all the way back to their ears. It was commonly known as 'The Chelsea smile' and Hall did not want this to happen to him... Slowly, he climbed awkwardly back into the car with his hands tied together.

"Yow get in the back with him." Scriven ordered and
 O'Leary got out of the driver's seat and sat down in the back next to the bruised and battered Ronnie Hall.

Scriven inspected the wheels of his car which were still lodged in the snow and then got back into the front and started the engine.

Slowly he accelerated and eased the car forwards. *Barry had obviously not driven in the snow before!* Scriven silently cursed himself for trusting Barry O'Leary to drive.

As he drove down the Bristol Road towards Longbridge Scriven could still taste the mixture of blood inside his mouth. He thought about what had just happened and he began to worry that in the heat of the moment, he could have actually cut Hall from ear to ear...

He had always prided himself on not being as ruthless as his cousin Bill, but there he had been, angry and covered in blood, ready to permanently scar another human being... He shuddered at the aggression inside of him and promised himself that he would show more control in future.

The car passed through the Austin motor works in Longbridge and the many large buildings and bridges looked quite menacing in their shadowy darkness.

Scriven took a left turn at the side of the works and pulled up in a dark and desolate corner of Cofton Park. The large park stood at the side of the factory and Scriven thought it was the perfect spot for inflicting their revenge on Ronnie Hall.

He got out of the car and walked around to the rear door and opened it. "Get aaht."

Ronnie Hall knew exactly where he was. The perfect spot for a gangland killing. "No please, I have children, don't kill me please I'm begging you." The once confident Hall was now begging for his life.

"Just get aaht of the fuckin' car!" Scriven raised his voice slightly and O'Leary pulled his own knife from out of his pocket whilst smiling menacingly at Hall.

It was a clear night and the soft light of the moonlight illuminated the knife making it look haunting and forbidding inside the darkness of the car.

Hall slowly shuffled along the back seat and stood up outside of the car. He looked helplessly at the stars that twinkled in the night sky and expected nothing but death.

This was it… He would never see his wife again, never hear the voice of his grandchildren. Here on this bitterly cold night in a snowy Cofton park he would meet his maker. In his mind he knew that with all he had done over the years, he probably deserved to die. He was going straight to hell and there was nothing he could do.

Hall closed his eyes and waited for the cold steel to slice open his throat, but instead Scriven dealt him a hard upper cut that raised him straight off his feet and landed him flat on his back.

"Right, this is retribution…" Scriven spoke with a smug satisfaction. "Pay back for what yow did to young Wilfie Dugmore. Yow deserve this and it is just that yow suffer this way." Harry Scriven aspired to think of himself as a good man and felt that these brutal actions were justified and worthy.

He raised his left foot and rammed it hard into Hall's neck, pinning him to the floor with his hands tied and unable to move.

He then lit a cigarette and proceeded to smoke two of them whilst Barry O'Leary went to work with a cricket bat. Blow after agonizing blow, O'Leary summoned up all of the strength and weight inside of him to batter and shatter Hall's legs. The cartilage and bones made awful cracking noises as they were reduced to mush.

Eventually Ronnie Hall's torment ended when the cricket bat shattered itself with the force that had been applied and its handle came away from the main body of the bat!

"That'll dew…" Scriven announced as he sucked the last dregs from his cigarette and then stubbed out the glow on Hall's forehead.

By this point, Hall had no feeling left in his legs and could hardly tell what was going on around him.

O'Leary and Scriven cursed at the weight of the large semi-conscious man as they lifted him back into the car.

"Here drink this." For a brief minute, Scriven took pity on their victim and handed him the remains of the whisky in his hip flask. Hall grabbed it and eagerly gulped down the fluid. His face was bruised and battered almost beyond recognition and his legs were dead to him.

Chapter 3

It had been three nights since Scriven and O'Leary attacked Ronnie Hall and dumped him outside The Wellington pub near Colmore row in the city centre area of Birmingham.

The Wellington was owned by Isiah Boswell, leader of The Brummie Boys and Billy Mucklow had hoped that this act of vengeance would send a clear message. Though as yet there had been no word from anyone and Mucklow and the rest of the gang were still anticipating their rival's next move.

They had sat about The Haden Cross drinking copious amounts of beer and smoking cigarettes whilst waiting for a reaction but nothing happened. "Fuck it. Ar'm a gooin over Tipp'n fer a pint!" Harry Scriven was bored of waiting around and he decided to venture out.

The snow had started to thaw and the region's roads were becoming much more passable as Scriven noticed when he got into his car and ventured over to The Fountain Inn.

The Fountain stood in the heart of Tipton in Owen Street and had enjoyed a particularly famous past locally. In the 1800s it had been used as a training ground for William Perry who was more commonly known as 'The Tipton Slasher.'

Perry was a Tipton native and a British heavyweight boxing champion between 1850 and 1857. He started his fighting career in 1835 and after defeating a number of highly rated contenders claimed his first heavyweight title by defeating fellow Midlander Tom Paddock after 27 rounds on the 17th of December 1850.

The Slasher would later loose his title to Birmingham fighter Harry Broome before reclaiming it and holding onto it until 1857.

After his boxing career had finished Perry went on to run various pubs throughout the Black Country before dying of alcoholism at his home in Bilston on the 24th December 1880.

Harry Scriven had been spending more and more time in The Fountain recently due to the Landlady Irene Miller. She was slightly older than him and was in her very early forties.

This was of no concern to Scriven at all, for him there was a certain allure of an older married women and he viewed their supposed unattainability as something of a challenge.

Irene Miller had shoulder length blonde hair which was straw like in colour and immaculately kept. Her eyes were heavily made up, big and blue with long black eyelash extensions.

She always dedicated a substantial period each morning to applying her 'Meck up.' Without fail it was always ever so slightly 'over-done' and exaggerating of her moderate natural beauty, though this did help to hide any lines that were beginning to appear on her face.

Irene Miller was about 5'4 and was no longer slim and slender, though she was by no means overweight. Harry Scriven liked the fact that she carried just a few extra pounds in certain areas and so did many of the regulars at The Fountain.

Her attractive 'older women' charm was very popular with the men that drank in her pub, though she was often overshadowed by her twenty-year-old daughter.

Irene's daughter Suzy also worked in the pub. She carried slightly more weight than her mother, but she had a stunningly pretty face with piercing red hair and a tendency to wear a seductive scarlet lipstick that accentuated her perfect lips.

Irene had been just twenty years old when she fell pregnant with Suzy and it was automatically expected that she would marry the father, which she soon did.

Her husband was a couple of years older than her and he had fallen for the young Tipton blonde in the early thirties when she was working at a pub he frequented in Sedgley.

They got married soon after and saved up enough money to purchase a pub of their own. That pub was the Fountain and at the time of purchase the young couple were not even aware of it famous past and its connections to the Tipton Slasher.

Over the years the couple had expanded their business with Irene running the Fountain in Owen Street and her husband Nigel moving to a new pub, The Tilted Barrel in Princes End.

Since the purchase of the second pub just after the war, the couple had started to drift apart and Harry Scriven had recently seen the opportunity and was making his move!

Irene Miller had not felt like this for many years. The butterflies in her stomach and the ever present gnaw she felt within her made her feel like a besotted teenager. She would constantly remind herself to 'act her age' and that she was a married woman and should not be giving into such adolescent behaviour. But she could not help it. Harry Scriven made her feel something her husband had long since ceased to do.

Whenever she bent down to pull a pint of beer, she would drop her shoulders a little lower to give Scriven a more than welcome glance of her generously proportioned cleavage.

She would hold onto his gaze just a little longer than she should, then flutter her eyelashes in a bid to reassure Scriven that his attention was more than welcome and reciprocated. Then, she would lean over the cash till at the back of the counter and give Scriven a glance of her large but perfectly proportioned rear end.

He wasn't the world's most handsome man. He was bald and slightly overweight, but he had eyes of a shimmering deep blue that revealed an inner sensitivity that contradicted his tough, masculine exterior. He was always immaculately well dressed in beautiful suits and he wore an impressive Rolex Tudor wristwatch.

Irene Miller wasn't quite sure what he did for a living, but she didn't really care. He had immaculate manners and treated her with a flirty respect she could not resist.

As Scriven sat at the bar, supping his pint of Holden's beer, he watched his love interest closely and chatted with her between the ever-present locals she was serving in the bar.

Out of the corner of his eye he noticed an unsavoury looking group of men sat in the corner playing cards. It was a long rectangular shaped bar room and a large art deco mirror hung on the wall just above the men's heads where Scriven could see his own image reflecting back at him.

Scriven thought that the men looked very old fashioned in their flat caps and drab suits. However, he also thought that it was very typical of the Tipton area in which they were in.

"Who am they?" Scriven asked, curiously eyeing the loud unruly group over his beer.

"That's Jimmy Danks. Stay well away from him, he's bad news... Seriously, stay well away!" Irene warned as she took payment for a round of drinks.

"He ay bin no trouble to yow as he?" Scriven asked with some concern.

"No, not really. They come in here, play cards, count their money and meck dodgy deals. I stay out of their way. They am good customers."

Jimmy Danks was a particularly unsavoury character. By trade he was a 'Rag un' boone mon,' dealing in (mostly stolen) scrap metal and junk, *just like most of the men in Tipp'n* so Scriven thought...

He was also involved in various other more criminal activities. Robbery, protection rackets, pimping and his particular favourite past time: dog fighting.

Danks was a cruel, heartless man who had been originally from Gypsy stock and Scriven eyed him intently over the rim of his beer glass.

"What the fuck yow lookin' at?" Danks suddenly noticed Scriven's intense stare.

He held his gaze for a few seconds then looked away. He was far from his home turf and neither himself nor even Billy Mucklow were known or respected in these parts.

Tipton was home to Gypsies, scrap metal dealers and some of the roughest, hardest people in the Midlands. Billy Mucklow's Police contacts had no influence here, this was Tipton…

As much as he fancied a scrap with Danks, Scriven knew that it would not end well. Besides, did he really need the Police coming out and finding the 'shooter' in the boot of his car?

Scriven turned away and averted his gaze back to his woman. His eyes drifting down past her face to her bosom that protruded slightly from her tight Polka dot dress.

"Ar said, what the fuck am yow lookin' at?" Danks started again. "Yow come in here wid yower fancy fuckin' suit and sit there and look at me!"

"Yow berra goo Harry." Irene pleaded. The rest of Danks' crew looked menacingly at Scriven. Every single one of them looked hard and mean and Scriven knew the odds were stacked well against him.

For a mad second, he thought of going out to the car and coming back gun in hand and smashing the shit out of Jimmy Danks. *But what would that achieve? Apart from putting Irene well off him!* Scriven collected his thoughts, nodded goodnight to Irene and shot Danks a cheeky wink across the bar. With that he picked up his Crombie coat and hat and left the pub.

"That's it! Fuck of ya bastard, dow come fuckin back or ar'll spread yower fairce all ova the floowa... Prick!" Danks sat back in his chair and enjoyed showing off in front of his friends.

Just as Scriven was about to get into the car, Irene came running out of the pub.

"Ar'm sorry bab." She said wrapping her arms around him. Scriven laughed. She really did not know him at all.

"It's ok Wench. Ar was a gooin anyway."

Irene kissed him full on the lips and Scriven wrapped his hands around her waist, lowering them to grab a feel of her firm buttocks.

"Yow better goo back inside. It's freezin' aaht here." He said, stroking her cheek affectionately.

She nodded in agreement and kissed him one more time on the cheek. Then he stood and watched her figure as she headed back into the pub.

Two more nights passed and Bill Mucklow had finally heard from The Brummie Boys. A messenger had been sent to The Haden Cross explaining that Isiah Boswell wanted to meet with Mucklow to discuss a truce. It was agreed that they would meet at the place where this had all started, The Royal Oak in Lapal.

Twenty-four hours later and the rear snug of The Royal Oak had been completely cleared of all regular customers and Boswell and Mucklow sat face to face at a large table in the middle of the room.

Behind Boswell stood two enormous men who Mucklow thought were probably armed with razor blades and pistols. In his mind, Mucklow worked out a strategy of how he would quickly try to disable the men should things turn nasty. He had killed bigger Germans! But in his heart of hearts he hoped that things could be resolved. Boswell's organisation was much bigger and more complex than his and there was only so long he could hold his own against the big boys from the city.

Behind Mucklow sat the ever-agitated Dick Hickman and Mucklow's cousin Harry Scriven who sat casually smoking a cigarette. Billy Mucklow sat back in his chair and looked at Boswell awaiting his proposals.

"You know Billy, what you did to Ronnie Hall was a fuckin' liberty kid… The poor bastard's never gonna' fuckin' walk again!" Boswell struggled to keep the anger from his usually calm voice. At that, Dick Hickman let out a sudden burst of laughter.

"Shut up Dick." Billy turned around and shot Hickman an angry look. Boswell gave Hickman a look of disgust and turned back to face Mucklow.

"Were such drastic measures really necessary?" Boswell asked.

Isiah Boswell was an older man in his late fifties. In the 1920s he had been one of the original Peaky Blinders running with the infamous Billy Kimber and his men. Like Boswell, Kimber had been born in Aston. For years he was the biggest gang boss in England and controlled the bookmakers and racecourses of the early twentieth century. His influence and control spread throughout the entire country and when he died at a nursing home in Torquay in 1942, the younger Aston native Isiah Boswell assumed overall control of the empire.

Boswell was originally from poor Gypsy stock but had fought hard and ruthlessly to rise to the top of The Brummie Boys gang. Now he lived in large house in the wealthy Birmingham suburb of Harborne and drove a luxurious Rolls Royce car. The city belonged to him and he was reluctant to involve himself with this 'tin pot rabble' from the other side of the Hagley road! He ran hundreds of pubs, betting shops and factories, *why was he wasting his time with this small-time gangster from Yam Yam land?*

"I feel that our actions were more than justified." Billy Mucklow explained. "Young Wilfie Dugmore had a career ahead of him as a footballer... He was the star player for Halesowen town!"

The two big men sniggered.

"Well, they may be just a little ode fudball team. But I happen to be the owner!" Mucklow raised his finger and narrowed his eyes. "We were in the middle of agreeing a deal to sell Dugmore to the Baggies! Ar would'av med a fuck load of money!"

Harry Scriven groaned inwardly at Mucklow's revelation. He was not aware that Dugmore was to be sold to West Bromwich Albion. He had thought that his attack on Ronnie Hall with Barry O'Leary was an act of vengeance for their friend and his young family, not payback for Mucklow being out of pocket... He said nothing.

Boswell looked deep in thought and then pulled out a box of expensive cigars and placed them down on the table.

"I just happen to have a proposal that could make you a lot more money Mr Mucklow." He offered Mucklow a cigar and took one for himself. One of the men behind stooped down and held a light as Boswell inhaled heavily, igniting the huge Cuban cigar. Mucklow lit his own cigar and listened intently to what Boswell had to say.

"I'm a very busy man Mr Mucklow. I have a city to run and I haven't got time to trade punches with small time boys such as yourself." Boswell paused to savour the flavour of his cigar. "With all respect.... Feuds are bad for business, I'm sure you will appreciate this Mr Mucklow?"

Mucklow thought for a minute as he smoked his cigar. "Ok.... What proposal do you have in mind to reimburse me for my loss?" Mucklow enquired.

Boswell laughed through gritted teeth. "You crippled a personal friend of mine!" Boswell stopped and calmed himself.

Isiah Boswell was usually a very calm and restrained character. He had power and had not been afraid to seriously hurt and murder men on his way to the top. But experience had taught him that he could achieve twice as much by being calm and totally in control of situations.

"Mr Mucklow. I want you to meet a friend of mine." Boswell beckoned over a middle-aged man who carried a briefcase and wore a pin striped suit.

The man sat down next to Boswell. He wore horn rimmed spectacles that hung on the end of his nose like those of a Victorian School master. Mucklow could tell instantly that the man was definitely not a gangster.

"This is Mr Williams and he represents the Austin Motor Company in Longbridge. I will let him explain the rest to you himself." Boswell sucked on his cigar and sat back in his soft, red leather chair.

"Hello Mr Mucklow. As Mr Boswell has just explained, I am from the Austin factory. We have a rather fortunate problem in our factory at the moment. It appears that our workforce are being somewhat over productive as of late." The nervous man was slowly becoming more confident and a small amount of spittle shot from his tight excited lips and onto the brown varnished table. "You may know that we have recently changed some of our construction methods for manufacturing vehicles?"

Mucklow looked disinterested and shook his head.

"We started building the A30 in 1951, it is our first car to feature monocoque chassis-less construction. Basically, this means that the car is cheaper and easier for us to produce as it does not have a separate chassis like our previous vehicles. As a result, we have found that we are currently having lots of surplus stock... We are more than meeting our quotas for production which puts me in a rather interesting situation." A twinkle appeared in Williams eyes as he looked up at Billy Mucklow from above the rim of his horn-rimmed spectacles. "The current sale price for a brand-new Austin A30 is five hundred and seven pounds. Now, if you were to arrange for some of your associates to come to our back gate near Cofton Park, I could let you drive away in several brand-new cars for just one hundred and fifty pounds each! You would have brand new cars worth five hundred and seven pounds for just one hundred fifty pounds! Just think of the money you could make! I could supply you with roughly ten cars a week." Williams opened his hands and turned them upwards in a questioning gesture.

Mucklow looked at Boswell and then back to Williams. "Ok... So why me? Why are you not selling them to him?" Mucklow asked, sensing a scam.

"At present. Mr Boswell buys fifteen cars from me each week. It is very lucrative for both of us, but Mr Boswell has found himself in a position where he cannot take all fifteen." Williams explained looking at Boswell.

"Yes, fifteen is becoming rather too much for me to handle. I do not wish to bring unnecessary attention to my business and besides, this is relatively small time for me. I would be happy to share the burden with newfound friends." Boswell smiled warmly, but Mucklow did not trust it.

Billy Mucklow thought hard about the proposal, smoked his cigar and sipped a small glass of Irish whiskey which Isiah Boswell had insisted on paying for.

"Ok." Mucklow finally spoke. "Firstly, I want to buy them at the same price he pays." Mucklow pointed to Boswell. "I'm sure it's less than what you have just suggested… And secondly, what is the catch? What do you want from me in return?"

"Firstly, I want you to stop attacking my associates and stop intimidating my businesses. This turf war ends today!" Boswell raised his voice and pointed an intimidating finger at Mucklow. "Then there is one other small detail we would need you to take care of for us." Boswell lowered his finger and smiled again.

"Go on." Mucklow took another drink of his whiskey.

"There is a workman who has been causing some problems in the factory. A real far left Commy prick! He has been stirring up problems with the unions and keeps moaning about workers' rights and all that shit. He has been handing out pamphlets around the factory and people are beginning to take notice of the fucker!" Boswell explained giving Williams a sideways glance.

Williams sighed. "If he continues, he will slow down production and our little arrangement will be off!"

"So what has this got to do with me?" Mucklow asked. "You have plenty of thugs, why do you need me to sort it out?"

"The orrible' little red bastard is from your neck of the woods. Cradley Heath or somewhere like that. We have tried threatening him and some of my lads gave him a bit of a slap, but it doesn't appear to have worked." Boswell leant back in his chair and looked relaxed.

"Now I could deal with it myself but like I said I am trying to avoid that sort of thing Mr Mucklow… I'm a businessman, I'm trying to get away from the old cloak and dagger… I'm getting too old!" Boswell looked at his cigar and shrugged. "Besides, he's from your Manor… Now you are a man much like myself in my younger days and I look at you and think: What could I use ya' for? A man of your…" Boswell paused for a second to think of a respectful description. "Talents should be working with me, not against me…" Boswell smiled revealing an immaculate set of teeth for a man of his age.

"So, you want us to have a word with him?" Mucklow asked. His strong Black Country accent disappearing for the duration of the formal conversation. He had been an army officer and was used to addressing different people with different voices.

"No. He needs to leave work permanently…" Boswell's voice lowered and his eyes narrowed.

"You are asking me to commit murder?" Mucklow raised his chin disapprovingly.

"No, just keep the bastard out of work for as long as you can…" Boswell downed his whiskey. His work here was almost done. "Mr Williams will give you the details of our man." Isiah Boswell extended his right hand for Billy Mucklow to shake. "Friends?"

"Just one thing." Mucklow drained his glass and placed it down hard on the table. "If you try to fuck me or do anything against me or my family or friends, then you will need to make sure you sleep with one eye open and spend the rest of your life looking over your shoulder…" Mucklow fixed his gaze strongly on Boswell and looked deep into his cold eyes. Boswell matched the intensity of the stare and was by no means phased.

Then he smiled and extended his arm towards Mucklow once again. "Friends?"

"Friends." Mucklow shook the Brummie's hand firmly. It was the dawning of a new era.

Chapter 4

When the three celebratory friends arrived back at The Haden Cross, the place was jumping! In the main bar you could hardly move for people drinking, smoking and chatting.

'Rags to riches' by Tony Bennett was playing on the pub's recently installed jukebox and even Billy Mucklow was content to leave the confines of his back room and sit at the main bar drinking his beer and smoking cigarettes. As he sat, he watched some of the younger members of his outfit dancing and making loud, drunkard fools of themselves!

Dick Hickman was jigging around the floor, clicking his right hand in time with the music, holding a pint of beer in his left and smoking a cigarette as he mumbled random song lyrics.

Harry Scriven was sat next to Billy Mucklow at the bar. The beer and whisky had started to go to his head and the whole world seemed to glow with intoxicated wonder. Scriven was very much in 'the zone' and every song that played was his favourite and everyone around him was his 'best friend.' With each drink the room seemed to shine a little brighter and soon Scriven knew that he would be in danger of crossing over from being pleasantly mellow to full blown 'kaylied.'

It appeared that some of their party had already crossed over… He downed the dregs of his ale and banged the glass down on the counter, more than ready for his next drink. Out of the corner of his eye, a drunken Dick Hickman appeared before him.

"Harry!" Hickman shouted, grabbing Scriven in a drunken hug. "We fuckin' tode em today day we?"

Scriven laughed, thanked the bartender for his freshly poured beer and nodded at Hickman. He didn't exactly share Hickman's optimism, but he wasn't in the mood to argue. One detail from the day's activities was playing on his mind especially. He would speak to Billy about it later, at the end of the night when the two cousins sat alone in the side bar and drank whisky together. But for now, he was happy sitting back and enjoying the atmosphere inside the pub.

Hickman turned around and went back to the party. "How much is that Doggy in the window? The one with the waggerly' tayul!" Dick Hickman joined in singing with the record that was playing, twisted himself as if to shake his 'tail' and nearly fell over! Billy Mucklow and Scriven burst out laughing.

"Hey Dick, yow better lay off them shandies aer kid." Billy Mucklow turned around to face Scriven. "I heard yow got yourself a new wench?"

Scriven raised his eyebrows and turned to face his cousin. "Who tode yow?"

'I believe' by Frankie Laine began to play on the jukebox and Scriven sat back and thought of Irene Miller in a drunkard moment of wonder.

"Ar just heard." Mucklow lit another cigarette.

Scriven knew that Mucklow had not 'heard' anything as he had not shared his personal details with anyone. He figured that Mucklow had surmised this all from the fact that Scriven had spent a few nights away from 'The Cross' as of late. He cursed himself for 'falling for the trap'and confirming the fact.

"It's about time yow settled daahn wid a bird mate. Yow ay a gettin' no younger… Me and our Mary av bin together for over ten years now!" Mucklow offered relationship advice.

Scriven knew that Billy Mucklow was a relatively good husband and a devoted father to his two children. But he also knew that his cousin had had numerous mistresses! His particular favourite of late being a half Jamaican girl from West Bromwich. Rumour had it that she was also involved with Lord Haden-Best who lived just across the park from the pub in Haden Hill house. Scriven figured that Billy Mucklow was not exactly the best person to be giving relationship advice.

"Fuck!" Billy Mucklow suddenly noticed that Dick Hickman had passed from being a 'happy drunk' and was now trying to pick a fight with one of the locals. "Sort him aaht…" Mucklow nodded towards Hickman and Scriven got up and walked over.

"Come on Dick, yow'm Kaylied Kidda." Scriven put his arm on Hickman's back.

"Fuck you Harry, just cus yam Billy's fuckin' blood, yow think yer can fuckin' order me abaaht!" Hickman squared up to Scriven. "Fuck you Harry!"

This often happened when Dick was drunk. Harry Scriven was not in the mood to fight. "Listen Dick, do ya want Billy to come over and sort this out? Yum best gooin home an sleepin it off. Be ready for that bit of business tomorra."

Hickman looked at Scriven, looked over to the bar where Billy Mucklow was watching intently and then back at the customer he was picking on. He came to his senses and burst out laughing before grabbing Scriven and hugging him again. "Yow boys am like brothers to me."

Richard James Hickman (Dick) had been born into a relatively stable family. His parents were not wealthy but he had been an only child and had been consequently spoiled rotten. From a young age, his parents had strived to give him everything he had ever wanted and he had grown up with a constant demand to be centre of attention.

He had come to Billy Mucklow's attention in the boxing ring where he had been a talented and extravagant showman. His boxing success had earned him a reputation as a tough guy and this was exactly the sort of man Mucklow wanted in his organisation. Reputation counted for a lot. In Mucklow's mind, if people already feared and respected you, you only had to hurt half as many people to get them to do what you wanted.

Dick Hickman eventually went home in a taxi and the rest of the clientele in The Haden Cross left in good time too. It was the end of the night and Harry Scriven and Billy Mucklow settled down in the side bar with a bottle of Jameson's Irish whiskey.

Mucklow lent over, produced his lighter and lit Scriven's cigarette. "Somethings on your mind Harry. Ar can tell."

Scriven lifted the cigarette from his lips and looked at his cousin, wandering which way to approach the conversation.

"What was the name of that chap from the Union?" Scriven eventually began.

Billy Mucklow pulled the cork from the whiskey and slowly poured a little into two glasses. "Ray Jones, he lives in Cradley Heath." Mucklow pushed one of the glasses in Scriven's direction.

"Yer want it done tommora?" Scriven picked up his glass.

"The longer we leave it; the more chance he gets to spread his Communist bull shit araahnd' the factory."

Scriven took a sip of his drink. "Do ya think he deserves to suffer this way?"

Mucklow paused, wiped his brow and then sat back in his chair. "If we allow this cancer to spread, then what next?" Mucklow banged his glass on the table angrily. "This is not fuckin' Russia!" He raised his voice knowing that he could not intimidate his cousin. "Business is business. Progress is progress. The progress of my, no our family…" Mucklow looked away in frustration. "If this fella stands in the way of what is mine and my children's destiny then I will break him with no remorse."

"But what about the chap's family? Their destiny?" Scriven wasn't convinced.

"Maybe they should realise that being a do-gooder is not going to get them anywhere and they should strive to better themselves." Mucklow laughed and poured more whiskey.

Politically Harry Scriven was inclined to agree with him, but he was used to fighting and hurting 'tough guys.' Picking on and seriously injuring a man whose only crime was to demand fair pay and conditions for himself and his fellow workers seemed a little harsh.

"Am yow a Bolshevik Harry?" Mucklow spoke with a mocking tone.

"Fuck no." Scriven responded. "Sounds like a great bit of business to me, but let's goo easy on the chap… Give him a slap and bung him a bit of cash?" Scriven looked at Mucklow pleadingly.

Mucklow respected the compassion in Scriven's eyes. They had been brought up to be good men. But ultimately he had an overpowering desire to achieve the best for himself and his family. Everything and everyone else came second and god help anyone who got in his way…

The next morning Harry Scriven woke up early. He always did when he had had a lot to drink the night before. He had a stinking headache and his mouth was dry, but he was awake.

He climbed down the steep stairway to his living room where he lit the fire, sat down and opened his cigarette case. The whole house was cold and damp as it had been throughout the night, but Scriven had been 'out for the count' in his drunkard state and he had been oblivious to the cold that surrounded him as he lay in his lonely bed. Now he sat enjoying the first cigarette of the day, contemplating what lay before him on this day of sin.

Billy Mucklow was also up at this hour. He sat alone in his large living room next to the grand fireplace and he too was smoking. He watched the flames as they engulfed the coal that crackled and burned inside the fire and he could not help but feel optimistic. He had agreed a truce with The Brummie Boys and now he was about to embark on another lucrative chapter in his family's history.

Dick Hickman would come to his house at ten to ten and then he would drive to the bottom of Barrs Road where he was due to pick up his cousin Harry Scriven. They would then drive to Cradley Heath, do the deed and then be back in the pub before opening time!

Raymond Jones lived in an old Victorian terraced house in Hollybush Street, Cradley Heath. It was cramped and pokey but inside was well kept and clean. Ray's wife Doris worked hard to make sure that

41

her home was as nice as it could be and that their two young children were well cared for.

Mr Jones did not drink alcohol and he had very little vices other than his occasional fondness for home rolled cigarettes. He was a good provider for his family, but in his time and affections they would often come second to his devotion and commitment to his political cause.

He was not a member of the Labour party, in fact he often disregarded members of the Labour party with scorn. In his mind, all they seemed interested in was the price of beer and fakes! His own beliefs went much further than that. *Why should he and his comrades spend all day slaving away in the factory whilst the suits upstairs earned more money and did less work! If everyone worked together for the greater cause, then they could all earn an equal amount!*

Ray Jones hated the British class system with a passion. As a child he had listened to his father moan about 'them upstairs' and as he had gotten older he had grown frustrated with his father's constant ramblings without action.

He had agreed with his father but could not understand why men with such strong political opinions sat back and did nothing! Men such as this sickened him even more than those who considered themselves to be his social and financial superiors. These men would sit around in pubs moaning about their jobs and their working conditions, but they did absolutely nothing about it! Ray Jones believed firmly that the lack of action from these men was what kept things as they had always been and it was his mission in life to help try and change the political and social face of Britain.

Each week he would meet with a small band of likeminded friends and they would discuss how they could put the world to rights. They called themselves the Rowley Regis Municipal Borough and North Worcestershire Communist Alliance. They would meet every Thursday night at the Worker's Institute in Lower High Street where Ray Jones would take meticulous minutes which would then be stored at his home in a row of lever arch folders.

These files took pride of place on a shelf in his living room and Jones would regularly recount the minutes to his wife as she sat and sewed. He would watch himself in the large mirror that stood above the fireplace as he paraded around the living room as if giving a political speech. Every so often he would pause for dramatic emphasis and to let the importance of his words sink into his own and his wife's mind whilst regarding himself with the utmost admiration.

He was a short and weakly built man with small, brown eyes that nestled above a rather large and almost comical nose. He sported a small but immaculately kept goatee beard that in his mind gave him a Lenin-esque appearance.

His wife was a skinny and particularly unattractive lady, but she hung on every word her husband said and was a devoted wife and mother.

On this cold Sunday morning in January, the Jones family were gathered inside the living room. Doris was busy shining her husband's boots for the week ahead and Ray was sat listening to classical records. He hated modern 'pop' music. To him it was all about love, romance and the acquisitions of superficial belongings! Ray had no desire to own a car or a big expensive house. All he ever wanted was to live a simple and meagre existence with equal rights for all.

His two children had very little toys and Jones believed that this was important so as not to fill their heads with superficial needs and desires. Christmas had never existed for the Jones children. It was just a commercial money-making tool that helped to feed the capitalist machine modern existence was a slave too! Besides, Ray Jones was a staunch atheist who in true Communist tradition believed all religion to be an unnecessary illusion and a hindrance to the human race.

There was a sudden knock at the door.

"Who on earth could that be?" Jones snapped at his wife.

"I don't know dear. I will goo an' find out." Mrs Jones stood up and went over to the front door, her two children following over to see who the mysterious visitor could be.

The Jones children were aged eight and nine years old and the couple had had them at a relatively young age as Mr Jones had not quite reached his thirtieth birthday. He had not served during the Second World War as he had been deemed to be in a 'Reserved Occupation' through his work in the factory. This was what he had told people but in reality certain medical conditions involving his heart had made him ineligible for national service. However, he had been secretly relieved at this as he would have found it very difficult to take orders from men who were considered to be his social superior!

Doris opened the door and was surprised to see three burly men looking back at her. At first she thought that they may be Police officers, but they were far too well dressed for that.

The man in the middle was about six-foot-tall and wore an expensive looking camel coloured Crombie with a fine black trilby which slanted slightly to one side.

To his right and slightly behind him stood a very similar looking man of almost identical height and build. He also wore a Crombie coat and trilby, though his coat was black.

To the left was a younger man who was shorter than the other two and of smaller build. He too was dressed in similar attire.

"Good morning Madam. Would it be possible for us to speak to a Mr Raymond Jones please?" Billy Mucklow spoke. He was the man at the centre of the trio and was polite and pleasant.

"Hang on one moment please." Mrs Jones came away from the door and called her husband over. "Please do come in out of the cold." Mrs Jones welcomed the three men into her house.

"Thank you Mrs Jones." Mucklow greeted as he climbed onto the doorstep and into the Jones' front room. There was no hallway in these old houses and the front door always lead directly into the first room.

Dickie Hickman followed and said nothing, but Harry Scriven flashed a nervous smile and muttered a small thanks.

Ray Jones looked at the men and took an instant dislike to them. Their clothes stunk of money and capitalist posturing. "What do you want?" He suddenly stood up and spoke impolitely to his visitors.

Bill Mucklow looked at the two children. "Mrs Jones. Perhaps you could take your children out for some cake whilst we discuss business?" Mucklow produced a one pound note from his brown leather wallet and handed it towards Mrs Jones.

"We do not want your stinking money!" Ray Jones erupted. "What right have you to burst into my home on a Sunday morning and order my wife around?"

"Mr Jones, we have urgent business we wish to discuss and would appreciate it if we could conduct such business in private." Mucklow was hiding his impatience well and turned to face Mrs Jones. "I apologise most sincerely madam for any inconvenience, but we really must talk to your husband alone. If you prefer we could take your husband out in the car for a chat?" Mucklow nodded towards the door where his cream-coloured Riley RM was parked outside.

"No, it's ok. I was going to walk the children raahnd' to me muthers' anyway." Doris Jones went over to a dark wooden hat stand that stood near the door. "Martin, Linda, come and put yer coots on. We'm a gooin to Nanny Pegs."

The two children walked nervously over and collected their coats before heading out of the front door with their mother.

"How dare you! I demand you explain the meaning of this at once!" Ray Jones had waited for his wife and children to leave before completely exploding in a fit of anger.

Mucklow looked at him and said nothing for a good few seconds. His eyes cold and emotionless.

"Mr Jones. Could I use your lavatory please? Is it through there?" Mucklow pointed to a doorway that led to the back of the house.

All of these old Victorian terraced houses were laid out pretty much the same way and Mucklow assumed that there would be an outdoor toilet and outer building. Ray Jones raised his eyebrows and looked at Billy Mucklow with a face of disbelief.

"Yes, it's out the back. This better be important!"

Mucklow went through to the rear of the house and walked across a small courtyard into a small 'outhouse.' There was still a light covering of snow on the ground and Mucklow was careful so as not to slip on the cold floor.

He had no need of the lavatory whatsoever but wanted to inspect the small room. He opened the door and looked around until he spotted, nestled in the corner, the contraption he had been looking for. He made a mental note of its location and picked up a small plant pot from off the side.

On the way across the courtyard he had spotted an overfull, semi frozen rain butt that had been used to collect rain water. He dipped the plant pot into the icy stagnant water and pulled up a full pot before placing it back inside the outhouse. He sighed deeply and then ventured back into the main house.

"Right… Now you tell me straight away what this is all about!" Jones demanded as Billy Mucklow entered back into the living room.

"I'm not here to debate politics with you Mr Jones. But I believe that men should be free to shape their own destiny through their actions and the paths that they choose. It appears that you have been and that you continue to be a hindrance to progress and Mr Williams at Longbridge has asked me speak to you regarding your attitude and activities at work."

Mucklow nodded for Hickman and Scriven to move in. Jones had feared already that this was another 'message' from the underhand 'suits' at Longbridge. *So I have to take another minor beating. So what, these people think they can bully people but they cannot break me!*

"This way please Mr Jones." Mucklow gestured to the door and the route he had just negotiated from the outhouse.

Jones walked slowly and mournfully through his own house as Dick Hickman stood in front and Harry Scriven followed behind him.

There was no point trying to fight. He thought. *That would only make things worse.*

On arrival in the outhouse, Ray Jones stood as tall as he could and held his chin up high. *He would not show fear!*

Bill Mucklow looked into his eyes and held his gaze for what seemed like an antagonizing age, then without warning he punched him hard in the stomach. Jones fell to the floor immediately, moaning in pain.

As he fell, he expected the other men to 'put the boot in' and give him a kicking. But it never came. Suddenly, Scriven pulled him up by the scruff of his neck and then grabbed hold of his hair, pushing him face down on to an old oak table.

With absolute horror, Ray Jones looked up and saw that he had been brought over to the old cast iron mangle that his mother had used to dry the washing when he was a child. As Scriven held him pinned to the table, Bill Mucklow grabbed his right hand and held it to the mangle.

"No, no, I will stop! I will stop!" Jones protested desperately.

"I'm afraid you have said that before Mr Jones." Mucklow began to turn the handle at the side of the old-fashioned contraption and Jones let out a horrifyingly disturbing scream.

Harry Scriven winced and almost vomited at the sickening sound of Jones' bones shattering and cracking inside the cruel device.

Bill Mucklow showed no pleasure in the torment, Scriven knew that there were others that would. This was strictly business and was much more agreeable than taking the worker's life, but Scriven could not help but feel sorry for the poor man. He did not agree with his political beliefs, but the man certainly did not deserve this.

Scriven closed his eyes to the horror and held the struggling man firmly in place as his cousin continued to turn the handle. With each dreadful turn, Jones choked and cried with the harrowing agony. He vomited his breakfast all over himself and then, when he could not bear the pain any longer, he passed out on the table.

"Wakey-wakey Mr Jones. I need you to be awake to enjoy and remember this special memory." Mucklow cruelly tipped the ice-cold water from the small plant pot over Jones' anguished face. This disappointed Harry Scriven and he gave his cousin a look of utter disbelief.

"Arrm' sorry mate, but you wouldn't listen to reason. Yow need to learn from this." Mucklow unwound the device as quickly as he could and Ray Jones collapsed back onto the floor in a pool of his own vomit. Mucklow now appeared to show a little more compassion and Scriven offered the injured Communist a sip of whiskey from his hip flask. Jones shook his head.

"Yow ay gonna be at work for a bit aer kid…" Hickman grimaced as he saw the shameful state of Ray Jones' right hand. He thought for a minute then smiled cheekily. "Which hand do ya wank off with?" Hickman asked as he erupted in fits of laughter. Mucklow sniggered and held back his laughter for the sake of his cousin.

Scriven was not impressed. *Here is this poor guy who no longer has a right hand, and these two am teckin' the piss!*

"Let it be a lesson to you Mr Jones. You will no longer be fit to work at Longbridge. I suggest you find other means of employment." Mucklow took out his wallet again, produced a crisp £20 note and placed it on the table. "Here, use this to help you get by for now." Mucklow turned around and went back inside the house and out to the car. Dick Hickman followed him but Harry Scriven stood routed to the spot.

"Yow gunna' be alright mate?"

"Fuck you!" Ray Jones lay crumbled and broken on the floor. Harry Scriven had no words for him. He left hurriedly and went out to the car, it was to be another afternoon spent in the pub…

Chapter 5

Harry Scriven lay alone in his icy-cold bed listening to the rain beat mournfully against his bedroom window. He closed his eyes and longed to be able to stand outside and feel the rain wash away the events of the previous day and cleanse his soul.

He was a hard man and this was the life he had chosen. But to Scriven it was all about being able to justify his actions in his own mind. Ronnie Hall was every bit as rotten as himself and after what Hall had done to Wilf Dugmore, Scriven had felt that his own actions towards Hall had been perfectly acceptable. He just wished he could feel the same way about his involvement with Ray Jones.

After leaving the Jones' house the previous day, Scriven, Mucklow and Hickman had done as they did every Sunday. Over to The Haden Cross for a bellyful of beer then back to the Mucklow household where Billy's wife Mary had cooked a ridiculously large Sunday roast.

There, the three friends and the Mucklow family had been joined by Hickman's fiancé Shirley before continuing to drink copious amounts of red wine, smoke cigarettes and crack distasteful jokes about the unfortunate Ray Jones.

Billy Mucklow had insisted there be no talk of business in front of the women and children, but Hickman had come up with smart remarks at every opportunity.

Later on that night after Hickman and his fiancé had left, Billy Mucklow had tried to justify the day's activities to Harry Scriven and had insisted that he would 'look in' on the Jones family from time to time and make sure that they never went short. *That was Billy Mucklow for you!* Scriven thought. *A ruthless gangster, but at least he had some kind of morale code.*

Scriven sometimes wished he could be more like his cousin. Billy Mucklow never felt guilt over anything and he did not apologise to anyone. Though he had not always been like that.

The Second World War had changed many men and Mucklow's position as a commanding officer in a heavy combat situation had given him the ability to make hard decisions for the greater good. Scriven often wondered about how he himself would have turned out if he had played a different role in the war. He had originally trained as a motor mechanic and had spent the war as an RAF technician, but if he too had killed people for King and Country, would he be colder now like his cousin?

It was 5:30 in the morning and it was still pitch-black outside. Harry Scriven cursed himself for drinking too much yet again as he lay in discomfort with a banging headache and gnawing stomach pain. He promised himself (as he did most mornings) that he would drink less alcohol that day, but he already knew that he would probably break that promise…

At least he had no work to do today and he decided that he would get up, have a big breakfast at the Café in Cradley Heath before heading over to the boxing club where he could take out his frustrations on the heavy punch bags.

Later he would drive over to Tipton and see Irene. She never expected to see him on a Sunday as he always had a familiar routine involving the pub and Sunday dinner at the Mucklow's. But Monday was different. Scriven allowed himself to fantasise for a minute about one day taking Irene over to the Mucklow's with him. They could officially be considered 'together' and Irene could sit with Mary and Shirley.

He had had many lady friends in the past but this time it was different. He had never wanted to take women to 'meet the family' before, *so this one must be special!* He thought to himself.

He knew that he was a long way from this though. Irene was a married woman and was still living with her husband and their adult child. Scriven found this incredibly hard to think about. Every night as he

lay alone in his bed, Irene was lay there next to *that man*… He wondered
if she would ever leave her husband and come and live with him.

Billy Mucklow had also woken early that morning and had
driven his children to school in the rain. After, he had called into a few
local businesses and chatted briefly with the owners. They had all tried to
offer him free goods, but he always refused and insisted on paying for
everything he needed. He knew that Dick Hickman and a few of the
other men that worked for him took advantage of the 'respect' that was
shown, but Billy always made sure he paid a fair price.

He genuinely believed that any business that paid 'protection'
money to him deserved something in return. He felt that he was giving
them a legitimate service and strived to achieve this. If a pub paid him,
he always made sure that there was never any trouble with rowdy
customers and that the Police never knocked on the door during a 'lock
in' after closing time… He really was quite a useful friend to have, but
naturally, this all came at a cost.

Of course, if any local pubs decided not to pay, then Billy
would always make sure that there was plenty of 'trouble' with fighting
and the Police would always pay a visit as soon as closing time had
come. It really was as simple as that.

Mucklow was also 'connected' higher up and had lots of
influence with the brewery and the unions. He could create and end
union problems for a price, though political devotees such as Ray Jones
were a real problem as they could not be bought and every so often they
would have to be made an example of.

Billy Mucklow, his wife and two children lived in a large nineteen
twenties detached house that stood on the brow of the hill on Barrs road
which led from Cradley Heath to Haden Hill cross. The house was raised
on a slight bank which led up from the road and a large garage in which
Mucklow could park his prized Riley saloon was nestled beneath.

On return to his home, Billy Mucklow had settled into his red
leather armchair and reached over for the black Bakelite telephone which

stood on a small circular table within his expensive, well-appointed living room.

He carefully turned the dial with his index finger and waited for Isiah Boswell to pick up at the other end. A maid answered the call and swiftly went and brought Boswell to the phone. Billy Mucklow explained that Ray Jones would no longer be a problem and that he was now ready to collect his first batch of 'surplus' cars from Longbridge.

The pair agreed the arrangements and Mucklow was pleased that things seemed to be going well with his newfound ally, though it was not the first time Billy Mucklow had made such arrangements involving 'surplus' materials.

In 1953 he had arranged a deal to sell army surplus guns from an old Army contact in Gloucestershire to some Cuban rebels he had been put in touch with through some friends.

Unlike many British people in the nineteen fifties, Billy Mucklow was not a racist and he had made good friends with some Black Jamaicans who had come to Britain in the late 1940s as part of the 'Windrush' generation.

They had contacts in Cuba who needed guns for their political cause so Billy Mucklow was happy to 'acquire' surplus weapons from the British army - for the right price! He thought that it was somewhat ironic now that only a few months earlier he had been selling guns to communist rebels and now here he was disrupting communism within the factories…

'Protection' rackets were the main source of income for the Mucklow family, but every so often, a lucrative opportunity would arise and Billy was always happy to take full advantage of the situation and sell to the highest bidder!

He wished Isiah Boswell good day, hung up the phone and settled back into his armchair to let his hangover catch up with him. He had always insisted that the best cure for a hangover was to get up early and throw himself into the day.

He reached into his suit pocket and pulled out a silver-plated cigarette case when there was a sudden and aggressive knock at the door.

Wondering who on earth it could be, Billy Mucklow placed the cigarette case on the grand marble mantel above the large art deco fireplace and walked purposefully into the hallway towards the front door. *Who the fuck could this be?* He thought to himself. *Ar bay got time fer coppers!* The intense hammering on the front door started again and Mucklow assumed that due to the ferocity of the knocking it was probably the local Constabulary.

He flung open the heavy wooden door and looked down to see a very agitated looking Dickie Hickman.

"What?" Mucklow asked impatiently. Hickman was literally foaming at the mouth with anger and could barely spit words from between his gritted teeth. Billy Mucklow went back inside the house and gestured for Hickman to follow before shutting the door. The two men walked through the hall and into the living room. "Sid daahn." Mucklow invited but Hickman remained standing, ready to burst from the anger that simmered within him.

"Here, drink this." Mucklow went over to the elaborate drinks globe that stood in the far corner of the grand sitting room and poured his friend a large Irish whiskey.

Hickman snatched the drink and downed it in one swift gulp. "Someone's gunna' fuckin' die!" he snarled. Mucklow poured another drink and wondered for a brief second if Hickman was angry with him? He certainly had no reason to be, an argument with his young associate was the last thing he wanted to do.

"What yow blartin' on abaaht?" Mucklow asked and poured a drink for himself.

"Some bastards blagged the Express and Star newsagent on the Halesowen Road this morning!" Hickman clenched his fists and failed to conceal his anger. Mucklow thought for a minute.

"Why blag a newsagents? It ay exactly crime of the century is it?" He shook his head and wondered why Hickman was so pissed off about it. "What's this got to do with us?"

Hickman looked at Mucklow with a livid stare. "Ma Missis werks theyur dow er!" he growled, raising his voice far louder than many men would dare to. Mucklow had forgotten that Hickman's fiancé Shirley worked in that particular shop.

"The bastards gid er' a good hidin' day they! An one of em' felt er' up!" Hickman clenched the cut glass tumbler so hard that it broke in his hands and blood started to trickle down his arms and onto his pristine white shirt.

Mucklow let out a long and deliberate sigh whilst trying to think of words to say. He was slightly annoyed for his friend's sake but in the grand scheme of things, the event was hardly significant. He wandered over to the fireplace and thought as he picked up his discarded cigarettes from off the mantel piece. *Everyone knew that Dickie Hickman got kaylied and went home and knocked is Mrs abaaht'a bit. What difference did it make if somebody else did it for a change?* On previous occasions Billy had even had to speak to Dick about it himself as he didn't agree with hitting women and Shirley's concerned father had asked him to intervene.

"It gets fuckin' better!" Hickman snarled.

"What?"

"They day teck nuthin'. They tode Shirley it was a message for us!"

Mucklow's heart started to sink. He had just silenced Ray Jones for Isiah Boswell and now things were kicking off again. Had he been a fool? *Had this all been some elaborate plan by Boswell to get Jones out of the way and get revenge for the Ronnie Hall attack? How could he have been so stupid!* Mucklow cursed himself under his breath.

"They said: Fuck yower ode mon, an fuck Billy Mucklow! We'm a cumin for ya!" Hickman explained, still raging.

Mucklow thought very carefully about his next move. He did not know for a fact that this was The Brummie Boys and he did not want to jeopardise his relationship with Isiah Boswell should it turn out to be somebody else behind the attack.

"Am the Police involved?"

"Ar" Hickman replied.

Mucklow swallowed down the last of his whiskey.

"Right. Yow goo and find Harry'. He will probably be at the boxing club." He walked into the hallway and grabbed his hat and over coat from the hat stand. "If he ay there, try the Raand a' beef pub in Colley Gate. He guz in there sometimes."

"Where yow gooin?"

"Ar'm gunna speak to ode Bill. See if Inspector Turner knows anythin."

Dick Hickman immediately left the house and went outside to his 49 Vauxhall Velox. He opened the front door and threw himself into the driver's seat. He opened up the choke and pulled on the starter. The car burst into life and Hickman engaged first gear and set off for the boxing club they all used in Halesowen.

As he drove he swore, cursed and pledged a violent and bitter revenge on whoever had dared touch his girl!

He arrived at the club and as soon as he walked through the tatty old wooden doors he was instantly met by a number of adulating fans.

Dickie Hickman was like royalty to them, a local boxing champion and one of their own! He loved the attention and despite the current situation and all of the anger he was feeling he couldn't help but lap it up and pose for the boys at the gym.

"Alright lads, ow bin ya? Ar'm a lookin' for Harry Scriven. As he bin in?" Hickman pushed back his immaculately side parted hair and flashed a cheeky smile.

"Ar, he's a beatin' shit arr't on heavy bags raahnd the back aer kid." A friendly local replied.

"Saahnd Kidda."

Sure enough, Harry Scriven was at the back of the boxing club, dripping in sweat and throwing hard punches at the heavy bags.

"What yow want?" Scriven saw Hickman and his heart sunk. Bang went his day off!

"Billy needs ya. Summets' a kickin off."

"Fucks sake." Scriven turned around and started walking towards the showers. "Whas gooin on?"

"Some fuckers blagged the newsagents on the Halesowen Road. They gid mar wench a slap!"

Scriven raised his eyebrows "Am yow the only one aloud to gid er' a slap then?" His joke was inappropriate but was said deliberately to wind Hickman up.

"Fuck yow Harry!" Hickman squared up to Scriven. "Me and yow in the ring, right now come on!"

Harry Scriven was tempted. Dickie Hickman was the prize fighter and a better boxer, but he was half the size and weight of him and the cocky little shit had long needed teaching a lesson… But now was not the time or the place.

"That ay gunna' help us sort these fuckers aaht is it?" Scriven joked giving Hickman a smile. "Ar'm a jestin' yer mate."

Hickman still struggled to accept the ill-timed joke but he half smiled and tossed his eyes upwards. "Ar'll see yer back at Billy's then mate. Saahnd."

When Hickman and Scriven arrived back at Mucklow's house, Billy was already waiting for them. The three men gathered in the living room and Bill Mucklow poured whiskey for everyone.

"Yow spake to Ode Bill?" Hickman was impatient for news. Scriven sat and listened quietly.

"Ar. It wore The Brummie Boys thank god! Inspector Turner reckons it was some chap from over Tipp'n way. Fella' called Jimmy Danks."

Harry Scriven's ears pricked up.

"How does Turner know?" Hickman asked.

"The shap keeper was shown a photo of Danks and he swore blind it was him. Apparently this Danks is trying to make a name for himself at the moment." Mucklow explained, relieved that his business with Isiah Boswell was not in jeopardy.

"Did mar Missis see the photo?" Hickman bit his knuckles.

"Ar. Danks was the one that interfered with her mate."

"Ar'll slit his fuckin' throat!" Hickman jumped to his feet.

Mucklow paused and thought for a few seconds. "We will need to meck an example aaht on him. We cor av folks thinkin' they can come raahnd' ere' and meck fewls aaht' on us like this!" Mucklow sipped his whiskey. "We just gorra' find the fucker first. The cozzers ay got no fixed address for him, other than that he's from Tipp'n."

Harry Scriven sat back in his chair and smiled. "Ar know where he drinks…" he said gleefully. Mucklow and Hickman turned and looked at him intently.

The three men hatched a plan and went to pick up Barry O'Leary. Scriven had remembered that Danks usually had three or four men sat with him in The Fountain so an extra man would come in handy.

During the drive to Tipton, Harry Scriven thought constantly about Irene Miller. *Would her pub get damaged? Would Danks hurt her to get back at him? Would Irene not want to see him again once she found out what he was really like?* A thousand questions drifted through his mind. He finally came to the conclusion that if things were to get serious between the two of them, then sooner or later she would have to find out about his 'professional' activities. He knew that she would be in the pub tonight. She always worked on Monday nights because they would usually meet up.

Scriven pulled up outside the Fountain on Owen Street Tipton and brought the Prefect to a halt.

"Right Harry, yow know what ter dew?" Mucklow asked as he turned to face Scriven from the passenger seat.

"Ar" Scriven replied. He was actually quite looking forward to teaching Danks a lesson. He got out of the car, entered the pub and was relieved to see that Jimmy Danks and his crew were sitting in their usual spot. He slanted his trilby over his face and turned his collars up so as not to alert them to his presence.

He walked over to the bar and saw Irene's daughter Suzy. Irene was busy serving another customer and had not noticed him.

"Can I have five pints of mild on a tray please wench?" he asked Suzy, being careful so as not to speak to loudly and attract attention.

In the meantime, Mucklow, Hickman and O'Leary had also snuck into the bar and had discreetly sat down at a table just around the corner from the gang so as to be out of view from Danks.

Scriven wondered for a moment about how accurate the Police had been. *Were they really sure it was Jimmy Danks? Or was he just a nuisance they wanted sorting out? Either way, Danks needed a kicking!* The idea went through his mind that maybe the Police were setting them up to sort Danks out, but then he remembered that the shop keeper had identified Danks and so had Hickman's fiancé Shirley. His biggest worry was if Dickie Hickman went too far and the noose would be beckoning!

Scriven took the tray of beer and carried it over slowly towards Danks' table, adrenaline and anticipation flowing through his body. He placed the tray down on the table in front of Jimmy Danks and waited for the Tipton thug to look up.

"A little peace offering after the other night lads." Scriven announced, referring back to the brief altercation a few nights earlier.

"Look who it is boys!" Danks sneered. "It's that flash bastard whose bin bangin' the ode slag from behind the bar!"

Scriven smiled and half laughed. Then in one swift move, he slammed Danks face down hard into the tray of beer glasses. Blood and beer sprayed across the table and before Danks could react, Scriven lifted his head from out of the glass with his right hand and smashed him in the nose with a hard straight left, breaking it instantly.

He then pulled back his right fist and followed up with his signature combo, one, two, three, four quick fire straight right punches that threw Danks back off his chair and onto the floor, semi-conscious and bleeding.

As the Danks gang got up to defend their leader, Mucklow, Hickman and O'Leary jumped in from behind. One of the gang threw a lazy punch at Dick Hickman but the boxer demonstrated his skills by neatly dodging the punch and countering with a lightning fast combination of jabs, hooks and finally an upper cut that dispatched the unsuspecting thug to ground just in time for Harry Scriven to volley him in the ribs as if he was kicking a football. The man screamed in agony clutching his ribs and was dazed by the quick-fire onslaught of boxing technique.

Just feet away, Billy Mucklow knocked a man to the ground with a violent head butt and then the whole pub gasped in shock and horror as Mucklow picked up a circular cast iron table and smashed it down on the man's face, ripping his jaw clean off!

Barry O'Leary was busy trying to fight off two men, but they were getting the better of him. Dick Hickman reacted quickly and within a matter of seconds, Hickman had knocked one of them to the ground with a master class in boxing technique. Barry O'Leary then cracked a beer bottle in the other man's eyes and proceeded to pummel punch after punch into his face as he lay on the floor.

Irene Miller had witnessed the whole occurrence. At first, she feared for her lover, but then she had been quite shocked by his casual ability to put down one of the fiercest men she knew. She couldn't quite work out if she loved him more or less as a result of his actions.

He looked over to her and smiled. It was a warm smile full of a love and tenderness that completely betrayed the presence of the other men's blood that was splattered across his shirt and face. At first, she did not quite know how to react so she averted her gaze before looking him in the eyes and returning the smile.

"Right, this is what yer get for messin wid mar bird!" Hickman pulled out a knife and moved towards Danks who was lay on the floor propped up against the wall.

"Leave it Dick! Think abaaht Ong' Mon's noose!" Bill Mucklow warned, very aware of the death penalty they would face for murder. "We dow wanna' dangle!"

"Ar'm a gunna slit his fuckin' throat!" Hickman raged. Mucklow and Scriven both knew that he wasn't joking. The two men grabbed their friend and Mucklow forced his arm behind his back, holding him in a solid lock.

"Drop the knife!" he yelled in Hickman's ear. "There is a line you cannot cross!"

"What good will yow be to Shirley dangling on the end of a rope mate?" Scriven reasoned with his associate and Mucklow applied more pressure causing Hickman to wince in pain.

He screamed out long and hard, venting a mixture of anger, frustration and pain from Bill Mucklow's hard lock. He took a deep breath and finally dropped the knife to the floor.

Scriven put a comforting arm around him and led him out of the pub followed by Barry O'Leary.

Bill Mucklow lingered for a minute before going over to Jimmy Danks who lay bruised and battered against the wall. Mucklow lowered himself and whispered casually in his ear.

"If yow try anything like this again, I will let him carve you up like a piece of meat in the fuckin' butchers shap!" Mucklow grabbed him by his heavily blood-stained collar. "Do you fuckin' understand?" he raged through gritted teeth. Danks nodded and mumbled an inaudible response through his broken teeth and bleeding face.

Chapter 6

Jimmy Danks awoke in a pool of his own blood next to an empty bottle of Scotch. Every bone in his skull was hurting and he was still bleeding from the various cuts that covered his bruised and broken face.

He had managed to crawl out of the pub before the Police and Ambulance service arrived but he had heard since that one of his gang, Pete Glover, had been taken to hospital and would probably have to wear a wire on his jaw for the rest of his life.

Apparently, the Police had been asking questions but nobody had told them anything. That just wasn't the way they operated. *It didn't matter now anyway.* He had been humiliated in front of the whole pub and his associates, there was nothing left for him here and he didn't want to be seen by any of them again.

He would make his way to Liverpool and then catch a boat over to Ireland. He had family over there and it seemed the ideal place for him to go and start all over again, he had failed. But before he went, he had some business to take care of…

He felt a shiver of excitement tremble through his body as he imagined exactly how he would take his revenge and visualised just exactly what he would do.

He had already taken payment from his boss for what he had done to the girl in the newsagents and now there were only two left on his list. Harry Scriven's woman and Bill Mucklow's wife! *But the boss would have to make do with just one more.* Jimmy Danks intended to do an 'extra special' job on this one.

Danks did not have a fixed address of his own but he tended to sleep in a disused council house on Laburnum Road on the Tibbington estate.

The 'Tibby' as it was known locally was first built in the late 1920s and early 1930s and had a particularly tough reputation. Danks had originally lived in the house with a young woman whose name the house was still registered to.

The two had been engaged to marry, but Danks' violence towards her had been relentless and horrific and she had eventually managed to escape.

Danks actually enjoyed hurting women, physically and mentally. It turned him on and on this day he planned to entertain some of his nastiest and most obscene fantasies in his quest for revenge.

He recalled memories of how he had beaten and sexually used his previous partner Margaret. It almost brought a smile to his aching face and certainly effected his body in other ways.

Danks got up from off the floor and walked over to an old dresser that was a solitary piece of furniture in the rundown living room. He opened the top drawer and pulled out a large hunting knife. Danks ran his fingers over the blade to feel the cold steel and then closed his eyes and imagined how he would use it later, his body continuing to stir. He placed the knife in his jacket pocket, reached up on to the top of the dresser and felt through the dust to pull down an old shotgun. He cocked it, checked that it was loaded and then snapped it back into place before pulling down a substantial wad of cash and shoving it in his pocket next to the knife.

He took his flat cap from off a rusty iron nail that hung on the wall as a makeshift hanger and ventured outside with his gun in his hands.

Out in the cold yard he found his only true friend. The one thing in this world he cared about other than himself. He extended his hand and stroked the main of his faithful horse. 'Jilly' had served him for many years as a 'Rag un' boone mon' and he spoke affectionately to the old girl.

"Ar gorra' goo away ode girl." He patted her nose lovingly. "Ar woe be back umm me babee." With that, he raised the shotgun to the horses head and shot her point blank between the eyes. The beast shuddered and brains spewed out over the yard. The body instantly fell to the ground and shook violently for a few seconds before turning permanently still.

Danks almost shed a tear as he wiped residue from his face and placed the gun back inside the house. He took one last look around and then went out of the door for good.

Irene Miller's twenty-year-old daughter Suzy listened to loud 'Rock n Roll' music inside The Fountain as she cleaned up after the events of the previous night. The pub was due to open at midday so she had three hours in which to get the place ready. She felt tired as she worked, the Police had stayed until late and had asked lots of questions about what had gone on. Nobody had said anything. Jimmy Danks was a notoriously bad man who had been involved with lots of other bad people, it was far safer to simply 'mind yer' own business!'

Danks was certainly not popular with the Police either and as he had disappeared quickly after the fight in the pub, it was unlikely that there would be any follow up. The Sargent investigating had even joked to his colleague that he would "like to buy the fuckers' a beer!"

Suzy had originally been assisted in the clean up by her mother, but Irene had had to pop over to the other pub for an hour so Suzy was now left alone.

She liked to have the pub to herself as she could play her music loudly and sneak the odd glass of gin and tonic!. What she did not know was that on this particular morning, an evil lustful pair of eyes were watching her intensely through a gap in the curtains.

As his eyes watched, the man's heartbeat raced with anticipation and he breathed loudly and deeply as he watched the young woman with evil intent. His hot breath on the cold windows smeared in front of him as he watched her buttocks move around the bar in exceptionally tight denim. Her red hair was tied up in a bun and he could see her full and impressive cleavage heave and bounce as she worked. He watched for a while but could resist no longer.

Jimmy Danks had originally intended to 'have' the older woman, this would hit Harry Scriven harder and was what his boss had specified, but the daughter would do nicely instead. He knocked the door and waited for an answer.

"We ay open yet bab." Suzy said cheerily as she appeared at the door. "Oh Mr Danks!" she was surprised to see the regular customer at the door after the events of the previous night. "I didn't see yer goo last night, am yow ok?" she asked with genuine concern.

Suzy Miller was mostly unaware of her mother's involvement with Harry Scriven and only knew Jimmy Danks as one of the customers in the pub.

"Ar'm a feelin a bit rough actually wench, was hopin' yow would let me in to warm up and have a glass of whisky?" Danks held his collars tightly to his chin and shivered with the cold.

Suzy instantly felt sorry for him, though by the smell she could tell that he had probably already had a more than his fair share of Whisky. She opened the door and gestured for him to come in. "Come an sit daahn a bit."

He sat down at the bar and waited as she poured him a large Scotch. The whole time he did not take his lascivious eyes of her curvaceous rump that was accentuated by her tight denim jeans that clung provocatively to her shapely young thighs. He was going to enjoy this.

She continued to make polite conversation, anxious for gossip about the previous night. Danks was barely listening, he watched her like a predator watches its prey in the jungle. Her deep scarlet lipstick on those big full lips, her heavily made-up brown eyes and her long teasing red hair, he could not take it no longer.

He got up and walked over to the cigarette machine. "Shit Bab, the fake machines bosted, goo and fetch me some from upstairs me wench."

"Is it a bosted' again? Bloody thing." She replied. "Ar'll goo and fetch some."

Danks seized the opportunity and followed her up the stairs to a large storeroom that stood above the pub.

"Yow cor cum up ere Mr Danks." She said, startled by his menacing figure which loomed in the doorway. He grinned a twisted lascivious grin of pure evil.

"Did yow know about yower slut of a mutha?" he asked, pulling the knife out of his pocket and blocking the exit.

"What, what do yer mean?" Suzy asked, gasping for breath, almost paralysed with fear.

"That bloke who comes in here, the chap who beat the shit aaht on me last night, he's bin avin an affair wid'yower Mom!" Danks sneered.

Suzy had had her suspicions, but her father wasn't a particularly nice person and she wouldn't have blamed her mother even if it was true, but right now she was more concerned with the current situation.

She desperately moved her eyes around and searched in vain to find an escape from the room, but the windows were bolted and Danks blocked the only exit.

"Yer see, ar cum daahn here to see yower mutha, and maybe ar still will once ar've dealt with yow!" His eyes penetrated her so deeply that she already felt violated.

His face was covered in scars and fresh dirty cuts that were still bleeding and he was missing most of his teeth, the ones that remained were black and rotting and his breath stank of whisky and decay. This was truly worse than her most horrid nightmares.

Danks laughed and then grinned his twisted evil grin again. "When yow woke up this morning Susan, did yer think for one minute that this may be your last day upon this earth?" He breathed heavily with excitement. Suzy's bladder gave way and she wet herself before starting to sob uncontrollably.

"This is the end for you Suzy..." Danks exclaimed with pleasure. "How bad it will be depends on how good a job yer do in yer last minutes. Now get over here and get daahn on yower fuckin' knees!" He moved closer and grabbed her hair as she knelt obediently, sobbing, the knife glistening in his hands. He could hardly bare the tension.

From outside the pub, something didn't seem right. Harry Scriven peered through the pub windows and could see Suzy's discarded cleaning materials on the floor, but no sign of Irene or Suzy?

He had struggled to sleep all night, worried about any reprisal from Danks against Irene after the fight in the bar. He had got up early and decided to drive over and check everything was ok at The Fountain.

Upon his arrival Scriven could not see anyone through the window so he discarded his cigarette, trod it into the floor and tried the heavy front door. To his surprise the door opened, *why wasn't it bolted?*

He walked a few steps into the pub. "Irene?" he called, completely unaware that Irene was not there and of what was going on upstairs.

He moved through the bar and forwards to the foot of the small stairwell that led to the upstairs storeroom. *There must be somebody here somewhere,* he thought. *Why would they leave the front door unbolted?*
Something was definitely not right...

He stood at the bottom of the stairs and listened hard. He thought he could hear muffled voices coming from upstairs so he began to climb the stairs, being careful so as not to make them creak. *Did Irene have another man up here?* He thought to himself, his heart beginning to sink with disappointment. As he climbed further up the stairs, the voice became a little clearer...

Suzy did not want to die, *she was far too young, and what about her mother? Would he really go after her once he had finished?* In the horror of the moment she could not comprehend her thoughts and was unable make sense of any of it.

Danks still held the knife to her throat as he stood in the middle of the room and continued to enjoy her ordeal, his head back and his eyes closed in total ecstasy. He did not hear the soft sound of leather winkle pickers approach stealthily from behind.

"You utter, utter bastard." The voice was that of Harry Scriven and Danks suddenly felt the intrusive barrel of a pistol pressed into the back of his head. "Drop the knife!"

Danks hesitated,

"I said drop the fuckin' knife!"
Danks dropped the knife to the ground and Scriven kicked it across the old oak floor.

"Get up Suzy."   Scriven could feel an intense anger burning inside of him and an overwhelming desire to punish Danks for his sick crime.

Suzy had never been so relieved to see another person, she hurriedly got up and turned her face so as not to see the man who would haunt her dreams for the rest of her life.

"Yow ok bab?" Scriven asked as he held the gun firmly to Danks head, knowing that she was probably far from ok. She nodded her head and suddenly burst into another fit of sobbing.

Scriven thought for a second and allowed the fire to build inside like a fiery demon he could pull out whenever the situation deemed necessary.

Danks began to mutter something under his breath and then started to chuckle.

"Yer know Harry, ar come here today for yower bird. Ya know, the ode slag, her mutha." Danks turned to face Scriven defiantly and stepped closer into the gun.

Scriven ignored the comment. "Get on yer knees ya bastard" Scriven smiled "Let's see how yow fuckin' like it…"

Suzy looked up, she didn't think for one minute that Harry Scriven would be into *that sort of thing!*

"Do yer like boys do ya Harry?" Danks began to laugh hysterically as he got down on his knees and then looked up at Scriven with a lewd perverted smile.

"Open yer fuckin' mouth" Scriven ordered and Danks obeyed, looking at Scriven the whole time, daring and goading him as he slowly opened his mouth to reveal the foul smelling remains of his black teeth.

Scriven lowered the barrel of the gun into Danks' mouth and pulled back the hammer. Danks closed his eyes and muttered a gypsy curse which was illegible with the gun thrust firmly into his throat.

As he knelt and waited to die he wished in that moment that he had never got involved in any of this. *He had been doing ok on his own, why did he take orders from someone else? Why had he been so eager to move higher up? He had been doing well on his own with his own little gang! He was only 38 years old, he could still have a life, in Ireland. He was not ready to die!*

"Wait" he protested, Scriven was just able to understand him.

"What?"

"This ay mar dewin" Danks, pulled his lips clear of the gun.

"What yow mean?"

"Ar was paid ter dew it."

"Yow tellin me that some fucker paid yer to attack Dickie Hickman's Wench and then this today?" Scriven doubted the story. "Bollocks."

"It's true, somebody much bigger than me is planning to make a move against the Mucklows." Danks' voice began to take on a slight pleading tone.

Scriven suddenly realised that there was a slight possibility that Danks was telling the truth. *Had Isiah Boswell put him up to this?* He thought to himself.

"Who put yer up tew it then?" Scriven demanded.

"If ar tell yow, ar'm as good as dead, yow might as well pull the trigger."

Scriven put the gun to Danks head, laughed and pulled the trigger. Danks closed his eyes and tensed his whole body and in what seemed like an absolute eternity he realised that the hammer had clicked and nothing had happened. The gun had not been loaded.

Harry Scriven laughed and kicked Danks hard in the face sending him sprawling across the room. Danks made a grab for his knife but Scriven stood on his hand, his smart leather shoes moving from side to side as if stubbing out a cigarette. Danks raised his free hand to try and pull Scriven to the floor but Scriven stamped down hard on his stomach, winding him terribly.

"Piece of shit!" Scriven snarled as he looked down at his victim and then turned and picked up the discarded hunter's knife. He raised it high and then rammed it straight through Danks hand and into the wooden floor.

Danks screamed like a wild animal as Scriven pushed and twisted it deeper into the floor, pinning him to the spot as if he was about to be crucified.

Scriven stepped back and pulled out his cigarette case. Danks remained pinned to the floor, wildly lashing out, unable to reach Scriven, hissing and spitting curses and insults.

"Suzy, goo an fetch us a cuppa' tay love. Bring the kettle up here, meck sure its red hot!" Scriven looked at Danks and smiled. "Yow want one tew dow yer Jim?"

Danks spat at him, missing.

"So." Scriven lit his cigarette and breathed in deeply. "Who put yer up to this?" the smoke escaped from his mouth as he spoke.

"Fuck you!" Danks replied. Scriven pulled up a nearby chair and sat down whilst enjoying his cigarette.

"Believe me, ar'm askin' yer a whole lot fuckin' nicer than Billy Mucklow will…"

Jimmy Danks did not doubt that this was the case. "Fuck you!" He spat again.

Scriven stood up and walked over to the window. It was a crisp cold January day and the sun shone brightly without giving off much heat. The remains of the recent snowfall still clung partially to the rooftops of the nearby buildings in Owen Street and Scriven noticed that some of the houses held substantially more snow than others. He figured that this was due to them being warmer and therefore melting the snow faster.

He had actually enjoyed beating on Jimmy Danks these last couple of days. *Danks was pure evil and deserved everything he got...* The more he hurt Danks, the more he felt the pain and guilt surrounding his involvement with Ray Jones melt away like the snow on the roof of the houses. It was all very therapeutic.

Suzy Miller returned to the room carrying the freshly boiled kettle of hot water and a cup of tea for Harry Scriven.

"Yow drink the tay love. Goo an wait for me daahnstairs, ar'll be daahn in a bit." Scriven took the boiling hot kettle from her hand.

Suzy gratefully accepted the tea and walked slowly back down the stairs, still traumatized by her experience.

Scriven looked down and noticed that Danks' flies were still undone. He casually walked over and poured a substantial amount of the boiling water onto Danks' crotch. Danks grunted through clenched teeth, swore and cursed some more. Then Scriven poured a small amount onto his face. The swearing and cursing continued.

"This could all be avoided." Scriven put the kettle down on a nearby table and looked down at Jimmy Danks who was suffering before him. "Yow've got two choices. We can get Billy over here with a big bag of tools, or yow can tell me who put yer up to it? Then yow can fuck off an' never come back..." Scriven stood beside him menacingly. "What do you say Jim?" Scriven kicked the knife gently and Danks winced and trembled with the pain. "Ar can pull this aaht right now." Scriven kicked it again, this time harder. "Was it Boswell?"

Danks shook his head "Nah" he said, his hand throbbing with the most intense pain he had ever experienced, the knife still pinning him to the ground.

He lay back slowly and rested his head on the floor, sweat flowing from his over stressed body. Jimmy Danks closed his eyes and thought about his childhood. *If his father had not beaten him with his belt every night of the week, maybe he would not have turned out like this? Maybe if his mother had not allowed it to happen, he would not hate women so much?* Danks' mother had been scared of his father, but she put her husband before her only son every time, she always allowed her husband to hurt him, *to use him.* He let out another loud shriek as Scriven kicked the blade again, tearing the nerves in his hand and reducing it to a bloody mess.

Scriven got down on his knees and grabbed the knife with his left hand and thrust his face into Danks' "Who put yer up to it?" he yelled, yanking the knife back and forth causing further excruciating pain.

Danks mumbled something, trying to speak. Scriven let go of the knife and got back to his feet.

"Ar wore gunna' kill her honest!" Danks lied, almost in tears at the memory of his mother. "Ar was just doing what ar was told."

"Just tell me who put yer up to it and yow can goo…" Scriven was losing his patience. "Was it Boswell?"

"I ay ever met the bloke." Jimmy Danks could take no more. He trembled and lay his head back again. The blood was running from his mutilated hand and he was on the verge of passing out. He mumbled a name quietly.

"Ar day hear ya!" Scriven lowered his head to hear the name.

"Brian Tanner" Danks repeated a little louder. Harry Scriven was surprised, he had been almost certain that it would be The Brummie Boys.

Brian Tanner was a feared and respected gang boss from Wolverhampton. He was in his mid-fifties but was still very much active on the gangland scene.

Most of the Wolverhampton underworld was under his control and so was much of the town of Dudley. For years Brian Tanner and the Mucklow family had tolerated each other. Parts of Dudley came under Tanner's control, other parts were run by the Mucklow family. Tipton had been a sort of 'no man's land' full of rough and ready tough guys such as Jimmy Danks who did not pay protection money to anyone.

"Why?" Scriven asked, unconvinced.

"He had heard that yow boys were gettin involved in some big business with the Brummies. He promised me something fer me an mar lads. He said that yow lot were a bunch'a Champagne Charlies and that yow had gone saft. He said yer weren't the same since Ode Mon Mucklow retired (Bill Mucklow's father) and that yow were all loved up wid yer wenches." Danks was struggling to talk with the knife in his hand. "He told me to meck a move on yer families and that would meck ya gid up the rackets raahnd Dudley." Danks stopped to breathe, the effort of talking was too much for the severely injured man. "Ar'm a tellin the truth, ar swear on the soul ov' me mutha."

The more Scriven thought about it, the more it all seemed feasible. He continued to question Danks until he could tell him no more.

Warily, he got back onto his knees and yanked the knife from out of Danks' grotesquely mutilated hand. He stood up quickly and readied himself for a swift attack from Jimmy Danks. But it never came.

Danks got up with difficulty, unable to use his shredded hand. Scriven thought that the damage would probably be permanent, *but that was just. Suzy Miller would have to live with the day's events for the rest of her life.* Danks was the scum of the earth and Harry Scriven had no pity for him.

He followed him back down the stairs and into the bar where Suzy was sat alone sipping a large gin and crying softly to herself. Danks had no remorse. That was just the way he was. That was the way he had been made. He grabbed a couple of bar towels, tied them tightly around his injured hand and left the pub without as much as a backwards glance.

Scriven went over to Suzy, sat down beside her and gave her a big hug. He held her there in is his arms and comforted her after the horrendous ordeal she had been put through. She felt safe there, reassured, she could see what her mother saw in this man and for a moment she felt slight jealousy.

"Ar'm so sorry for all of this Suzy. If it weren't fer me, none of this would ever of happened." Scriven felt bad that this young girl and her mother had been dragged into his world of violence. She did not answer him, partially because she agreed with him and partially because she just did not want to speak.

The Fountain did not open that day. On Irene's return to the pub, Scriven and Suzy explained what had happened. Though Suzy had omitted a lot of the details. There were certain things a mother should never know about her daughter and she could not bear the shame of her mother's pity.

Chapter 7

Brian Tanner banged his fists down on his desk "What do yer mean yer dow know where Jimmy Danks has gone?" He was the sort of man who wouldn't have looked out of place sitting suspiciously on a park bench watching children play.

He was short and round with wiry unkempt hair and always wore a pair of half-rim spectacles which covered small, pig-like, goggled eyes. He spoke in a high pitched nasally timbre and when he spoke spittle would often fly from his mouth. He was in his mid to late fifties and was not the typical charismatic, dapper gangster.

Brian Tanner was certainly not a tough guy, but he was utterly ruthless and a master of manipulating people into doing exactly what he wanted them to do. He surrounded himself with men who were more than capable of fighting for him and he carried each and every one of them in his pocket alongside much of the local Police force and anyone else that was of any use to him.

He had several cruel methods of getting to people and was not afraid to do whatever it took to achieve his aims.

Not long after The Second World War, a wealthy scrapyard owner had refused to pay protection money, so Tanner arranged for his thirteen-year-old son to be badly beaten as a warning. On another occasion a local restaurant owner had also refused to pay, so Tanner arranged for thugs to viciously attack the Restaurateur's Eighty-year-old mother.

That was Tanner's way, he knew exactly how to scare people and would play on their insecurities and the innocents around them to get whatever he wanted.

He wasn't like Jimmy Danks, he took no sick and twisted pleasure in hurting defenceless vulnerable people, it was just business and it gave the otherwise physically weak and unintimidating manpower.

Until recently, Brian Tanner had been content with his life. He had complete control of most of the underworld in Wolverhampton, its surrounding towns and also most of the town of Dudley.

But just recently he had become more ambitious. He had plans to drive the Mucklow gang out of Dudley and then make a move on their territories in Netherton, Old Hill, Blackheath and the various parts of Halesowen and Cradley Heath.

Tanner had had an understanding and a relatively respectful relationship with William Mucklow senior since the 1930s but since the Old man had retired, Tanner was beginning to feel that it was his right to become 'top dog!'

He had heard that Billy Mucklow junior was a tough character who was more than capable of looking after himself, but he had also heard that the younger Mucklow was negotiating deals with businessmen in Birmingham and was losing interest in the day-to-day business of protection rackets, bookmaking and unlicensed boxing.

On this day, Brian Tanner sat in his expansive Tettenhall townhouse in a grand office which occupied one of the downstairs rooms. Sat before him at his large oak desk was Sidney Walker, a member of Jimmy Danks' outfit who had taken a beating at the Fountain a few nights previously.

"He's gone Mr Tanner, we ay sid' him since Billy Mucklow an that lot gid us a lampin' in the Fountain th'utha night!"

"Yow bin to his house?" Tanner demanded.

"Ar, some fuckers av shot is oss!" Walker had been round to Danks' house in Laburnum Road and had found nothing apart from the dead animal in the yard.

Tanner paused for a second and clenched his face in bemusement "What der'ya mean somebody shot is oss?"

"Somebody shot is oss wid a gun Mr Tanner, med a right fuckin' mess!"

"Was it Mucklow?" Tanner asked with a little concern. "He cor know it was me who told Danks to attack them women?" Tanner was beginning to get a little nervous and was starting to regret his actions.

"Ar dow know Mr Tanner." Sid Walker wasn't the smartest individual and his stupidity was beginning to test Tanner's patience.

"Just remember, we never ad this conversation…" Tanner got out of his chair and went over to the door. "If yow do see Jimmy then tell him I want a word with him." Tanner flung the office door open. "Now, fuck off!"

Walker picked up his cap sheepishly and scuttled out of the door. "Thank you, Mr Tanner." He said, doffing his cap as he went across the hall and out to his old Austin truck that was parked outside.

Tanner felt the icy cold of the January day brush against his cheeks and decided he would like to go for a walk in the fresh air to think things through.

He picked up his sand-coloured mac and put it on before shouting a brief goodbye to his wife and striding purposefully down the path that led from his house. *What should he do next? Leave things be? No, his daughter was expecting her fourth child and his son was soon to be married. His family was expanding and he wanted to provide more wealth for them. He would make sure his instructions were acted upon and he would soon have Billy Mucklow right where he wanted him!*

As Brian Tanner walked briskly across the pavement and away from his house, he had not noticed the jet-black Ford Prefect that rolled slowly along the road behind him, stalking his every move, its occupants dressed in long black coats like reapers of death.

Tanner suddenly realised that he was being watched and froze to the spot. In front of him stood an old oak tree that was dripping thawing snow onto the dark pavement. He was too old to try and run and he had recently been diagnosed with a serious heart condition.

He stood rooted to the spot and waited for the car to pass by, but it did not. It came close behind him and he could hear the clattering of the side valve engine before two doors opened in almost unison.

"Hello Brian..."

Tanner recognised the voice. "Billy Mucklow, we dow see yer raahnd ere' much, how am ya son?"

Mucklow smiled and opened the rear door. "Get in Brian. We would like a little chat."

Harry Scriven stood on the other side of the car next to the driver's door, watching the small, overweight and quite pathetic older man with discontent. *This sick bastard ordered the rape of mar' wench!* He thought to himself as he struggled to hide the seething anger from his expression.

"Oh, ok Bill, can dew." Tanner waddled slowly towards the car and dropped nervously into the passenger's seat. He knew that if he tried to escape he would give up his guilt, he had no choice but to try and 'front it out' and act like nothing had happened. Billy Mucklow closed the front door and got into the back whilst Harry Scriven started the engine.

"Where we gooin boys?" Tanner asked, trying to remain calm. There was no reply. "Hows the ode mon?"

"Yeah he's good ta Brian." Mucklow replied pleasantly.

The car passed through the towns and streets of Wolverhampton until eventually coming out into the Shropshire countryside.

As they drove, Tanner continued in his attempts to make polite conversation as if everything was normal. Scriven remained deathly silent and Mucklow was polite but short in his responses.

Scriven drove the Ford deeper and deeper into the remote countryside, the sky appearing to darken instantly at the setting of the sun. The temperature began to drop drastically and Tanner watched his breath cascade rapidly into the icy cold atmosphere of the car.

"Whas this about lads?" His voice quivered, giving away his guilt.

"We want to have a chat Brian." Mucklow sat in the back seat and admired the countryside at dusk. The remnants of snow on the trees and the miles and miles of vast white fields looked somewhat spectacular in the clearness of the night sky. There was not a single cloud visible and Mucklow thought that it would be a long cold night.

The car slowed and turned onto an old track, the Ford's headlights barely lighting the way as they moved through the eerie darkness.

It took what seemed like an age for the car to slowly rise up and down across the bumpy terrain before coming to a halt outside a derelict farmhouse and outbuildings.

Tanner trembled with cold and fear as a darkly dressed Billy Mucklow opened the door and invited him to get out of the car. As he stepped out into the night the cold air surrounded him and he wished that he was back in his warm house with his wife.

The men then proceeded to walk towards the old farmhouse and Harry Scriven followed as Mucklow led Tanner into the dirty abandoned building.

The trio walked slowly through corridors of darkness and Tanner felt quite nauseous at the decaying odour of the foul-smelling rooms. Rats scuttled across the floor and a bat nearly touched them as it was disturbed by the visitors. Tanner began to fear the worst and cursed himself silently for ever speaking to Jimmy Danks.

They stopped at the entrance to a small room at the very back of the building and Tanner shielded his eyes against the light as Mucklow pulled an ancient cord, illuminating a single bare light that hung and swayed in the middle of the dingy room.

There was a small table at one side of the room and four rotting chairs were placed either side.

"Sit down Brian." Mucklow pulled back a chair and gestured for Tanner to sit down. He then picked up three porcelain cups and placed them around the table before taking out a large bottle of Jameson's Irish whiskey.

He poured a generous amount into each cup and pushed one across the table towards Tanner before sitting down in the chair opposite. Harry Scriven pulled up the chair next to his cousin and sat down, fixing his gaze upon the older man opposite.

"So." Mucklow paused, sipped his whiskey and stared coldly at Tanner as the single light bulb rocked back and forth casting menacing shadows in the dimly lit room. "Things were gooin so well Brian." Mucklow shook his head and looked disapprovingly at the table.

"What yow a talkin' abaaht?" Tanner laughed uncomfortably, frantically searching the other men's faces for signs of humanity.

Mucklow stood up slowly and retrieved a small brown briefcase from a dark corner of the foul, damp smelling room. He placed it on top of the table next to the whiskey and used painstakingly slow movements to open the bronze catches and reveal its contents to a distraught and horrified Brian Tanner.

Inside were a variety of sharp, rusting tools. A manual hand drill, various pairs of pliers and a hammer and chisel. Tanner looked at the torturous instruments and breathed deeply before urinating and feeling the warm liquid flow steadily down his leg and soaking his trousers.

He had failed to convince the men of his innocence; his nerves and worried manner had been scrutinized the whole time and it was obvious to Billy Mucklow that Brian Tanner had something to hide.

Mucklow took out a piece of rope and meticulously wrapped it around Tanner's waist, securing him to the chair whilst Harry Scriven tied his hands firmly behind his back. Tanner looked to the heavens and struggled to regulate his breathing.

Mucklow opened up his cigarette case, offered his cousin one and then they both lit up as they continued to stare intimidatingly at Tanner.

"What the Fuck is gooin on!" Tanner was getting agitated. "Do you know who I fuckin' am! Yer cor do this to me!"

Mucklow took a long drag of his cigarette before beginning to speak.

"Do you think it is acceptable to hurt innocent civilians Brian?"

Tanner looked up and stammered. "Ar dow know what yum talkin' about Bill."

"Do you think it's acceptable to order men to rape and assault women?" Mucklow remained calm. "Harry's Mrs? Dickie Hickman's bird?" Mucklow raised his voice slightly before screaming in Tanner's face, "My wife! My fucking Kids!"

Tanner looked at the floor and closed his eyes. He tried to speak but could not. Scriven watched calmly as the cigarette burned away in his fingertips. *How far would Billy go? He wouldn't go too far?* He hoped silently.

Billy Mucklow stood up and extinguished his cigarette on the floor. *If Tanner was allowed to get away with this then what would happen? It was an unwritten rule that you could not hurt civilians, people's families could not be put in jeopardy. He would have to make an example of the man.*

"Please Bill." Tanner pleaded in vain.

Mucklow sat down again and took a drink of whiskey.

"In France and Germany, I killed young boys." Mucklow took no pleasure in recounting the memories, he was not showing off and he was not proud of what he had done. "Young lads, eighteen years old with their whole lives ahead of them. We fixed our bayonets and carved them up in all sorts of horrific ways." Mucklow paused and let the horrific, traumatizing memories flood back to him. "I killed some of them with my bare hands... Young German lads who cried for their mothers when the cold steel cut into their flesh and spilled their guts all over the fucking floor... Some died very slowly, praying that they could see their mother one last time." A tear almost appeared in Mucklow's eye. "Do you think I won't fucking hurt you Brian?" He put his face into Tanner's and stared at him with haunted agonized eyes. He downed his Whiskey and poured some more. "Is it fair that those young men had to die whilst an utter bastard like you continues to breathe? Plotting the rape of young girls?" Mucklow slammed the cup down on the table and gave Tanner a back handed slap with such force that the chair flew onto its side. He turned to the briefcase and took out a pair of pliers which he held high so that Tanner could see them clearly.

"Danks took things too far Billy!" Tanner pleaded again as he lay tied to the chair on the floor. The swinging lightbulb cast a ray of light straight onto Mucklow's face and Tanner could see a man haunted by his past, haunted by the horrors of the Second World War and livid with the actions of a man who had threatened his family! Brian Tanner felt afraid.

Harry Scriven continued to watch, casually smoking his cigarette. He wanted to hurt Tanner, wanted to punish him for what he had planned to do to Irene, but Billy had told him not to. He did not want him knocked out, Billy Mucklow had other more disturbing plans and he always wanted his victims to be conscious and awake for as long as possible.

Tanner screamed as the pliers tore through his bone, ripping a toe from his foot, blood flowing frantically onto the floor, the sound of gristle and fracturing bone filling the air. Tanner reeled violently with the pain and pure rage filled his head.

"Fuck you!" he screamed as Mucklow went to work on another toe.

"This little piggy went to market, this little piggy stayed at home, but this little piggy..." Mucklow mocked him cruelly and applied the force again. Tanner spat more curses then shouted over to Harry Scriven.

"Hey you, quiet one, Scriven!" Mucklow stood up so Scriven could see their prisoner. "Yeah you!" Tanner started again. "I paid Danksy to hold a knife to yower Wenches throat! Ar told him to fuck the shit aaht' on er!" Tanner laughed hysterically as his toeless foot continued to bleed heavily onto the floor. Mucklow stepped back, took a sip of his drink and gestured for Scriven to take over.

Scriven stood up and looked at the tools. He was not as cold as Billy, he was not as haunted and deranged as his cousin. He was a brawler, he did not need tools. He heaved and pulled the chair back upright, Tanner spat and cursed as he did so.

"Hello Brian." Scriven mocked before hitting him with a hard right upper cut that broke his jaw and sent the chair reeling backwards onto the floor. Tanner erupted in laughter, partially trying to show his captors that he was not afraid and partially accepting that it was too late for him. His time had come.

"Ar bet she loved it the little slut..." Tanner spat his words and stared at Scriven, his eyes taunting him and daring him to go further.

Harry Scriven clenched his teeth so tightly in rage that his tooth chipped, he had seen how badly Suzy Miller had been affected by her ordeal and Tanner's lack of remorse enraged him.

He stood up and kicked Tanner continuously in the ribs and face, the older man coughing and spluttering on his own blood as broken ribs splintered into vital organs.

Just then, Bill Mucklow stood up and put a hand on Scriven's shoulder. Scriven stopped his onslaught and they both watched as Tanner lay strapped to the chair and proceeded to have a massive heart attack.

As he died, his grandchildren's faces passed quickly before his eyes, then he looked into the vengeful eyes of Bill Mucklow and Harry Scriven and they watched him take his last breath upon this earth.

Upon realisation of what he had done, Harry Scriven immediately ran outside and vomited into the remnants of the snow. His life would never be the same again and as he stood hunched against a tree, he heard the door open and the shadowy figure of Bill Mucklow emerged through the darkness.

He stood still for a minute or two and then finally began to speak. "Ten years ago, I stood on a landing craft just off the French coast... I waited and watched as countless men before me got out onto that beach and were butchered and blown to pieces. Their blood and body parts mixed with the frothy foam of the sea. Do you think ar was scared?" Scriven said nothing as Mucklow lit another cigarette.

"Ar was bloody shittin' meself… But I was an officer in the British army, stiff upper lip and all that bollocks. Ar couldn't let the men around me see that ar was just as scared as they were…

We got onto the beach and I saw a lot of good men, good men who were following my orders killed, like lambs to the fuckin' slaughter. Somehow, I survived and med it off the beach. But that was just the beginning of it mate." Mucklow sighed as he smoked his cigarette.

"That was June 1944 and for the next ten months we fought our way through Belgium, Holland and into Germany… The Krauts were pretty desperate by now but they refused to surrender. They started sending young kids, teenagers and ode blokes to the front line alongside men who had previously been considered unfit to serve. They put up a good fight but we killed and killed and killed and killed." Mucklow hung his head to the floor and composed himself. "Like I said earlier, young lads who cried for their mothers… We fought through forests, towns, rivers, everywhere! I saw many good friends killed and every day I wondered if that one would be my last…. Anyway, one day, April 1945, we entered a town in Northern Germany, Bergen." Mucklow shuddered at the mention of the name and blew smoke from his lungs. He took a long deep breath and continued to speak. "That afternoon we entered a concentration camp that had surrendered without a fight…. We went inside and what ar saw that day will stay with me for the rest of mar life…" The slightest of tears appeared in his right eye and proceeded to roll down the side of his face and dampen the collar of his meticulous white shirt. "Over about an acre of ground lay the dead and dying. People so skeletally thin that I could not tell who was alive and who was dead. I could not tell who was male, who was female, who was young and who was old…" Another tear emerged from his eye and his voice almost quivered. "I could tell children, babies, toddlers… Literally thousands of them, bodies, endless bodies… The smell was unbearable. I can still smell it now… Absolute hell on earth…" He raised his eyes from the floor and waited for a reaction from his cousin that never came.

Harry Scriven remained slumped against the tree staring deep into the forest, listening intently.

"From that day on, I felt less guilt for the things that I had done, the men that I had killed..." Mucklow discarded his cigarette and grunted a sarcastic laugh. "Ten years agoo, they gid us medals for killin' sick bastards like Brian Tanner. Today they'd dangle us on the end of a fuckin' rope!"

Scriven turned to face his cousin, Mucklow handed him the bottle of whiskey and he took a long hard drink.

"That fuckin' animal in there paid blokes to hurt our families." Mucklow raised his voice. "That is against the rules! And if we'd have let him get away with that, then what next? Would you go and hurt his kids for revenge?"

Scriven shook his head, his gaze still fixed firmly on the floor.

"No... Nor would I... That sort of thing simply cannot happen... Hurting civilians is not acceptable mate... Brian Tanner has bin a bastard for years, he deserved everything he fuckin' got... Besides, we day kill him anyway. He had a fuckin' heart attack!" Mucklow raised his right arm and placed a firm hand on his cousin's shoulder. "It's moments like this that either make you, or break you... Because of what happened here tonight, our families can sleep safer in their beds at night... Ar bin tellin' meself' that for the last ten years and its bloody true!"

Billy Mucklow went back into the room, ignoring the deceased that lay on the floor, he grabbed two shovels from a far corner and took them out to his cousin. "Dow talk. Just dig..."

The two men walked deeper and deeper into the woods until they came to a remote spot that would haunt Harry Scriven for the rest of his life.

He dug deep within himself to find the strength to cut through the icy ground with his shovel, with each stroke he pushed himself further as if the physical activity of what he was doing could dissolve the recent memories from his mind.

The mud stained his expensive leather shoes and cast dirty streaks across his suit. He watched in envy as Billy Mucklow treated the whole experience with a professional, mundane normality. He had done this all before. Buried comrades and enemies.

Scriven wished that he too could accept the magnitude of all that had happened and he wished that he did not fear the burning guilt and responsibility that would haunt his future dreams.

Chapter 8

Eleven months later and 1954 had proven to be an eventful year. Questions had been asked about the disappearance of the once feared and hated gang boss Brian Tanner, but his heartless, controlling and bullying methods were not missed by many other than his close family.

Tanner had always opted to pay as little as he could to the Police. He preferred to use black mail and threats of violence towards innocents to get people on his side. As a result, he was of no great loss to a lot of people. Maybe a rival gang had taken him out? Maybe his disappearance had something to do with Jimmy Danks? Who cared?

The Mucklow organisation had risen from strength to strength, they prospered in their dealings with Isiah Boswell and as the end of November neared, Billy Mucklow could not help but feel proud of a successful and lucrative year.

In fact, the whole world seemed to be finally on the road to recovery after the horrors of World War 2 just 9 years earlier. Even the musical landscape of the airwaves and The Haden Cross Jukebox was changing and embracing the new exciting teen phenomenon of 'Rock n' Roll!'

Rock Around the Clock by Bill Haley and his comets had been blasting out in the main bar along with other popular hits of the year, Shake Rattle and Roll, Earth Angel, Sh-Boom and of course, the arrival of the revolutionary and cutting-edge super star Elvis Presley with his trendsetting hit That's Alright Mama had made its mark on the youth of the day.

It was quite the soundtrack to the activities of the ever-successful Mucklow crew who stalked the locality in their sharp suits, gold jewellery and big flashy cars.

Every 'Teddy Boy' from Hagley to Netherton, Kingswinford to Oldbury was under the influence of the Mucklow family and every bit of criminal activity they were involved in paid tribute money to Billy Mucklow. With Tanner gone and Boswell on side as a friend, it appeared that there were no limits to the successes and wealth that were available to Billy Mucklow's band of merry men.

Despite the intense guilt he felt over events earlier in the year, Harry Scriven had also prospered alongside his cousin. He had upgraded the old Prefect to a gleaming 1951 Ford V8 Pilot and Irene Miller had finally left her husband, sold The Fountain pub and used the profits to buy a nice 1930s semi-detached house in the respectable suburb of Haden Hill for herself and Scriven to live in. At first, Irene's husband had protested and had tried in vain to regain the love of his long-overlooked wife. It had all come to a head one night and Harry Scriven had been forced to give him a 'bit of a hiding.'

The marriage was well and truly over and it was agreed that Irene could sell the Fountain on Owen Street and her husband would keep the Tilted Barrel in Princes End. He still saw his daughter Suzy occasionally, but she had opted to live with her mother and Scriven at their house on Beauty Bank Road, Haden Hill.

On this cold rainy Saturday evening in November, Suzy Miller was in the kitchen of the Beauty Bank house dressed in a sleeveless red and white polka dot dress that rose just above the knee.

She looked at her reflection in the kitchen window and she liked what she saw. She had applied her make-up and her big seductive lips pouted with a piercing shine and shimmer. Her eyelashes extended long and elegantly above her big brown eyes and her red hair was immaculately styled in the bouffant fashion complete with elaborate curls.

She no longer worked for her father in Tipton and she had now got a job working behind the bar at The Regis Club in Old Hill. It was a small night club that was run by a small-time businessman by the name of Albert Hackett.

Hackett fancied himself as something of a 'Billy Mucklow wannabe' and was looking to make a name for himself. He wore the sharpest of suits and was always flanked by his two imposing brothers who both had reputations as being particularly useful in the event of a fight.

"Where yow gooin?" Harry Scriven appeared in the kitchen and instantly noticed the alluring figure of his lady friend's daughter as she turned to greet him.

"Ar'm workin' tonight Harry. Could ya' gid me a lift to the club? It's throwin' it daahn aaht theyur!"

Scriven checked his watch and raised his eyebrows. "Ar. I suppose so. I've gorra' meet Billy up The Cross in a bit."

She looked at him and smiled. "Thanks Harry."

He could see why she was so popular with the lads at the club. She was stunningly attractive with lovely thick curves in exactly the right places. He couldn't help but look her up and down, admiring her beautiful brown eyes, curvaceous thighs and those red lips... But then he reminded himself that this was the daughter of the woman he had fallen in love with. Still, as she pulled herself into the lavish, lush interior of the Ford Pilot, he could not help but sneak a glimpse of her full thighs as she lent sidewards to pull the heavy door shut.

Suzy Miller knew exactly what she was doing and she loved it. Ever since Scriven had saved her from the evil clutches of Jimmy Danks she had held a soft spot for the older man. The way he dressed, his immaculate manners, his respect towards women and the way he could handle himself against bad men such as Jimmy Danks! *Everyone was scared of Harry and his cousin Billy and he was her hero!* He had saved her from the big bad wolf and now she tried so hard to make him notice her even though she knew in her heart that it was wrong. He was her mother's man. She had left her father for him so she knew exactly how much he meant to her. *But some innocent flirting would not hurt would it? Her own father had been one big let-down and this ruggedly handsome older man was only fifteen years her senior anyway.*

Scriven pulled up outside the Regis club and watched Suzy as she got out of the car and scurried up to the entrance whilst trying to protect her hair from the rain. He waved goodbye then put the Pilot into gear and drove back up the hill towards The Haden Cross.

He usually walked to the pub as it was only a few hundred yards over the brow of the hill from his new home, but tonight he took the car on account of the rain. He probably could have telephoned Billy and asked him if he wanted a lift, but it was too late now and Bill would probably have taken his own car.

Scriven parked on the car park and walked hastily into the pub so as not to expose his expensive suit to the rain. He had forgotten his over coat and the cold November rain caused him to regret this instantly.

He entered the main bar through a side door and noted that it was particularly full for an early evening. The smooth sounds of Dean Martin caressed the airwaves over the monotone hum of voices in the bar and Scriven strolled through the room to the Latin rhythm of 'Sway' which had been a hit for Martin in October.

He was greeted with cautious friendliness by many of the regulars in the pub and he responded with brief pleasantries as he passed through the bar and into Billy Mucklow's side room.

"Yow alright Harry?" Mucklow rose out of his chair and extended his right arm to shake his cousin's hand.

"Ar." Scriven smiled warmly at Billy. "Yow got me a beer?"

"Here mate." Dick Hickman was stood in his usual spot at the fireplace and gestured to a tray of ale that rested on the table.

"How's yower Suzy gerrin' on daahn the Regis club?" Mucklow enquired about the daughter of Scriven's lady friend.

"Mmmmmm, lovely Suzy…" Hickman butted in, referencing the fact that Suzy Miller was rather popular with local men.

"Fuck off Dick!" Scriven laughed, well aware of Miss Miller's popularity. "She seems to be gerrin' on ok as far as ar know Bill… Why yer ask?"

"That chap who owns The Regis is gerrin' a bit out ov hand." Mucklow stretched back in his chair thoughtfully.

"What, Bert Hackett?" He seems ok to me mate?" Scriven lent back against the window and took a generous gulp of his beer.

"Ar, I thought he was ok too, but aer kid Barry came raahd' the house today. Told me that Bert Hackett wasn't gonna pay protection money anymore... He reckons he can handle things himself!" Mucklow explained as he thumbed a beer mat.

Scriven couldn't hide the disappointment on his face as he pulled out his cigarette case. Things had been going well these past few months and he had hardly had to resort to using violence.

Every so often he would remember events from earlier in the year and he would freeze with the guilt as memories came flooding back. Sometimes he would awaken in a cold sweat in the middle of the night after the same reoccurring nightmare.

In the dream he was always strolling through woodland when suddenly he would find himself in the exact spot where he and Billy had buried Tanner. The hole would suddenly appear in the ground and the stench of rotting flesh would fill the air. Then as he peered into the grave he would see Irene and Suzy huddled together, dead and skeletal as Mucklow had described the victims in Germany. As he watched, a decaying Tanner would then appear from behind him, laughing as he had done on the night of his death. The laughing spectre would then push him into the hole and he would fall endlessly before bolting upright in bed. Scriven shivered at the thought of his dream.

"That fuckin' prick needs a good kickin'!" Hickman offered his thoughts on the Albert Hackett situation and was ever eager to overreact.

"Dow be saft Dick." Scriven did not share his over enthusiasm.

"Yow gor a better idea?" Hickman responded. His eyes deadly serious.

Bill Mucklow laughed, relaxed in his chair and put his hands behind his head. "Let me think abaaht it boys. I wanna' prove a point, but let's be subtle. Ar'm sure we can meck Hackett see sense without havin to hospitalise the bastard!"

Scriven appreciated his cousin's words. *Was it possible that Billy was mellowing slightly?*

The three men spent the rest of the night drinking beer, smoking cigarettes and talking about mundane everyday subjects. Women, boxing and football.

Every so often, Dick Hickman would suggest some ultra-violent solution to the Albert Hackett situation, but Mucklow and Scriven would always laugh it off and tell Hickman he had been watching "too many movies!" Mucklow just needed a few hours to think of a subtle and effective way to deal with the problem and make Hackett see the error of his ways.

At the end of the night, the three friends wished each other good night and arranged to meet back in the pub at twelve the next day. It would then be back to the Mucklow's after a few hours hard drinking for the traditional Sunday roast. It was a weekly tradition that was hardly ever missed.

Feeling slightly worse for wear, Scriven swung the V8 Pilot onto the driveway of his semi-detached house and fumbled for the front door key.

He assumed that Irene would be in bed fast asleep but was surprised to find Suzy still awake and stood up in the kitchen smoking a cigarette.

She was lent provocatively against the pastel blue work surface and Scriven couldn't help but notice her short dress creeping revealingly up her rear thighs as she gazed forwards out of the kitchen window.

"What yow doing still up?" He enquired as he entered the kitchen and placed his keys on the side.

"I only just got in. It was a busy night down at the club. Do yer want a cuppa' tay?"

Scriven had forgotten that he had dropped Suzy off at the Regis club earlier. "Ar. Goo on then." He lent backwards against the kitchen cupboards and steadied himself as he semi-soberly watched her pour the tea. "Good night at the club?"

"Was busy, thought they'd never goo home!" She added a splash of milk to Scriven's teacup and handed it to him.

"Hackett's dewin alright daahn theyur then?" He nodded a thanks for the tea.

"He always has a few punters in." She gave him a cheeky flirtatious smile and fluttered her lashes.

"Suppose he likes to goo on servin' ale after chuckin' aaht time?" Scriven sipped his tea and watched her eagerly.

"Ee' dow arf, bet them a still servin' daahn theyur now!" Suzy poured herself a fresh cup. "They said ar could come home at eleven though."

Scriven made a mental note of her revelation. "Be careful walkin' the streets by yerself Bab." Scriven's concern was genuine.

Suzy smiled again and looked at him with her big brown eyes. "Dow worry, ar got yow ter teck care of me now..." She winked seductively and Scriven blushed.

Was he imagining it? Was this ridiculously attractive twenty-year-old girl actually flirting with him? He passed it off as wishful thinking on account of the beer and was disappointed in himself for yet again lusting after his partner's daughter!

She raised a fresh cigarette to her full scarlet lips and he reached forward with his silver plated lighter and lit it for her. She sucked hard and took a long drag before exhaling provocatively into his face.

He stood mesmerised, breathing in and savouring the thick smoke, resisting the urge to pull her closer as they stood face to face in the small kitchen.

"Where's yer mutha?" Scriven broke the tense silence.

"She's in bed fast asleep." Suzy continued to breathe smoke into his face that mixed with the sickly-sweet smell of her inexpensive perfume. He blatantly held onto her gaze far longer than was necessary.

This was the same girl he had saved from the evil clutches of Jimmy Danks but she was no longer just a girl, she was maturing and he was beginning to find her totally irresistible. Suzy knew exactly what she was doing. *Why should her mother have 'her' hero?*

"Suppose ar better goo up ter bed." Scriven took a step back and took a large gulp of his tea. "I wanna give the car a wash tomora before I meet the lads up The Cross."

"Dow yer ever get bored of that place?" Suzy half laughed at the thought of Harry Scriven constantly going to the same pub with the same close-knit friends. "Yer could always come and see me daahn the Regis club?"

"Maybe I will pop in sometime?" Scriven slung the remnants of his tea into the sink and turned to leave the room. "Night Bab."

She put her cigarette to her mouth, took a drag and slowly withdrew it, narrowing her eyes sultrily before blowing more sweet smelling smoke in his direction. "Night Harry."

He took one last look at her and subtly glanced her up and down, taking in her full figure and heaving chest before half staggering out into the hallway and up the stairs to bed.

Harry Scriven awoke the next morning later than he had intended. He was instantly greeted to the alluring vision of his lady friend Irene who lay scantily clad next to him in a lacy silk nightie. She may have been approaching middle age, but she was still an attractive woman.

Scriven put a loving arm around her and silently cursed himself for his lascivious thoughts regarding her daughter.

"I day hear yer come in last night?" She enquired as she nestled within his big arms.

93

"Ar wore that late love." He couldn't quite explain why he was feeling the slightest pangs of guilt. Her blonde hair cascaded onto his chest and he felt happy and still very much in love with the marginally older woman.

"Ar'm gonna' pop raahd me muthas this morning before we goo over to Bill and Marys later." Irene raised her head and looked at him with her piercing blue eyes as if seeking permission. "Yer dow mind do yer?"

Scriven felt a mixture of fear, guilt and excitement at the idea of being alone in the house with Suzy. "Course not Bab. I need to pop over and see Bill in a bit. I need to have a chat with him."

"What about? Cor it wait? Yer gonna see him up the pub in a bit!"

"It's important Irene." He slipped away from her and sat up on the side of the bed.

"Cor yer teck me over to me muthas fust?"

Scriven groaned at the thought of having to drive her over to her parent's house in Tipton. "How yer gonna get back?"

"Me Dad can run me back."

Scriven smiled at the thought of Irene's ageing father driving her home in his old 1930s Austin. He hadn't had much involvement with her family as he had been regarded as the 'home wrecker' and the reason for why Irene had left the security of her husband.

He tapped her shapely thigh playfully and smiled. "Goo on then, but hurry up and put yer meck up on. I've got to see Bill after I drop yer off."

It was an intensely cold Sunday morning; the rain had eased off in the night and had been replaced by a weather front of high pressure that had brought a chill to the late November air.

Billy Mucklow had eaten breakfast in his large dining room with his family and was now sat reading the Sunday papers and enjoying the warm glow of the grand fire that stood within an intricate marble fireplace.

It had been a nice morning spent with his young family and Mucklow had all but forgotten the situation with Albert Hackett and the Regis club. He sat at the head of the vast dining table and read a newspaper article about a shipwreck in the Irish Sea on the previous day where six sailors had lost their lives. A Nat King Cole record span on the turn table in the corner of the room and Mucklow appreciated the peaceful cosy atmosphere.

The doorbell rang and Mucklow heard his wife Mary go through the hallway to answer it. "Oh hello Harry." Mucklow heard her greet his cousin. "Billy is just in the dining room reading the paper. Go on through."

"Bit early ay yer?" Mucklow joked as Scriven entered the room. "Pub dow open til twelve!" He stood up and gestured for Scriven to come and sit down at the table.

"Sorry to disturb yer mate. I wanted to talk about this business with Bert Hackett daahn at the Regis club." Scriven sat down next to his cousin.

Mucklow put down his paper and returned to his seat.

"Yer could'a told me up the pub in a bit?" Mucklow looked at him curiously.

"Ar found aaht summet useful mate. Thought I'd pop over, sorry." Scriven looked a little sheepish.

"Dow apologise, yum welcome here anytime, yow know that."

Scriven smiled a thank you. "I heard that Hackett's bin avin' lock ins! Late night boozing sessions at the club."

"Interesting." Mucklow looked into the fire. "How der ya know?"

"I av mar sources mate."

Mucklow laughed. "She a bit tasty? Yower source?" He knew exactly who had told his cousin about the late-night drinking sessions. Scriven ignored the comment. "Do yer want a cuppa' tay Harry?"

"No tah, be beer time soon!"

Mucklow laughed. "Ar." He looked at the fire for what seemed like an age, deep in thought. *Things had been going well. The last thing he needed was trouble and any unnecessary attention from the Police. Whatever he did, it would have to be subtle and low key.*

"Who's the best house burglar you know?" Mucklow suddenly looked up from the fire and caught his cousin's gaze.

Scriven didn't need to think about the question. A name came into his mind straight away. "Ar know someone. Why?"

"Have your man break into Hackett's house, place a bouquet of black lilies on his bed whilst he is asleep with a note that says: Best regards from Billy M." Mucklow thought again then laughed. "The bastard will shit himself knowing that somebody was in his room as he lay sleeping. He will know that his life is in my hands and that he needs to behave himself..." Mucklow smiled smugly. "In the meantime ar will goo an av a chat with the Cozzers. Meck sure they goo raahd his club every night at eleven! No more late night drinkin sessions! He will lose more money in revenue then what he has to pay me..." Mucklow shrugged. "Ar dow even need the money Harry, but it's the principle. If yer let one chap get away with it, next thing is everyone thinks they dow av ter pay!" To Billy Mucklow it was the ideal suggestion. *No unnecessary violence, nice and subtle.*

If Hackett dow respond to this then he deserves a kickin! Scriven thought, relieved to hear that Billy had opted for a relatively peaceful solution.

"Oh, one more thing Harry." Mucklow sat upright in his chair. "Meck sure yower mon dow steal a thing! This is about proving a point. We ay stealing from the bastard! I want Hackett to trust me again."

Scriven nodded.

"I mean it Harry! Give yower mon ten pound and ten shillings for his trouble, but meck sure he DOES NOT touch a thing in Hackett's house. This is important!" Mucklow over emphasised that nothing should be taken.

"When der yer want it done?"

"As soon as possible."

Scriven nodded as he looked at his watch. "Ar will pop raahd and see mar bloke now before we goo up the pub." He stood up as if to leave then suddenly stopped. "Where am we gunna get black lilies from on a Sundee?"

"Goo up to Gaunt's Underteckers at the top of Powke lane, tell em ar sent yer."

"Ok, get me a beer in for when ar get back to The Cross…"

The two men exchanged farewells and Scriven walked back over to his own house where his car was parked on the drive. He pulled out the choke, tugged the starter and the V8 fired into life. He tickled the throttle and smiled at the thunderous roar of the engine. He reversed off the drive and set off to find Chad Cooper.

Chapter 9

Chad Cooper lived in a modest workers house at the top end of Cokeland place Cradley Heath near the junction with Congreaves Road. The road had originally been named to commemorate the fact that in the early nineteenth century the Congreaves works of the New British Iron Company used this area to convert the coal to coke in preparation for its use in their blast furnaces.

Despite being a 'workers' house, Chad Cooper was a young man who did very little honest work. He was a master thief and his youthful dexterity and small size meant that he was perfect for sneaking stealthily into properties and stealing anything of value.

Chad Cooper was an almost loveable rogue. A likeable chap who was friendly, talkative and devoted to his young wife and daughter.

He was twenty-two years old, about five-foot six-inches tall and had short, scruffy hair. He wore thick spectacles and had a lazy left eye that had a tendency to look in a completely different direction to his right. He was not a wealthy man and this was reflected in the way that he dressed, but his proven abilities within his chosen field meant that his family were not starving.

He had previously served short prison sentences and the Police were constantly on his back, but he was good at what he did and was generally very careful not to get caught. However, deep down within him, Cooper harboured ambitions and a desire to make a name for himself and rise up the criminal hierarchy.

He was a short man, weighed less than nine stone and had no aptitude whatsoever for violence. But he looked upon men such as Harry Scriven and Dick Hickman with a mixture of respect and envy. He wasn't 'tough' enough to be part of a gang, but he lusted after the glamour, respect and fear these guys cultivated. He wanted to wear the sharpest suits and drive around in a big posh car! He had to start somewhere and when Harry Scriven knocked on his door on this cold Sunday morning he was almost thrilled that such a man had chosen to visit his home. He eagerly opened the door and invited him inside.

"Mr Scriven! Please come in. What can ar dew for yer?" Cooper stood aside and gestured for Scriven to walk into the front room of his house.

It was a small room with a high ceiling. A small, tiled fireplace stood on the far side of the room but was currently unlit. The Cooper family were gathered in the back room and it was economical to heat only one room at a time. Scriven noted that the room was simple but relatively modern and clean in its appearance.

He followed Cooper into the back room where the family spent most of their time and was instantly greeted by a quite adorable little girl who could not have been more than four years old. The little girl smiled warmly and Scriven noticed that a tooth was missing from the front of her mouth but she appeared healthy and well-loved.

"Hello" Scriven said, bending down onto his knee to speak to the child. She proudly showed him a picture she had drawn but he had no idea what it was supposed to be. "What a lovely picture." He lied uncomfortably and the girl ran to fetch her treasured Rosebud doll to show the gangster.

"Mr Scriven dow wanna see that Linda!" Cooper lovingly corrected his child and placed an affectionate hand on her head. "Sorry Mr Scriven."

"Dow be sorry mate. What a lovely dolly." Scriven smiled at the girl and pulled a shilling out of his pocket to give to the youngster. She eagerly took the coin and Cooper insisted that his daughter thank her benefactor.

"Jean… We have a guest." Cooper excitedly called his wife from the kitchen and a petite unattractive girl of about twenty years of age appeared in the doorway. She was scatty and looked rather unintelligent, she nervously extended her right arm to shake Scriven's hand.

"Hello sir." She said, surprised that such a smartly dressed important looking man was standing in her living room. Her first thoughts had been that he must be a Policeman, but he was too well dressed for that and appeared to be better mannered.

"Get Mr Scriven a cuppa tay Bab." Chad Cooper placed a loving hand on his wife's shoulder.

Jean looked at her husband with love-filled eyes and went back into the kitchen to make tea for the two men. Scriven could tell straight away that despite Cooper's dishonest line of work, he lived in a happy caring home and that he treated his family with respect and love.

"What can ar dew for yer Mr Scriven?" Cooper sat down in his armchair and invited Scriven to sit opposite him on the settee.

"It ay fer me mate. It's fer Billy Mucklow."

Cooper quivered silently at the mention of Mucklow's name. He was excited at the prospect of doing a job for the local boss, but at the same time he felt a little apprehensive about working for the feared gangster. *But maybe this was it? His opportunity to move up?* For a second or two he lost himself in his thoughts and he imagined himself wearing a suit whilst sat at Billy Mucklow's table in The Haden Cross smoking a big fat cigar.

"What can ar dew for you boys?" Cooper oozed confidence without being 'cocky.' He took out a packet of cigarettes and offered Scriven one. He accepted and the two men lit up.

"Before I explain." Scriven took a drag of his cigarette and gave Cooper a hard serious glare. "I trust that you respect confidentiality?" He exhaled smoke and watched it rise slowly to the ceiling. "Basically, keep yer fuckin' marf shut abaaht anything ar tell yer and anything yow do fer us!"

"Dow worry Mr Scriven. Ar'm kinda attached ter me legs!" Cooper joked and Scriven felt confident that he had made his point.

Cooper's wife brought in the tea and the two men talked for over twenty minutes about exactly what had to be done and how it would be done.

Scriven repeated Billy Mucklow's instructions meticulously and instructed Cooper on how important it was that he followed these instructions exactly. He had already called in at Gaunts undertakers at the top of Powke Lane and had picked up the flowers. He paid Cooper in full for the job and the two men shook hands. Cooper thanked Scriven for thinking of him and promised not to disappoint.

"Just do exactly as ar explained and do it tonight..." Scriven stood up to leave and gently rubbed the little girls head in a friendly gesture before shouting farewell to Cooper's wife and thanking her for the tea. He took one last look at the happy family and walked out to his car. He opened the door, got inside and set off towards the pub.

The rest of that Sunday passed as it always did. The familiar faces gathered around the Mucklow dinner table had begun to speak of plans for the ever-nearing Christmas time and the end of an eventful year was in sight.

In a quiet moment, Harry Scriven had informed Billy Mucklow that everything was arranged and that his man was set to do the job that night. Mucklow had already met with the local law enforcement and they were going to put some extra pressure on Albert Hackett and The Regis club. Both Scriven and Mucklow hoped that the plan would work.

The year had started violently but things had now settled down lucratively. They enjoyed their Sunday dinner, sipped Port and smoked fine cigars. Life was good and the last thing they needed was some new vendetta to spoil things.

At nine thirty, Harry and Irene bid their hosts farewell and walked the short distance down the road from Mucklow's house to their own home. They walked arm in arm and Scriven was quite surprised at himself for such a sentimental gesture.

On arrival at his home he went straight upstairs and collapsed on the bed, tired from the busy day and the vast accumulation of alcohol that he had drank.

Two days passed and there was no word from Albert Hackett. Billy Mucklow was biding his time so that Hackett could feel the financial pinch of being forced to close his club early. There was no rush though and Mucklow was continuing to live in his own little bubble whilst retaining, in the words of his idol Frank Sinatra, "The world on a string."

It was Wednesday 1st of December 1954 and Harry Scriven was busy in Cradley Heath high street.

The area had originally been an open landscape of heathland between Cradley, Netherton and Old Hill in the Parish of Rowley Regis but as cottages were built in the early 1800s the town and its industries began to develop and the area took on the name of Cradley Heath.

During the industrial revolution in 1830, Cradley Heath developed two prolific industries, chain making and nail making which would become synonymous with the town for many decades to come.

A distinctive signal of the growth in the community came in December 1833 when the Cradley Heath Baptist church was constructed. This Church became famous throughout Britain when in 1837 the Rev. George Cosens became the countries first Afro-Caribbean Minister.

As Harry Scriven had ventured through the town on this frosty morning he had noticed that the very first signs of Christmas had begun to appear and for the first time in many years he felt a slight warmth and anticipation inside of him at the appearance of the Christmas lights that twinkled in the early morning darkness.

As a child he had loved Christmas, spending time with family, the food, the music, the lights, but as he had gotten older things had changed. This year he would be spending Christmas in his wonderful new home with his beautiful lady friend Irene. For half a second the ridiculous idea of a marriage proposal even entered his mind!

On this morning Scriven was calling in to see the owners of several business' who paid protection money to Billy Mucklow. He was explaining that as a gesture of good will, the family would be demanding slightly less money for the duration of December.

It was all part of a plan to ensure that people did not follow Albert Hackett's example and stop paying their protection money. Mucklow also figured that it may also help to encourage Hackett to re-start his payments before too much fuss had occurred and others started to follow suit and refuse to pay!

Even Harry Scriven thought that maybe his cousin was going too soft, but he was more than happy to spread the word as he called in on the various business' for a drink and a chat.

As midday struck he found himself sat in a café in the centre of Cradley Heath eating a rather delicious bacon sandwich. He finished his food, insisted on paying his bill then put on his trilby and Crombie before venturing out into the cold air.

As he was unlocking his car he was surprised to see Billy Mucklow pull up behind him in his cream coloured Riley. He wound down the window and instructed for Scriven to "get in."

"What's gooin on?" Scriven asked as he walked over to the Riley and lowered himself down to the window.

"Get in. I will bring yer back to yer motor afta. Ar dow wanna' talk here. Summets happened…"

Scriven opened the passenger door and climbed in next to his cousin. The plush leather interior was ornate and luxurious and he always enjoyed the luxury and comfort of Billy Mucklow's Riley RM series.

Mucklow put the car into gear and accelerated rapidly away from the high street towards Old Hill, from there he continued through Halesowen and up the hill to Romsley where he pulled over and stopped the car.

From where he had parked high upon the hill, the two men could see the distant buildings of Birmingham city centre in front of them and to the left Halesowen and deeper into the Black Country. The vast array of factories belched black smoke into the atmosphere and the constant hammerings from the Somers forge in Halesowen could be heard clearly when the wind blew in the right direction.

Mucklow got out of the car, pulled his Crombie collars up around his neck and lent back against the bonnet. Scriven followed him and the two men looked at the view. Mucklow lit a cigarette and his failure to offer his cousin one alerted Scriven to the fact that something wasn't right. He pulled out his own cigarettes and waited for Mucklow to speak.

"Yower mon fucked up." Billy Mucklow eventually broke the silence.

"What yow on abaaht?"

"Chad Cooper." Mucklow spat the name with a good deal of content. "The thieving little bastard did exactly what he was asked, but he also took twenty quid from Hackett's house!" Mucklow spoke through gritted teeth. "Do yer know how that mecks me look?"

Scriven shook his head apologetically.

"It mecks me look like a pathetic little tramp who sends blokes raahd to nick money like ar'm sum kind of fuckin'pauper!"

Scriven looked at the floor in utter disappointment. His time spent in the Cooper household had touched him and had had an effect on his own outlook on life. The amount of love the father, mother and daughter shared was special and had made Scriven realise that he needed such relationships himself! He had hoped that Cooper would do a good job.

"And now Hackett is fuckin' raging too!" Mucklow slammed his fist down on the bonnet of his car. "He ay gunna' pay an he's gooin around saying Fuck Billy Mucklow to any bastard that listens to him!"

Scriven looked up and saw the anger in his cousin's eyes.

"I cannot afford to be belittled like this. Cooper needs to be punished as an example to show people that orders need to be obeyed! In the army, if men disobeyed orders they were punished! An army marches on its discipline. I will not be made to look a fool."

Scriven could tell that Mucklow was serious. His thick Black Country accent would often fade in moments of seriousness and he would revert to his wartime British Army Officer's voice.

"Ar will speak to him Bill, sorry." Scriven tried to appease him.

104

Mucklow looked at Scriven with frustrated eyes. "A shoutin' at and a slap is not going to cut it Harry… Ar want yer to break his thieving fingers! Properly break every fucking one so that he and every other fucker else can see what they get for being a thieving little bastard who disobeys fucking orders!" Spit flew from Mucklow's lips as he ranted and cursed. "This will also show that fucker Hackett that we mean business and that we never intended for Cooper to steal from him."

Scriven laughed sarcastically. He did not want to seriously hurt Chad Cooper and cause sorrow to his idyllic young family. "Fuck you Billy." He squared up to Mucklow and flung his face so close to his cousin's that their noses were practically touching.

Mucklow swiftly lost his cool and grabbed Scriven aggressively by the scruff of the neck. "Do as you are fucking told!" he screamed in his face.

Harry Scriven matched the intensity of Mucklow's stare, grabbed his throat and yanked him with full force sending them both plummeting to the floor. Neither man was prepared to go as far as throwing a full punch and Mucklow let go of his grip and got up on one knee.

Scriven quickly adopted a similar stance and gazed angrily at his kin. "Fuckin' come on then Soldier boy!" He gritted his teeth and readied himself for Mucklow's attack.

Mucklow took a deep breath and stood up. "Look at us!" He said mournfully. He reached into his pocket and pulled out a hip flask filled with Brandy. He took a long drink and then handed it to his cousin.

Scriven was relieved to see that Mucklow had calmed and apprehensively took the flask before Mucklow spoke again.

"If we dow meck a stand then folks u'll start to teck the piss!" Mucklow's cigarette had rolled down the hill in the struggle so he took out another, this time offering one to his cousin.

Scriven understood where Mucklow was coming from, he was right. *But Chad Cooper was just a kid with a young family!*

"If yow dow do it ar will have to ask Barry O'Leary or Dick Hickman…" Mucklow paused to let the suggestion sink into Scriven's head and then continued. "Do yer think they give a fuck? Do yer think they will show as much restraint as yow?"

Scriven rubbed his eye lids with his fingers and let out a long sigh. He had no choice. "Fine." He could not believe how quickly he had been reduced and brought around to his cousin's way of thinking. "When der yer want it done?"

"Today. I will drive you back to your car. You will need to use a hammer or something to do a proper job."

The two men got back into the Riley RM and drove silently back to Cradley Heath High Street. Scriven got out of the car and trudged sadly over to his own vehicle. Neither man said a word to each other. Billy Mucklow was still terribly angry about the whole occurrence and Scriven was attempting to ready himself for the violence by wiping all human consciousness from his thoughts.

He knew that he was capable of extreme cold violence and he knew that there was a dark place deep within him that was equally as aggressive, nasty and depraved as his cousin. He also knew that alcohol would help him reach this point of oblivion so upon picking up his car he drove straight to the Hand of Providence Public house in Hollybush Street.

He spent the next couple of hours drinking strong ale and straight London Dry gin until he looked out through the pub window and saw a slight darkening of the sky. He would have to make a move before it became dark. He went out to his car, opened the boot and found a claw hammer that was nestled amongst an array of other tools. He placed it inside his deep Crombie pocket and set off for the Cooper household in Cokeland place.

Chapter 10

The Black Ford Pilot pulled up outside the house in Cokeland place. It was mid-afternoon and the lateness of the year meant that daylight was soon to cease.

Harry Scriven sat at the driver's seat dressed in black as he watched the house and slowly smoked a cigarette. He smoked the last dregs from out of it, making it last as long he could to put off the deed for which he had been sent to commit.

He eyed the house with reluctant intent and when he had finished his cigarette he slung it out of the window, stepped out of the car and trod the butt into the pavement with his black shoes which were polished to the point that he could almost see his own reflection in them. He removed all emotion from his eyes and expressions and slowly approached the front door.

Scriven knocked loudly and the door was eventually answered by Chad Cooper's young daughter Linda. Scriven found it hard not to smile at the youngster. "Hello… Is your Daddy home please?" Before the child had a chance to speak, her mother approached and scolded her daughter for answering the door on her own.

"I am so sorry Mr Scriven! Her should not be openin' the doowa erself!" Cooper's wife was apologetic and nervous in her mannerisms. "Please, do come in sir."

"No thank you, I would like to see your husband please. We have business to discuss."

A confused look came over her face. *Mr Scriven was definitely somewhat colder than on his previous visit* and she worried that her husband may be in some kind of trouble. Before she had chance to call him, Chad Cooper appeared in the doorway.

"Hello Mr Scriven. What can ar dew fer yer?"

"I need you to come with me Chad. I need to speak to you." Scriven stared at Cooper with a mixture of anger, disappointment and pity.

Cooper could smell the gin on Scriven's breath and the menacing cold look in his eyes sent shivers down his spine. Chad Cooper knew exactly what this was about and he instantly regretted his actions on the night of the break in. The colour drained from his face and his spirit changed. "Hang on one minute." He ducked back into the house, picked up his flat cap and put on his heavy over coat. He kissed his wife and daughter, lingering a little longer than usual as if concerned he might never see them again.

They could both sense that something was not right and his wife tried in vain to protest but Cooper held a tender finger to her lips. He placed his right hand on her cheek and whispered "Don't worry... I love you." Tears of concern began to fill her eyes and she felt the need to suppress her emotions for the sake of her daughter.

She clung tightly to the child and tears began to stream down her cheeks as she watched the love of her life being led away to the big black car. Cooper sat in the passenger seat and turned to look at her for one last time. For one torturous second she saw a look on his face that she had never witnessed before. *He was usually so confident, so happy.* It was a look of pure terror and in that instant she broke down and sobbed uncontrollably, her young daughter not understanding what was going on. *Why was her mother crying? Why was her Daddy being taken away from her?*

Scriven said nothing for the duration of the journey, his eyes fixed on the road in front of him. Chad Cooper occasionally tried to engage the older man in conversation but he was met with brief responses.

The car travelled through Cradley Heath, Old Hill and then over the canal bridge towards Blackheath. It bared right and began to ascend the hill on Powke Lane before turning off to the right in front of a row of houses that stretched further on up the hill.

The Ford drove across a small plot of wasteland and stopped alongside the canal that had once been so busy transporting goods and materials from the Black Country to the rest of England.

"Yow gunna' dump me in the cut?" Cooper anxiously turned and looked at Scriven. His lifelong fear of water playing disturbingly on his mind. For a second, he thought of getting out and running. Harry Scriven was older and much heavier than him. *There was no way that he could catch him, but then what? Would his family be safe?* All he could do was face up to what he had done and see what Scriven had to say.

"Why would ar dump yer in the cut Chad? Yow got summet ter hide?" Scriven knew the answer to the question. "Get out." Scriven did not look Cooper in the eye. The younger man opened the door and they both got out and walked over to the canal. Scriven stood just behind Cooper and Cooper could feel his presence on his right shoulder.

He looked into the water, watched the ripples pass and thought of his wife and daughter. Scriven spoke as little as possible. He was watching for signs of guilt. For all he knew this could be some kind of 'bluff' by Albert Hackett.

"What is this abaaht 'Mr Scriven?" Chad Cooper eventually spoke.

"Yow tell me."

"Ar dow know!"

Scriven took a long deep breath. "I need to know the truth Chad." He took out another cigarette and lit it. The whole time, his eyes burning a whole in the back of Cooper's head.

"What do yer mean Mr Scriven?"

Scriven took a step closer and Cooper could feel his smoky breath and the smell of gin on the back of his neck. Scriven jabbed him hard underneath his rib cage and he fell to the floor in pain. "Tell me what happened at Hackett's house?"

"Ar left the note by his head like yow said Mr Scriven."

Scriven pulled out a small flick knife and opened up the blade. "Ar'm gunna be honest with yow Chad. Ar dow wanna hurt yer. But

Billy Mucklow has got it in his head that yow took twenty quid from Albert Hackett on that night when yow were tode not too. If yow keep fuckin' lying to me then I am going to fuckin' hurt you, do you understand?" Scriven spoke words of anger with reluctance.

"Ar know yow took that money mate... If yer tell me the truth then maybe we can find a way aaht of this mess. But do not fuckin' lie to me!"

Cooper looked at the knife and tried to decide what he should do. As soon as he had left the Hackett house he knew that he had done wrong. *He should have never took the money. But it was just lay there upon the table. He could not resist, and now he was going to pay the price. But there was something about Harry Scriven that was not all bad... Maybe if he cooperated and told the truth, Scriven would help him sort things out?* He looked back at the canal and then up at the ever-darkening sky.

He figured that he would probably end up floating face down in the murky water either way, so all he could do was put his trust in the man who had treated his little girl with such kindness only a few nights previously. He had nothing to lose. He dried his eyes and began to speak.

"It was just twenty quid... Ar left the flowers as yer asked and was on me way out." Cooper stared at the knife and struggled to co-ordinate his breathing in panic. Scriven handed him the half-smoked cigarette and Cooper took a long drag. "Then ar saw the twenty quid on the side... Ar picked it up... I'm sorry Mr Scriven... I'm sorry."

Scriven closed his eyes in relief. *Cooper was not innocent and he deserved to be punished. How disappointing.* Scriven had hoped that Chad Cooper would have proved to be a useful associate. He pulled the claw hammer from out of his deep Crombie pocket and grabbed Cooper's hair with his free hand, holding his head up so that he could see the torturous instrument. Cooper's eyes widened in pure fear.

"No Mr Scriven, please no!" He begged, then relaxed himself in readiness for the fatal blow. He listened to the rippling water of the canal and fully anticipated that he would soon be floating in the dirty water, never to see his beloved family again. He thought of his young child and quietly began to sob.

Eventually the hammer struck, but not on his head where he had been expecting it. Scriven brought the hammer down hard on Cooper's left hand, the pain was intense and he cried out. Scriven raised the hammer again and continued to rain down blow after excruciating blow on Cooper's left hand.

After what seemed like an age Scriven stopped to get his breath from the ferocious intensity of his activity and Cooper lay on the floor near the edge of the water whimpering.

His hand had turned almost completely black, was swollen beyond recognition and blood oozed from the cracked remnants of his fingernails. Scriven walked to the rear of the car and slung the hammer into the boot.

He returned with his open wallet. "Here. Get yerself a drink... It will help... And get yer kid summet fer Chrismus." He threw two-pound notes onto the floor next to where Cooper lay sobbing and then got back into his car and drove off. Chad Cooper, despite his intense physical pain, felt relieved that it was over and he was not floating face down in the canal.

Harry Scriven drove the short distance home morbidly. He didn't feel like going to the pub and he knew that Irene was staying out that night to look after her ill mother. He didn't want to face anyone, all he wanted was to get home, open a bottle of Scotch and sit in the bathtub to 'cleanse' himself.

Nothing could wash away the guilt of the things he had done, but at least a long soak and the 'oblivion' of the whisky would help him to get through the night. He could have gone to the boxing club, but the last thing he wanted was to run into Dickie Hickman!

He couldn't quite work out why it all affected him so much. In his line of work it was quite usual to be around violence and he had never had a problem with hurting people who he felt deserved their punishments. In fact, the whole Jimmy Danks scenario had been quite therapeutic and Ronnie Hall had also deserved his beating on account of his treatment of Wilf Dugmore, but only days earlier Scriven had been somewhat touched by his brief time spent with the Cooper family.

Chad Cooper was just a kid with a cute young family who had made Scriven begin to think about the things that were missing from his own life. *A man in his position should not suffer such sensitivity* he thought to himself, but it was no use. His stomach ached with the pangs of guilt and he found himself pondering whether or not to go back and drive Cooper home to his family. He decided not to.

On his arrival home, Scriven was relieved to find the house empty. He did not know if Suzy was working at the Regis club that night but he was still not in the frame of mind to speak to anyone.

At his old house in Talbot Street, Scriven had taken baths in an old tub that was made of tin and had to be placed in front of the fire to warm up. But here in the new house there was a plush modern bathroom suite with the luxury of hot running water. He walked into the house, collected a bottle of Scotch from the pantry, a small cut glass ashtray from the kitchen and headed up to the bathroom where he turned on the hot tap and removed the cork from his whisky.

He watched the water level slowly rise as he 'necked' Scotch straight from the bottle. He placed it on the floor next to the enamel bathtub and placed the ashtray and his cigarette case alongside it.

As he removed his fine clothing, he folded it carefully and placed it in a neat pile next to the Belfast sink basin. He had been trained since childhood to look after his possessions, but on this day he regarded them with disgust and scorn. Symbols of his criminal successes. *How many people had he hurt for these luxurious items that surrounded him? He had spent his whole life following the orders of his cousin Billy Mucklow, he alone was nothing, insignificant, a slave to the orders of others. Even the impressive house in which he lived had been paid for with the money Irene had made from selling The Fountain pub in Tipton. He was a pathetic nobody of a man who was living off the successes of his woman. What right did he have to cause pain and suffering to men such as Ray Jones and Chad Cooper? His violence was getting out of control and what sickened him most of all was that a small part of him actually enjoyed the thrill of it!*

He eased himself into the steaming hot water with feelings of complete and utter self-loathing, the more alcohol he drank the more self-pity he felt.

He saw his reflection in the metallic tap at the opposite end of the bath and his features appeared to distort into the image of a grotesque monster he could hardly bear to look at. Often, these feelings of self hatred would make him angry. Anger was good, he could use this total rage against anyone Billy Mucklow told him too. Violence was a drug, like alcohol, like nicotine, like sex. But what bugged him most of all was the fact that his younger cousin had complete and total control over him. On this day he had defiantly refused Mucklow's instructions to hurt Chad Cooper. But within minutes Mucklow had manipulated the situation and made him carry out the terrible task. He caught another glimpse of his monstrous reflection in the tap once again and he kicked out at it, hitting it hard with his naked foot.

At first the heat of the water stung, but then he thought that the pain was just what he deserved. He took another long drink of whisky and then almost passed out with the intense heat of the water. He lay back and closed his eyes as he felt the hot water pass over him, the image of Cooper's young daughter entered his mind and he thought about the kind of Christmas she would have with her father unable to work.

Then he thought about Ray Jones and his family! He placed the bottle on the floor at the side of the bath, the alcohol loosening his inhibitions and emotions as tears began to run slowly from his eyes. He fumbled for a cigarette, lit it then desperately sucked in the nicotine. It briefly calmed his nerves and he started to relax a little. *This was the life he had chosen. He would pay for his sins in hell!*

Just then he heard movement on the landing outside the bathroom. For a moment he imagined it could be men sent for him and intent on revenge, but the alcohol had made him paranoid.

The hot bath had risen his body temperature and he could feel the intense alcohol pumping through his veins, his heartbeat rapidly and he almost longed for the attackers to be on the landing... He needed a release and he imagined the crushing violence he would inflict on whoever had invaded his home. His teeth clenched and his body shook with adrenaline as he sat upright in the bath.

He stared at the door and continued to smoke his cigarette. *Maybe it was Irene? Maybe it was Suzy?* Suddenly the bathroom door flung open.

"Hello Harry." Suzy Miller appeared in the doorway dressed in only stockings, suspenders and red, lacy knickers. The entire of her top half was completely exposed and Scriven could hardly believe his eyes!

She slowly approached the bath, her large perfectly formed breasts moving up and down slightly as she walked. Through the hot steam of the room he could see her voluptuous 'hour glass' figure move slowly towards him, her deep red hair flowing over her naked shoulders, her full scarlet lips pouting and those beautiful brown eyes staring provocatively at him. Any thoughts of guilt and self-loathing quickly disappeared from Scriven's mind and he instantly jolted forwards to cover himself up.

"What's wrong Harry?" She knelt at the side of the bathtub and slowly stroked his face, the feel of her breath on his face and the smell of her perfume caressed his senses. "I can tell there is something wrong Harry. Let me help you feel better." She cupped the bath water in her hands and slowly and sensitively began to pour it over his body, running her hands over his shoulders and across the top of his chest. He tried to protest but she raised her finger and held it to his lips before lowering her face to his and kissing him slowly, her mouth lingering next to his as he breathed in her warm breath and savoured the sweet smell of her perfume that had stirred him on so many previous occasions.

He sat back in the bath and relaxed as she continued to pour water over him and wash his naked body. She could feel the tension in his muscles and as she reached over to massage the back of his neck and shoulders her large shapely breasts pushed intently into his more than accepting face. She rose up and lowered her face close to his.

He continued to breathe in her hypnotic perfume and admire the sight and feel of her body so close to his. She was only twenty years old but was already so mature and womanly. She was also the daughter of the woman he loved. This was truly wrong and he knew it.

"I ay a good man Suzy."

She shook her head and pulled his face into hers. He could resist no longer, he reached out his arms and embraced her before pulling her into the bath with him. If he was going to hell, then he might as well make the most of his time upon this earth...

Chapter 11

It was Christmas Eve and throughout December Suzy and Scriven had stolen every opportunity they could to be together. Irene had been busy tending to her sick mother and this had enabled her daughter and her partner to be alone.

Suzy had become Scriven's confidant, to her he had confessed his many sins and each time she had sought to reassure him. They sat face to face inside a booth in the King Edward pub on Stourbridge Road Halesowen and Scriven could not help but admire her beautiful face as he looked into her eyes. He had been supposed to drive her to work at The Regis club but instead he had brought her over to one of his regular pubs which stood next to the Halesowen town football ground.

"Yum not gunna be able to work at the Regis anymore Bab." He touched her hand apologetically as he spoke.

"Yer what?" She pulled her hand away and looked surprised.

"Things ay bin good between us and Bert Hackett lately. Things could get rough. Billy reckons it ay safe fer yer to work there anymore."

"Oh..." She raised her eyebrows in annoyance. "So Billy Mucklow sez ar av to gid up me job and that's it? I just do as he sez?"

"It ay safe bab."

"Yow do everything that man tells yer!" Suzy laughed sarcastically and glared at Scriven. "Yer his fuckin' puppet! Why do you follow orders like some pathetic little dog? Ain't yow supposed to be the older cousin?" She took a deep breath and frowned before lowering her nasally Tipton voice "One day, yum gunna dangle on the end of a rope for that man!"

Harry Scriven looked at her unable to say a word. He knew deep down that she was right. *He had paralyzed men, severely beaten men, arranged robberies, beaten a man to death and even held a man down as Billy*

Mucklow fed his hand through a fucking mangle! Sooner or later, he would hang for his crimes and that was nothing less than he deserved. The large clock on the wall chimed the hour of one o'clock and Scriven returned his gaze to Suzy as she put out her hand again to touch his.

"Come away with me Harry." Her love filled eyes frantically searched his for recognition and reassurance. She feared rejection and in her young twenty-year-old mind she was madly in love with the older man. "Come to Scotland, I have family there on me Dad's side. Come away with me Harry, we can be together and not have to creep around anymore." She looked at him pleadingly. "You will be free from this life of violence, yer can be free from that man!" She clenched his hand tightly. "I love you Harry, choose me, choose love… Choose life!"

He let go of her hand and raised his own to his forehead as he gazed at the half empty glass of beer in front of him. He looked at her and wished that he could accept this opportunity for salvation. He thought for the words to say, but for a moment or two words escaped him and he remained speechless.

He brought his fingers to his eyes and closed them as he recalled a childhood memory. It was a Christmas day, many years in the past. He must have been about seven years old, the mid nineteen twenties. His parents were not wealthy people and as a gift that Christmas he had received an apple, a tangerine and small tin spinning top that never really did work properly. He had been overjoyed with what he had received but when he met up with his wealthier cousin later that day, it soon became clear that Billy had been given significantly more in his Christmas stocking. A tear almost came to his eye as he recalled how Billy had instantly insisted on sharing his gifts with him and how Mucklow had repeated this gesture every year. He then remembered a later Christmas in 1944 when Billy was not present and the whole family had worried for their loved one who was fighting fiercely in Europe. The bond had always been strong between the two cousins, as deep as that of brothers and there was no way that Scriven could simply abandon him.

"Ar'm sorry Suzy. No matter how much ar would love to come away with yer Bab and start a new life, we both have to think of family loyalties." He took a long drink of his beer and stared at her with sad remorseful eyes.

She looked up at the ceiling and tears began to flow down her cheeks causing her heavy make up to run. "I ay bin very loyal to me mutha."

"Neither of us have Bab." Scriven stroked her face and wiped away her salty tears. For a moment, he had felt torn. Here was a perfect opportunity for him to escape the life that Billy Mucklow had created for him, but it was not going to happen. He could not abandon his family and he could not cause such hurt and suffering to Irene, especially after she had so readily given up her own husband to be with him. He had no choice but to stand by his family and to stand by Irene and if that meant that he had to be Billy Mucklow's puppet then so be it, even if it meant that one day he would dangle on the end of a rope…

A few miles away in Old Hill, Barry O'Leary waited patiently inside The Regis club. Billy Mucklow had continued to apply pressure on Albert Hackett and his brothers by ensuring that the Police came down hard on his alcohol serving hours, but Hackett had continued to hold his nerve.

It had been several weeks now since Hackett had made his last 'protection'payment to the Mucklow family and each week Barry O'Leary had been sent to ask for the money, but each week he had been abruptly told to "fuck off!"

On this cold Christmas Eve, O'Leary had been surprised to be invited into Hackett's office and given a cup of tea. He sat there waiting to see what Hackett and his two brothers had to say, casually smoking a cigarette and wondering about his chances with the club's favoured barmaid Suzy Miller.

"Yow keep coming back dow ya!" Albert Hackett spoke in a mocking tone as he walked into the room with his two burly brothers. He was a smug looking man in his late thirties, about five foot ten inches tall with dark brown hair that was combed into a smart side parting with well-groomed sideburns that extended just below his ears. He wore a smart three-piece suit and fancied himself in every way.

Albert Hackett could handle himself in a fight and both he and his thicker built twin brothers had served in the Royal Navy during World War Two but they had reached a point in their lives where they were sick of taking orders from other people. *Why should they pay money to Billy Mucklow? They were as tough as anyone else and it was about time that somebody stood up to the Mucklows. The Hackett brothers were a force to be reckoned with and they would not bow down to anyone!*

O'Leary relaxed in his chair and smiled. "Billy Mucklow wants his money mate."

Albert Hackett laughed and took a step closer. "Billy Mucklow can gew and fuck himself! Now it's abaaht time yow fucked off and stopped bothering us every week!" With that Hackett hit O'Leary with a hard right hook straight across the jaw.

Instantly, the young second-generation Irishman lunged forwards to counterattack, but it was no use. Hackett's brothers jumped in and proceeded to kick, punch and stamp on him until he lay bleeding and unconscious on the floor.

His face was a bloody mess and his body was covered in bruises and broken bones. Albert Hackett stood over him and spat onto his face. "Teck this piece a shit raahnd ter Billy Mucklow's house and dump him outside!"

Harry scriven had by this time returned home and was sat next to the warm fire in his newly decorated living room reading a newspaper. He was reading about a recent scandal involving the American President Joseph McCarthy and was only half paying attention.

His thoughts were of Suzy Miller who was in the kitchen next door with her mother preparing food for the Christmas festivities. All three of them were due to attend Christmas dinner at the Mucklow's but they were to host the evening celebrations at their house.

It was all somewhat awkward for both Scriven and Suzy due to the nature of their illicit relationship, but neither of them wanted to upset Irene so they simply had to carry on and make what they could of the situation.

Suzy felt immense guilt but was also confident in her love for Harry Scriven. Scriven on the other hand was making the most of having two attractive ladies in love with him and was using alcohol regularly to medicate against any feelings of guilt he was suffering with. He sat with his feet up and was looking past the Christmas tree and out of the bay window at the fading light of the day.

"Billy Mucklow was just on the phone Bab." Irene suddenly appeared in the doorway with a tea towel in her hand. Scriven hadn't even heard the phone ring.

"He said yer need to get round there straight away!" She sighed in disappointment at the prospect of Harry being forced out to work late on Christmas Eve. "It sounded important. He sounded pretty angry on the phone."

Scriven stood up and kicked his slippers off in annoyance. He fastened his top button and pulled his tie off the back of his chair and put it back on. "Ar will see yer later then Bab." He pulled on his suit jacket and walked out to the hallway where he put on his shoes, grabbed his trilby and put on his black Crombie. *Somebody was probably going to get hurt!* He thought to himself.

"Try not to meck it too late Harry, ar thought we were gooin up the pub tonight?" It wasn't often the women had the rare honour of accompanying their men to The Haden Cross and Irene Miller fully intended to make the most of her Christmas time treat.

"Me too." Scriven shrugged as he left the house and made the short walk over to Billy Mucklow's house.

"Come in." Mucklow barked as Scriven waited patiently on his doorstep. He walked into the grand hallway and Mucklow slammed the door in anger.

"What the fucks gooin on?" Scriven asked, annoyed that his relaxing Christmas Eve afternoon had been interrupted. He knew that most men worked on Christmas Eve, but he hadn't done so since he had worked as a motor mechanic just after the war.

"Look in there!" Mucklow opened the living room door and Scriven peered inside.

"Fuckin' hell!" Scriven saw Barry O'Leary lying barely conscious on the settee being tended to by Mucklow's wife Mary. His face was battered, bruised and swollen almost beyond recognition. "What happened to him?"

"Them fuckin' Hackett brothers did it! They dumped him outside about twenty minutes agoo!" Mucklow looked at Scriven with intense angry eyes. "We'm gooin daahn there now! These fuckers need sortin' aaht right now!"

"Hang on Bill, there's at least three of them an just two of us, ant' we better wait til Dick gets here?"

"Ar dow give a fuck! We'm gooin daahn there right now!" Mucklow spat his words through gritted teeth as he grabbed his Crombie. He rushed out to his car and Scriven followed.

Mucklow pulled up abruptly outside the Regis club, he kicked open the car door and the two men jumped out. A tall thin man stood on the door to the club dressed in a trench coat and trilby. "Yer cor come in here gents sorry. We'm closed."

"Harry, put this bastard through the fuckin' winda!" Mucklow growled as they neared the glass doors that led into the club.

Scriven instantly grabbed the man by the scruff of the neck, punched him hard in the stomach before slamming his face through the glass door. The door exploded as glass shattered everywhere and mixed with blood as the man lay dazed and covered in cuts. A small, jagged piece of glass lodged through his cheek and blood ran through his teeth and onto his clean shirt.

Mucklow and Scriven walked into the club and were instantly greeted by the three Hackett brothers who were stood smugly at the bar drinking whiskey. The eldest brother Albert stood in the middle and turned to face the two unwelcome visitors.

"Look what the cat dragged in..." He sneered as his two burly brothers turned to stand alongside him.

Mucklow said nothing. He strolled straight up to the brothers and swiftly pulled a pistol from his left pocket and shot the first brother point blank in the knee cap.

The brother's knee exploded as blood and cartilage sprayed across the newly polished floor. The man dropped instantly to the ground in utter agony. Mucklow pulled back the hammer of the gun and shoved the barrel into Albert Hackett's face, forcing him to take a step backwards. He screamed a protest and held his hands in the air as Mucklow pressed the weapon deeper into his cheek.

"Who gets the next fuckin' bullet?" Mucklow demanded in anger. "Yow or yer other fuckin' brother?" Mucklow thrust the gun further forwards.

"Billy, Billy, ar day know yow had guns mate, come on kidda, let's talk about this?" Hackett mumbled in sheer panic.

"You or yer fuckin' brother?" Mucklow screamed, his eyes filled with aggression and hate.

Hackett looked at him, tears rolling down the side of his face. "Him." He said quietly as he shamefully looked at the floor. The second twin instantly protested and Mucklow seemed to find the whole thing quite amusing.

He shifted the gun from Albert Hackett's face and promptly blew the other brother's knee cap off, blood exploding over his tan-coloured Crombie as the man fell to the floor in agony. Mucklow continued to laugh loudly in an eerie almost psychotic tone.

122

"Fuckin' hell lads, some fuckin' brother yow got here! Yow bunch a bastards think it's acceptable to beat the shit aaht on mar bloke? Ar'v ad'a fuckin' nuff 'of this now..." Mucklow raised the pistol again and pointed it at Albert. "You." Albert Hackett flinched and twitched. "Goo to yer fuckin' safe right now and fetch me every ha'penny yer' got! Ar'm collecting." Mucklow lowered the gun to the second brother's forehead who was lay on the floor crying in pain. "If yow ay back in two minutes ar'm gonna shoot this bastard..." Mucklow pulled back the hammer again and looked at his watch.

Harry Scriven said nothing. He had realised by now that he was probably going to hell anyway and would probably dangle on the end of a rope at some point no matter what he did.

Albert Hackett soon returned from his office with a wad of notes. Scriven took the money and shoved it into his coat pockets as Mucklow continued to hold the gun to the brother's head. He pulled up the gun and stepped closer to Albert. "I hope I have proven my fuckin' point mate?" He held his left hand behind his back and gestured for Scriven to give him the money. Scriven handed it over and Mucklow took out an amount roughly equal to how much he had been owed for the last few weeks' protection money.

He handed the rest back to Hackett and instructed him that he should use it to get his brothers urgent medical attention for their wounds. "Ar know a private doctor on the Hagley Road in Harborne. Teck the money to him and tell him Billy Mucklow sent yer. He will sort em' aaht."

Mucklow put the gun back into his pocket. "If ar get any more trouble from yow lot, ar'll put a bullet straight in yer fuckin' heads, bury yer outside and teck a fuckin' piss on yer graves." He meant every word... He stepped forwards to the bar and drained the last of Hackett's whiskey into his mouth before turning and walking towards the exit.

"Merry fuckin' Christmas boys!" Mucklow laughed as he and Scriven triumphantly left the club, got into the Riley and drove home to celebrate Christmas with their families.

Chapter 12

January 1955 was a generally cold month with severe frosts and some heavy snowfalls.

The president of Panama, Jose' Antonio Remon' Catera, was assassinated at the beginning of the month and closer to home, a rail crash occurred on the 23rd of January in Sutton Coldfield killing seventeen passengers.

Harry Scriven had done 'the decent thing' by Irene and ended his illicit affair with her daughter Suzy. Suzy had then decided to embrace this as an opportunity to make a new life for herself in Scotland and an emotional farewell had occurred at New Street station in Birmingham. This had been a particularly dramatic occurrence due to the nature of the situation and the presence of both her mother and the man she loved! What made things even more difficult was that her mother was completely unaware that any affair had taken place, so she had to remain discreet throughout.

It was an awkward affair and Suzy could not help but feel a touch of jealousy as the steam train pulled out of the station. She watched her completely unaware mother left standing on the platform with the man who had saved her from the clutches of evil and with whom she had fallen completely in love…

However, the heart ache was short-lived as not long after her arrival at her paternal grandparent's home in Scotland she had proceeded to embark upon a series of new relationships!

Suzy Miller's grandparents lived on a farm near Dunbarton on the banks of the Clyde some fifteen miles northwest of Glasgow. This was the birthplace of Suzy's father who had remained in Scotland throughout his childhood and until he left for England at the age of 21.

Not long after Suzy's arrival at the farm she had begun an affair with an older, married man. Then, less than a week later she had made the acquaintance of a younger man which had resulted in the two men fighting viciously over her.

Suzy Miller had no problem attracting men and it appeared she had very little morals when it came to her conduct with them. Maybe it was due to some psychological disturbance after her ordeal with Jimmy Danks? Or some bitterness related to her affair with Harry Scriven? Either way, she had stirred up problems in Scotland so by the end of the month she was back in The Black Country and living with her mother and Harry Scriven at their home in Haden Hill.

Scriven had noted that she had appeared to return with a brattish arrogance and scorn that was of a significant contrast to her previous attitude towards him as she continued to drift further and further 'off the rails.'

Harry Scriven had continued to work for his cousin and did everything he was 'told' to do! The Hackett brothers had appeared to 'learn their lesson' after having bullets removed from their kneecaps over the Christmas period and Barry O'Leary had made a full recovery from his viscous beating on Christmas Eve.

It was a Wednesday dinnertime and Scriven sat alone at the bar in The Haden Cross. He had been having a conversation with the barman about the quality of the mild, but he was equally as content with his own company as he sat and pondered whether he should stay and have another pint, return home to Irene or call in at The Rose and Crown on the way home.

Just then a familiar face entered the pub. It was Suzy Miller accompanied by a young 'Teddy boy' with sharp sideburns and a black leather biker jacket that was similar to the one Marlon Brando wore in the 1953 movie 'The Wild Ones.'

Scriven could not deny, Suzy still looked good. Her tight blue denim clung voluptuously to her impressive figure and her eyes were as intoxicating as ever. Of course, he still felt jealous every time he saw her with a different man, but this in turn brought about feelings of guilt and shame. *She had been a foolish mistake and had proven herself to be a troublesome little slut who had caused problems wherever she went! But damn, she looked hot…*

He could not quite bring himself to say hello to the couple but instead blurted out a short, sharp sarcastic laugh at the sight of her with yet another man. *Fuck, ode' Danksy really had messed her up!*

"Yow gor a problem pal?" The Teddy boy combed back his long quiff with attitude and Scriven found the whole thing quite ridiculous.

"Ar bay got nare a problem Kidda…" he said as he turned on his bar stool to face the youngster. Scriven reckoned the lad was slightly older than Suzy, but no older than 23. *At least she was gewin for chaps her own age now!*

"Leave it Jack." Suzy held the Ted's arm. "That's Harry, he's me mutha's fella."

The Ted gave Scriven a knowing look and Scriven knew instantly from the look in his eyes that Suzy had told him everything. *A twisted one-sided account where he had probably been made to look like some sick perverted old uncle! Maybe that was true?* He reflected on his actions for a while and continued to drink his beer.

Suzy and the Ted sat down at a circular table at the back of the bar next to a large open fireplace. He soon had his hands all over her and the pair proceeded to kiss and smooch publicly.

"Disgusting behaviour in public…" The barman muttered under his breath. "An they ay even brought a drink! Cor yer say sumet Harry? If Billy catches um' behavin' like that in eyur' he'll goo mad!"

Scriven watched the couple with a mixture of jealousy and embarrassed shame as he wondered how he had once lowered himself to be in love with a trampy little kid like this. The more he thought, the more he began to realise that her behaviour was probably partly his fault. *He should not have played with the emotions and heart of an impressionable young girl.* Then he remembered how she had been a quivering wreck in his arms after her atrocious treatment at the hands of Jimmy Danks. *That bastard sure had a lot to answer for!*

"This ay a fuckin' knockin shap yer know!" Scriven finally spoke. "If yow ay gunna' buy a drink, fuck off!"

The Ted stopped, stood up and straightened up his jacket collar. He approached the bar coolly and ordered a pint of bitter and a gin and tonic for Suzy. He opened his wallet and flashed an impressive wad of notes that caused Scriven to wonder about the lad's occupation. *Suzy clearly had a thing for bad boys…*

The Ted left his pint on the counter, walked over to the jukebox and put 'That's Alright Mama' by Elvis Presley on before walking back over to the bar. He picked up his pint, took a sip then looked calmly at Harry Scriven.

"Yow speak to me like that again ode mon an ar'll smash yower face all over this bar!"

Scriven looked at him and smiled. "Ar think it's time yow left kid. We dow av no trouble in here."

The Ted combed back his quiff and raised his voice so that Suzy could hear him. "Come outside with me then!" he beckoned to the door with a flick of his immaculate hair.

"Get yer fuckin' hair cut kid." Scriven laughed and turned around to finish his beer.

"Ar'm fuckin' serious!" The Ted forcibly shoved Scriven back around to face him and beer shed all over the older man's suit.

Scriven was beginning to lose his patience. "What is yower fuckin' problem kid? Ar dow know yer from Adam and yer want me to goo rollin' abaaht in the car park?" Scriven stood up to face the Ted. The younger man was a good inch taller than Scriven, but he was of smaller stature. "If yow'm trying to impress her over there, it ay necessary mate. She ay that hard to get…"

A ferocious anger appeared in the Ted's eyes, his 'girl' had been insulted and he instantly demanded an apology. "Teck that back!" he bellowed in Scriven's face. "Teck that back right now or come outside with me!"

Scriven had no choice. The pub was partly owned by Billy Mucklow and if it got out that he, Harry Scriven, had been pushed about on home territory by some Teddy boy, what would Billy say? He had the family's reputation to think about and the kid was starting to get on his nerves…

Scriven followed the Ted outside to the rear car park, took off his jacket and tie and rolled up his sleeves.

Suzy followed too. Of course, she was still in love with Harry Scriven, but he had hurt her by choosing her mother over her, plus, he had initiated all of the trouble with Jimmy Danks, though she could still not bring herself to think about that. She stood at the side of the car park and watched on as her latest lover took off his leather jacket, rolled up his shirt sleeves and flicked back his impressive quiff.

Scriven stood and waited for the advance. The Ted adopted a boxer's stance with his left foot pointing forwards and his right foot behind him facing outwards to create a perfect ninety-degree angle. He moved forwards slowly and feigned a couple of jabs.

Scriven flinched slightly and took up a similar boxer stance. *The kid seemed to know what he was doing, what had he let himself in for?* Dancing around like a boxer was not his style. *Where was Dick Hickman when you needed him?*

The Ted dodged to the side and caught Scriven with a neat right-left combo. The older man composed himself and smiled. Then came another perfectly executed combination, a quick left-hand jab followed by a straight right. Scriven immediately tasted blood in his mouth and winced in pain as one of his teeth fell out.

"Give up ode mon?" the Ted sneered as he raised his arms and danced in a showboating, mocking manner. Scriven could feel the rage beginning to build inside of him as he looked over and saw that Suzy was watching. He could not allow himself to be humiliated like this in front of her! He lunged towards the Ted and threw a 'full pelt' right hook, the younger man stepped back and confidently dodged the punch before throwing a counter hit that caught Scriven on his right cheek.

The Ted laughed and continued to mock his tiring opponent. At this moment, Scriven began to realise that the punches he was receiving were relatively weak. He began to laugh as he stepped forwards taking further blows as the Ted frantically tried to beat him back. As Scriven got closer he suddenly reached out and grabbed the Ted's arm, kneed him hard in the testicles and thrust an almighty upper cut hard into the Ted's chin. The younger man fell backwards with the blow and was dazed as a now raging Harry Scriven grabbed the quiff of his hair, yanked it forwards and inflicted three straight right-hand punches.

The first punch broke the Ted's eye socket, the second dislocated his jaw and the third broke his nose in several places spraying fresh blood across Scriven's expensive shirt.

Scriven let go of his hair and laughed as the pathetic younger man fell to the floor in pain. Suzy rushed to tend to her most recent lover and screamed obscenities at Scriven as she ran.

"Sort him aaht' Bab…" Scriven laughed as he walked back towards the pub to finish his pint. What he did not notice was that the Ted had pulled a flick knife from his pocket! He got up and moved towards Scriven, he pulled back the blade and readied himself to stab his opponent in the back!

The Ted hit a patch of gravel on the coarse car park floor and Scriven immediately turned around to find the man about to stab him, he lunged forwards and grabbed the man's knife wielding arm, forcing the knife away. Scriven used his free hand to grab the Ted by the scruff of the neck and push him backwards towards the fence that separated the pub from the houses next door. The Ted tried to throw left hand punches but the force with which he was thrust onto the fence made it impossible. He still held the knife in his right hand and the two men grappled as Scriven held onto the Ted's arm in an attempt to stop himself from being cut! He lowered his face to the Ted's exposed right arm and bit down hard, the skin instantly broke and Scriven could taste the younger man's metallic blood in his mouth. The Ted instantly tensed in pain, dropped the knife and Scriven picked it up.

"Ar'll taych yer to pull a fuckin' knife on me!" He raged, his face grotesquely twisted in anger as blood dripped from his mouth.

In that moment, Suzy felt afraid and would never look upon Harry Scriven in the same light again. She looked at the man she had once been in love with and saw that his face, mouth and shirt were dripping with blood and an intense anger radiated from his crazed, narrowed eyes.

Scriven forced the Ted face first over the fence so that his rear end rose up into the air. He then took the knife and violently stabbed him twice in the fleshy rump of his buttocks. He pulled out the knife, wiped it on the Ted's trousers and then put it away inside his own pocket. The Ted screamed in pain as he instantly raised his hands to his wounds and dropped to the floor.

Harry Scriven stepped back and opened up his wallet. He pulled out two one-pound notes and thumbed bloody marks on them as he tossed them to the floor. "Get yerself some whiskey and dow sit daarn' for a few days!" He laughed as he spat blood from his mouth.

"You bastard!" Suzy screamed as she rushed to help the Ted up. "Yow am pathetic!" She spat the word with anger. "Yer live in that fancy house, paid for by mar mutha and all yow am is a fuckin puppet! Yum Billy Mucklow's puppet and yum turning into him! Difference is, he holds the strings and yow ay capable of thinking fer yerself! Yum gunna hang Harry Scriven!" Tears flew from her eyes, she had tried, but she could not save the man who had saved her, the man she loved so desperately. Harry Scriven was lost to the violent ways of his cousin.

She helped the Ted to his feet and across the car park to his 1937 Ford Model Y. He managed to pull himself into the driver's seat and winced as he sat down. Suzy got in alongside him and the pair sped off erratically leaving Scriven stood alone in the car park, covered in blood and thinking about what Suzy had said.

He went back into the pub and turned right into the toilets. He stood looking at himself in the mirror for what must have been at least ten minutes. The intense self-loathing returned… He was turning into his cousin, he even looked like him! *There had to be more to life? Something for him? Something away from Billy Mucklow…*

Chapter 13

C had Cooper's wife adjusted his tie and straightened his collar. He still had limited use of his left hand and needed help with tasks that required the use of both.

"What am yer gettin all dressed up for Bab?" Cooper's wife rarely saw her husband in a suit and tie and was naturally inquisitive. His suit was old, at least second hand and was ever so slightly too big for him, but he could not help but feel a slight tinge of pride and anticipation as he looked at himself in the mirror.

"Am yer gooin to get a proper job?" Mrs Cooper questioned further.

"Ar mar lover… Yow could say that ar'm trying to get a PROPER JOB!" He smiled at his own pun knowing that it would waft straight over her head. He loved his wife dearly, but she was far from being the most intelligent of women. He looked at her, stroked the hair from her face with his un-injured hand and kissed her tenderly on the brow of her head. She looked at him with her unknowing childlike eyes and he felt all the more eager to give his wife and child a better life.

They had both been born and bred in Cradley Heath at a time when poor people really suffered in poverty. As children they had both known times when they had neither food in their bellies or shoes on their feet, but they had found each other and the commitment and love they shared was enough to cause them to marry young. Chad was a slight man and was genuinely not 'cut out' for manual labour. In his determination to provide for his family he had switched to a life of crime.

It was his deepest desire to 'better himself' and achieve a better future for his beloved daughter and right now he was excited about a 'big job' he was planning.

Chad Cooper had made the acquaintance of a maid who worked in a large house near Himley. She had informed him that the owner of the house was an old army colonel who had a hoard of gold he had stolen from natives whilst serving in India. The gold was supposedly hidden in a locked building at the rear of the house and was enough to make anyone fabulously rich!

It was too big a job for Cooper to undertake on his own so he would need the help of a small gang. On this night he had arranged to meet an associate at The Railway pub which was just off five ways in Cradley Heath. There he hoped he would be able to 'sell' his plan and gain some support to help him carry out the 'job.'

"Where am yer gooin?" His wife persisted with the questions.

"To see a mon abaaht' a dog" he joked as he gave her a playful slap on the backside. She blushed and brushed a patch of dust off his jacket with her hand.

"Yer' do look handsome' aer Charlie… Just like the day we were married!"

"And yow look even prettier than yer did that day me wench." He kissed her again and turned to leave for the pub. "Ar'll see yer later love. Not sure what time."

He left the house and set off on the short walk through Cradley Heath towards Five ways where the Railway pub was situated. He wanted to get there early to create the right impression, so he hurried nervously along the road until he reached the pub.

He went inside, ordered a pint of bitter and sat down in a quiet corner where he knew they would not be disturbed. He took out a cigarette to calm his nerves and lit a match. He breathed in the smoke and instantly felt the calming effect as he sat back in the chair and closed his eyes. *What was the worst that could happen?* He told himself as he smoked and fixed his gaze on the entrance to the bar, waiting for his associate to appear.

Several people entered the pub and not one of them was the person Cooper was waiting for. He checked his watch and began to feel anxious. Just as he was about to walk over to the bar and order another pint, the man he had been waiting for walked in.

It had been two nights since his altercation with the Teddy boy on the car park of The Haden Cross and Harry Scriven still sported a badly bruised face. Chad Cooper could not quite decide whether the bruises made him look more intimidating or less so as he had obviously taken a few punches! Cooper had also heard on the 'grapevine' that Scriven had viciously beaten the other guy and had left him needing urgent hospital treatment. Either way, he breathed in deeply as Scriven approached the table and tried not to think about that fateful day when Harry Scriven had broken his hand and left him broken and sobbing at the side of the canal.

"What yer drinkin' aer kid?" Scriven smiled and Cooper immediately felt a little easier.

"Pint of bitter please Mr Scriven."

Scriven returned from the bar with the beers and opened a packet of his much-favoured Pork Scratchings. He placed them in the middle of the table and invited Cooper to "Help himself."

"What can ar dew fer yer then Chad? Yer said it was important?" Scriven had debated whether or not to come but he still felt guilty over his treatment of Cooper and thought that a quick pint was more than what he owed the simple thief.

"Err, yes Mr Scriven..." Cooper took a gulp of his beer and suddenly began to feel a little more confident. "Ar got a proposition for yer... Ar know that ar fucked up before and ar want to meck it up to yer Mr Scriven."

Scriven found it hard to hide his amusement. He placed his beer on a well-thumbed Banks's beer mat and took a pork scratching from the open packet. "I think yow settled yer debt mate." Scriven nodded towards Cooper's injured left hand. "Besides, yow let Billy daahn. There ay no way he's gunna' wanna' use yer again." He shrugged and took out his silver-plated cigarette case and lighter. He lay them flat on the table and gestured for Cooper to take one. Cooper gratefully took one and lent forwards so that Scriven could light it.

"It ay Billy ar wanted to spake to Mr Scriven… This is a private matter that I would like to keep between us two and one other person…"

Scriven instantly felt a little intrigued. He was desperate to become more independent and begin to make moves on his own, away from the ever-commanding presence of his cousin Billy Mucklow.

"What's that then kidda?" Scriven laughed. Despite his intrigue, Scriven could not help but find the whole thing slightly amusing. Here was this young lad, coming to him with a business proposition after what had happened! *Fuck, the kid must have some balls!*

The pub was dimly lit and the darkness of the late January evening meant that Scriven could barely make out the expressions on Cooper's shadowy face.

"Ar've gor a contact." Cooper relaxed and began to explain. "A maid who works in a big house not too far from here… Now this place is owned by an ode Army Colonel… This chap was in India with the army, fuckin' years agew, before the war."

Scriven nodded and waited for Cooper to continue.

"This chap was a right bastard to the locals over there. He took thousands of paahnds of gold off these Indian folks! He sent it back to England on a ship and now he's gor it stashed in a locked building at the back of his gaff!" Cooper adjusted his tie with a hint of smugness. "Nobody knows about it, apart from this maid ar know… He was bangin' er' yer see Mr Scriven." Cooper laughed and removed the cigarette from his lips so that he could take a drink.

Scriven's expression had changed somewhat. He sat smoking a cigarette and was now listening intently to the young thief. "Goo on."

"That's where we come in Mr Scriven… We drive up there, hold a gun to the ode mon's head, knock him abaaht' a bit and get him to give us the keys! We load up the wagon then drive off. He ay exactly gunna phone the law cus he nicked it in the first place!" Cooper took a smug drag of his cigarette and waited for Harry Scriven's response.

"What do yer need me for?"

"Mr Scriven, we both know that I ain't no tough guy… Ar need a couple of hard cases there to sort this fucker aaht an load the stuff onto the wagon. Ar'm askin with all respect Mr Scriven. Yow will be the gaffer, ar'm just coming to yow with mar contact and plan."

"Why come to me after what happened?"

"Ar fucked up Mr Scriven. Yow always seemed like a decent bloke to me and ar want to meck it up and gain some respect… Whatever we meck, yow teck 40 %, me and the other bloke get 25% each and 10% fer the maid. We will meck a fortune!" Small particles of spittle flew from his lips as he spoke excitedly. Scriven was surprised that the young man understood percentages!

"Robbery ay really mar style Chad." Scriven shook his head and gazed at the tip of his cigarette which glowed orange in the dim light of the pub. Every so often, headlights would appear in the window and sweep the dark bar as a car made its way to Five ways and down Cradley Heath high street.

"Yeah, but this ode Army chap is a real bastard… He stole it in the first place so he dow deserve it any more than we do!"

Scriven thought about it. Here was a perfect opportunity to do something for himself and not have Billy on his back. It would also give him the money he needed to pay Irene for what she had spent on the purchase of their home. He could feel like a man again!

"Yow got anyone else in mind?"

"No Mr Scriven. Like ar said, ar'm just coming to yow with the idea. Ar dow wanna get above me station or anything."

Scriven had somebody in mind. "Right… Ar'm interested Chad… Ar've got an idea of who could help us too… Leave it with me." Scriven drained the last of his beer and gave Cooper a threatening look. "Now if this turns aaht to be a set-up, or if yow breathe a word of this to anyone, ar will do a dam sight more than bost yower hand with an omma!"

Cooper held up his hands and nodded nervously. "Ar promise yow Mr Scriven, cross me heart!"

As Scriven drove through Old Hill towards The Haden Cross he thought of nothing other than Chad Cooper's suggestion. Armed robbery was really not his style, but if Cooper was right and the gold had already been stolen, then there was no chance of the Colonel going to the law! Of course, the Mucklow's paid the Police to keep them on side, but the last thing Scriven needed was Billy finding out about the robbery! If the Police thought that the Mucklow's business was armed robbery and not 'protection' rackets then the 'special' relationship the family held with the law would not last much longer! Scriven thought about how his cousin would react, but unlike everyone else in the local area, he was not scared of Billy Mucklow. *It was about time he did something for himself. Plus, if this Colonel was as much of a bastard as Chad Cooper had suggested, it would not be a problem to give him a bit of a slap!*

The V8 Pilot pulled into the darkness of the pub car park. It was now nine o'clock and Scriven knew that Bill and Dick would probably be wondering why he had not arrived yet.

The car headlights illuminated the elaborate front wing of Billy Mucklow's Riley RM and Scriven reversed the Ford into the space next to it. He switched off the lights and glanced across the car park in search of Dick Hickman's Vauxhall. Out of the corner of his eye he was relieved to see that it was tucked away in a quiet corner of the car park.

He locked the door and hurried across the dark car park towards the warmth of the pub. As he entered through the side door Scriven noticed that it was just like any other Friday night, not a free seat in sight and absolutely heaving with people. 'Mr Sandman' by Dickie Valentine was blasting out of the jukebox and a murky fog of tobacco smoke floated throughout the bar. He breathed in the familiar atmosphere and lent against the wooden bar as he waited to be served. It didn't take long as less 'respected' customers (who had been waiting patiently) watched on with a hidden mixture of fear and annoyance. Scriven could not help but feel embarrassed that he had been served before them.

"Get these boys a drink on me too please mate" he said as he eagerly took his pint of mild and smiled warmly at the disgruntled regulars. The men nodded their thanks and suddenly their opinions of him were not so bad…

Scriven weaved through the crowded bar cradling his beer and thanking the revellers who were all eager to move aside for him as he moved towards Billy Mucklow's private room. He opened the door and went inside.

"Where the fuck yow bin?" Mucklow joked as Scriven entered the room. Both he and Hickman were already on their fourth or fifth pint.

"Bet ar know where his bin!" Hickman winked and then laughed. "At home giddin' his Missis a portion!"

Billy Mucklow almost spat out his beer with laughter. "Ar wouldn't say no to er!" he laughed as he placed his beer on the table.

"Fuck off!" Scriven laughed as he sat down next to his cousin. "How come yow pair am being miserable sat in here? Is eavin' aaht theyur."

"Dick was just tellin me abaaht Amy Francis." Mucklow seemed somewhat amused. Amy Francis was a local prostitute who was well known by many a man for miles around. She was by no means unattractive but was 'rough and ready' and had lots of 'attitude.' Scriven smiled and wondered what had happened.

"Her's bin avin' some problems with her ode pimp from over Walsall way. She's from there originally." Mucklow looked at Hickman for further clarification on the story.

"Apparently he faahnd her werkin raahnd ere' and has started demanding money, and more from her!" Hickman raised his eyebrows in mock concern. Scriven grimaced.

"What were yer dewin' raahnd her in the first place?" Scriven laughed and took a long gulp of his beer, he had catching up to do…

"Her come over to me in The Gate Hangs Well last night."

138

"Ar dow mind giving some pimp a kickin?" Scriven looked at Mucklow enthusiastically and waited for his opinion. This was the perfect opportunity for some 'justified' and ethically 'right' violence…

"Naah. It's a dirty business mate. We av to keep on side with the law and ar cor see them putting up with us messin' abaaht with hookers!" Mucklow drained his glass and Scriven could not help but think about what Mucklow would say if he knew about his plans with Chad Cooper!

"Right, ar need a whizz, yow pair want another pint?" Mucklow stood up and picked up the metal beer tray that lay in the middle of the table. Scriven and Hickman nodded and Mucklow went off to the toilet.

Scriven waited for Mucklow to leave the room and began to speak. "How yow fancy meckin a bit of serious cash?" Scriven seized the opportunity to speak to Hickman alone.

"What yow on abaaht' Scriv?"

Scriven explained all about his meeting with Chad Cooper and the opportunity that had been presented to him. He had originally considered Barry O'Leary for the job (it would have been cheaper!), but O'Leary could be a liability at times and the last thing Scriven wanted was for the old Colonel to end up seriously hurt or worse! Scriven even thought that he might donate a small proportion of the money from the robbery to the local Sikh community that had started to emerge in Smethwick. After all, the Colonel had stolen the money from India in the first place! Being something of a 'Robin Hood' character justified the ethics of the job in Scriven's mind further. Scriven and Hickman were not exactly best friends, but they trusted each other and shared a mutual respect through their respective connections to Billy Mucklow.

"What would Bill say?" The opportunity was appealing, but the last thing Hickman wanted to do was upset the boss!

"He dow need to know. I'm askin' yow mate cus ar trust yer and ar want someone there who ar know ar can rely on!"

Hickman took a deep breath and looked at Scriven. "When?" He asked.

"Ar' dow know, Not yet. We'm gunna' do this properly and plan things carefully... We ay Jimmy Danks an' his band of amateur fuck ups!"

"Ar thought this Chad Cooper fella fucked up before?" Hickman lit his cigarette and took a drag.

"He did mate... But he wants to try and meck it up to us..." Scriven wasn't convinced himself, but he was desperate to try and achieve something for himself, away from his cousin.

"What's gooin on in here then?" Mucklow suddenly appeared in the doorway with a tray full of beer and pork scratchings. The two men had suddenly stopped talking and Mucklow was instantly suspicious.

"Ar reckon we should sort this pimp aaht!" Scriven thought quickly to cover any suspicion.

"Yow ay still a gooin on abaaht that am ya?" Mucklow handed the men their beer and they thanked him.

"We dow want no pimps from Wassul' pokin their bloody noses in raahnd' here!" Scriven took the top of his beer and placed it on the table with a slight bang.

"Yow bin bangin' Amy Francis or summet?" Mucklow laughed as he settled back into his chair.

"Fuck off" Scriven smiled.

The three friends laughed and joked the rest of the night away. None of them really cared about the whole Amy Francis issue but it was a good opportunity for banter and masculine teasing.

Billy Mucklow had definitely had more than enough to drink and this was confirmed when he entered the main bar, cigar in one hand and whiskey in the other singing along loudly with Frank Sinatra records. "Ar fuckin' love Fronk" he slurred as he displayed his admiration for the music.

On the other hand, both Dickie Hickman and Harry Scriven found it very hard to think of anything other than their impending bit of potential business. If Cooper was right, both men stood to make a considerable amount of money and Harry Scriven could finally look

Irene in the eye and feel like he was a man making financial commitments to their relationship.

The two men had little opportunity to discuss things properly but the seeds had been sewn. All Scriven had to do now was give Hickman a couple of days to think about things and hope that he would not breath a word to Billy!

The next morning Scriven lay alone in bed. He wondered where Irene had got to but he could not quite face leaving the warm cosy confides of his bed covers to go and look for her.

It was relatively light outside and a quick glance at his watch on the bedside table confirmed that it was nearly half past eight! He was pleasantly surprised by the lack of a hangover as he vaguely remembered polishing off a bottle of Scotch with Billy and then leaving the car on the pub car park so he could walk home.

Irene had been fast asleep when he had got in from the pub and was unappreciative of the bag of sweets he had slung at her as he entered the room worse for wear. The 'Suck mon' always came around the pubs on a Friday night and Scriven would always buy a bag of liquorice and take it home for Irene.

He sat up in bed and reached for his cigarettes.

"Here's yer cup'a tay' Bab." Irene appeared in the bedroom doorway with a tray of tea. She handed Scriven a cup and sat down next to him on the bed, her well-endowed thighs exposed through the shortness of her night dress.

"Thanks Bab." Scriven gratefully accepted the drink. "Ay yow cold?" He asked, gesturing towards her scantily clad attire on a late January morning. Before she had chance to answer there was a loud knock at the door.

"Who the fuck is that at this time?" Scriven moaned as he placed his cup on the bedside table and swung himself out of bed. As he got up, the sudden movement reminded his head that he had been drinking heavily on the previous evening and the hangover finally caught up with him. He pulled on his house coat, slipped into his slippers and made his way down the stairs, a cigarette hanging out of his mouth as he moaned and cursed the earliness of the visitor. He stopped at the front door and pulled it open.

"Hello Harry." It was Dickie Hickman, suited and booted and up early. "Can ar come in?"

Chapter 14

A Waxing crescent moon hung wearily in the early morning sky illuminating a small area of the junction that connected Redhill Lane to Halesowen Road at the top end of Old Hill high street.

Lurking within the darkness of the shadows sat Chad Cooper who was nervously smoking cigarettes. It had been well over a month since he had first approached Harry Scriven with the idea of robbing Colonel Henry Harris and the pair had soon teamed up with Scriven's associate Dickie Hickman to spend the next five and a half weeks meticulously planning the 'heist.'

Harry Scriven was in charge and had insisted that they do things properly and prepare for the job in detail. They had studied maps of the target area and had made several reconnaissance journeys to the locality to ensure that they each knew exactly what they were to do and that the plan would not fail.

Cooper had engaged in no criminal activity throughout the preparation period and his finances were dwindling. The last thing he needed was to get arrested for some-small time job and jeopardise the 'golden prize', besides, if he 'fucked up' again, he knew that Scriven would not be quite so forgiving this time.

He watched as the dying embers of his cigarette glowed orange as it burned out on the floor in front of him and he wondered if Scriven and Hickman would actually come and pick him up. His biggest fear was that now he had told them everything he knew about the target; they would cut him out at the last minute and keep the spoils for themselves.

He lit another cigarette and glanced down at his watch through the dim light of the match. *Five past Six. They were late.* They had arranged to meet at six and be in Himley before seven so that they could surprise the Colonel as he slept off the remnants of the previous night's whisky. They also knew that the Colonel's wife and adult daughter would not be home as they were out of the area visiting family. Harry Scriven had been particularly eager to ensure that no innocent bystanders were involved.

Cooper exhaled tobacco smoke into the dark early morning sky and felt his heartbeat rapidly with a mixture of nerves and anticipation. He had been a thief and small-time crook throughout most of his short life, but he had always specialised in breaking into shops and other small-time robberies. Violence, weapons and robbery that involved the intimidation of people were completely new to him and he was well aware that the potential punishments for such crimes were much more severe than for that of his previous endeavours.

The not-so-distant rumble of a motor engine sounded through the stillness of the early morning and a set of headlights emerged from the direction of Old Hill high street. Cooper squinted as they got closer and looked to see if it was Scriven and Hickman.

The car drew closer and motored past him as it carried on towards Netherton. *Fer Fucks sake, where am they?* He thought to himself as he seriously began to suspect that he had been dumped so that the other two could take a bigger share of the gold. He had done nothing for five weeks and his wife's cupboards were bare. Suddenly, he felt a fool.

Another car passed by and then a couple of bicycles carrying their riders off to work at one of the many chain making factories in Cradley Heath passed him as he checked his watch again. *Quarter past.*

He had been betrayed and there was absolutely nothing he could do about it… Just then, another set of headlights appeared and he told himself that if this wasn't them he would make his way home.

The vehicle was loud and cumbersome and appeared to slow down as it reached the junction. It was an old Austin K3 van that had been made just before the Second World War and as it got closer Cooper was able to make out Harry Scriven sat in the driver's seat, his face like thunder.

The van pulled up and the hydraulic brakes squealed as it ground to a halt. The passenger door flung open and without uttering a word, Chad Cooper climbed up onto the bench seat alongside Dick Hickman before shutting the door.

He sensed an atmosphere and was reluctant to speak before finally muttering "Mornin' Mr Scriven… Mornin' Mr Hickman." There was no response for a minute or two until Scriven finally spoke.

"At least someone stayed fuckin' sober fer today!"

Cooper glanced at Hickman and noticed that he looked slightly worse for wear. Now was certainly not a good time to be suffering from a hangover but Cooper was certainly not brave enough to make a comment.

"Give it a rest Harry" a red eyed Dick Hickman began to speak. "Ar just ad' a few last night to get me some Dutch courage fer today day I!"

Scriven did not look impressed. "Is that why I had to sit aahtside yower house fer ten fuckin' minutes waiting!" Scriven clenched his teeth so hard in anger that another small piece of enamel chipped off inside his mouth. "Ar bay gooin to jail cus' yow cor hold yower ale!"

Hickman looked at Cooper and raised his eyebrows. Cooper remained silent.

Harry Scriven was feeling particularly stressed this morning. The van had been stolen by an associate and had been taken from a company in Hockley. It was not due to be used until the next day and Scriven had switched the plates giving them a good few hours until the truck would be missed. But a plan had been meticulously drafted and it annoyed Scriven that the entire operation had been put back by ten minutes due to Dick Hickman's ill-timed drinking session on the previous evening.

As he drove closer to Himley, a small village four miles west of Dudley, the sun began to slowly rise and Scriven began to have some doubts about the whole thing. *What was he doing? He wasn't no armed robber! What would Billy say? What would Irene think?* A million questions drifted through his mind but still he continued on the road ahead.

Despite his hangover, Dick Hickman seemed confident enough. He smoked cigarettes and made loud coarse jokes about the task ahead of them. Chad Cooper stared at the floor and wandered if his wife would leave him if he ever faced a long prison sentence.

Finally, the van slowed up as it arrived at the gates of Colonel Harris' property. The men had visited the site on several occasions and had played out the scenario several times in their minds, but nothing had ever felt as real as this. This was the big event and their minds were filled with a mixture of adrenaline, fear and guilt.

It was still dark enough to approach the house remaining unseen and the three men cast their eyes upon the shadowy mass that stood in front of them as Scriven slowed the van and ascended upon the house as silently as possible. He switched off the headlights and strained his eyes to make out the driveway in front of them.

"Here we goo then boys." Scriven turned and looked at the other two as he drove past the house on the left side and slowly reversed the Austin down a path that led to an outer building which was supposedly where the Indian gold was kept. "Remember what we planned and do not fuck things up!"

Chad Cooper silently exited the truck first and stealthily made his way across the rear gardens to the side of the house whilst holding a small pair of garden shears. He knew exactly where to go and what he had to do and in no time he was at the rear corner of the old building where a telephone cable ran along the wall. He raised the shears and in one swift movement cut the wire ensuring that it was impossible for whoever was inside the house to telephone for assistance once the robbery started!

Then, like a silent spider stalking across the bedroom floor he crept around to the rear entrance where he met up with Scriven and Hickman. The three men had already stretched their black balaclavas over their faces and were wearing black Crombies with their collars turned upwards.

As Cooper worked on the lock with impressive silence, Scriven pulled out his Webley pistol and held it in his sweaty palm. As usual, the gun was not loaded, but only Scriven knew. Dick Hickman was not quite as subtle, from beneath his coat he pulled a sworn off shotgun which had been loaded with two cartridges with a further four stuffed into his coat pocket. Through the excitement and adrenaline of the moment his hangover had all but ceased and he took a deep breath as he savoured the anticipation of the moment. Hickman's plan had been to storm into the house loudly and announce their arrival, but Scriven and Cooper had managed to convince him that it would be much more appropriate to creep into the Colonel's bedroom early in the morning and take him by surprise.

The lock clicked open and the three men crept into the kitchen. It was dark and deserted with the faintest smell of the previous night's cooking.

Slowly, the three men made their way across the old oak floor to the doorway where they stopped and peered into the equally as deserted hallway.

For Chad Cooper, this was his natural environment and he was relaxed and professional but Harry Scriven felt sick. He could hear his own heartbeat pounding and his brain screamed at him to get out of there as fast as he could, but he ventured on, deeper into the darkness of the home he had no right to be in. He stopped, closed his eyes and reminded himself that the victim *had no rights to the gold they were taking and that he (The Colonel) was a cruel bastard who deserved everything that was coming to him!*

Scriven opened his eyes and felt a little giddy. He took a deep breath and continued to make his way slowly across the floor. It was starting to get light outside and he could see the gradual daybreak emerging through the grand windows that stood at the front end of the large hallway.

Cooper made out the shape of the staircase several feet in front of them and gestured for the other two to head towards it when suddenly one of the main lights in the hallway flickered and slowly came on!

The three men quickly ducked back around a corner and Scriven peered out to see what was going on when to his horror and surprise a woman appeared on the staircase with a cricket bat in her hand.

"Who goes there?" She asked in a stern well-spoken accent. She was of about thirty years of age and was tall and slim with long dark brown hair. She was a particularly attractive woman and all three men could not help but admire her as she stood in a long silk nightdress, her pale white arms exposed and her small but well-proportioned breasts sporting cold erect nipples which were visible through the silk of her attire.

Scriven and Cooper looked at each other in silent confusion. *What should they do now?* Before they could react, Dickie Hickman darted across the hallway, grabbed the woman and yanked the bat out of her hands. She briefly screamed but soon quietened down when Hickman thrust the shotgun in her face and gestured for her to be quiet.

Scriven's heart sank. He really should have anticipated that something like this would have happened and he should have known that bringing Hickman was a bad idea! *There was no going back now!*

Hickman dragged the poor woman into the kitchen and shut the door. He threw her hard against the table and through gritted teeth and in a hushed voice he told her to "Shut the fuck up and not utter a fucking word!"

The light from outside began to seep in through the kitchen windows and the three men could now make out the woman's features as she lay back against the table and looked at them with stubborn eyes. Scriven felt his anger building inside and his natural reaction was to give Hickman a slap and tell him to pack it in, but he stopped himself. The last thing he wanted to do was incriminate them by mentioning any names and Hickman may just scare the woman into handing over the keys to the outer building. The door was heavily bolted and there was no way in other than by locating the key. Scriven was not prepared to intimidate a woman with violence so he happily left it to Hickman. He would just have to keep an eye on him and make sure he didn't go too far!

Chad Cooper was well out of his depth. He looked on with horror and regret.

"Where are the fucking keys?" Hickman demanded as he thrust the shotgun in the woman's face.

"I don't have a clue what you are talking about..." She spoke to him with utter contempt and her stubborn, upper-class defiance turned Hickman on.

"The keys to that fucking building outside you slag!" He pointed in the direction of the outer building and took a step closer to the woman.

"Only my father has the keys to that building and he is not around... So I am afraid gentlemen, that you have wasted your time... Now please fuck off!"

Hickman slapped her hard across the face and cast his eyes over her night dress as she fell back onto the table. He was feeling increasingly aroused by her defiance and had an overwhelming desire to have her right now as he held the shotgun to her face.

Harry Scriven noticed what was going on and quickly intervened. "I must apologise for this inconvenience Madam, but we urgently require those keys."

"And I told you that I do not have them!" She spoke in a highly patronising tone as she tossed her eyebrows in defiance.

"Ar think this bitch needs taychin' a lesson!" Hickman pushed himself closer and grabbed her by the neck.

Scriven could take no more. He moved to stop Hickman when suddenly an older man appeared in the doorway with a huge German shepherd that foamed and snarled at the mouth revealing huge, powerful jaws. The man held the dog firmly by the lead and in his eyes was the same confident, upper class arrogance that was present in his daughter's.

Colonel Henry James Harris was a tall man in his mid-sixties with balding hair that had been pushed into an awkward well-groomed comb over. He sported an immaculate military style moustache that completed his aura of authority and entitlement.

He had spent much of his military career in India as a senior officer in the British Indian army before retiring as a result of the Partition of India in 1947. He had seen plenty of action in The Second World War and had fought in the Middle Eastern campaigns from June 1940 until May 1945.

"What the devil do you think you are doing?" The Colonel demanded as he teased his dog by pulling its collar tight and angering it even more.

"Give us the keys to the outbuilding or we'll blow her fuckin' head off!" Hickman raised his gun to the woman's head and waited for a response.

The Colonel stared at Hickman with an intense irritation that reminded him of his old school master. Then, without any warning, the older man let go of his dog's lead and yelled a command that was incomprehensible.

The dog sprang forwards and made to attack Hickman, but his boxer's reactions were too fast and he simultaneously span and blasted the dog in the head at almost point blank range. Blood instantly splattered across the room and the dying animal fell to the ground. Most of its brains were splattered across the kitchen and its body shook violently for a few seconds before coming to a complete and eternal rest.

Hickman burst out into hysterical laughter and brought the blood covered barrel back into the Colonel's daughter's face. The Colonel was almost visibly distressed by the death of his beloved pet but he retained his 'stiff upper lip' and made no further movements.

"Dow meck me fuckin' do this!" Hickman screamed as he pressed the bloody gun into the daughter's breasts.

Harry Scriven hated to see a woman treated in such a manner, *even if she was a stuck up cow!* He swiftly approached the Colonel and slapped him hard across the face. Before he could fall to the floor, Scriven caught him by the scruff of the neck and shoved him with force against the frame of the door. The Colonel met his gaze and equalled its ferocity with furious defiance. Scriven lowered his voice to a whisper so as only the Colonel could hear.

"We both know yum a bastard Harris! We both know that yer stole from innocent folks in India!" Scriven lowered his voice further. "We both know that yer raped and murdered over there!" He grabbed the older man by the chin and gripped so tightly that the Colonel feared his jaw would crack. Scriven's breath smelt heavily of tobacco and whisky and his eyes exuded violence. "Did yer think it didn't matter cus they had brown skin?" He gripped even harder and pushed his face so close to the Colonel that their noses were practically touching. "Does yower kid over there know what yer got up to?"

A look of concern suddenly came over the Colonel's face. His daughter had no awareness whatsoever of his 'activities' in India!

"Ar thought not." Scriven still spoke in hushed tones. "Yow dow deserve no gold… Maybe we should tell yer pretty wench over there all about it?" Scriven withdrew his hand from the former Army officer's face and held his hand open. "Keys."

The Colonel continued to gaze intently at Scriven, his eyes remained cold and evil and Scriven could tell that the awful stories Chad Cooper had told of him were completely true.

"I have no idea what you are talking about." The concern had all but gone from the Colonel's eyes and his lips even suggested the slightest of a smirk. The man was clearly not scared of Scriven and his defiance was beginning to make Scriven's blood boil! They were supposed to be working to a strict time frame and the sooner they had the gold out of there the better. He searched his brains for the subtlest method of persuasion he could use. *What would Billy do?*

"Don't tell them anything Daddy!" The Colonel's daughter was still pressed against Hickman's shotgun as droplets of nervous perspiration trickled down the spine of her back.

"Is he a good Father is he?" Scriven raised his voice considerably so that the Colonel's daughter could hear.

She looked at him with a mixture of confusion and fear and told him to "Fuck off."

"Did he ever tell yer about a young girl called Karishma?"

The Colonel instantly reacted to the mention of the name and told Scriven to "Shut his insolent mouth!"

Chad Cooper had previously told Scriven about a young Indian girl by the name of Karishma. It had appeared that during his intense love affair with his maid (Cooper's contact), Colonel Henry James Harris had confessed all in an effort to try and free his mind from the intense guilt that had plagued his existence for many years.

Whilst serving in India Harris had made the acquaintance of a stunningly beautiful twelve-year-old girl by the name of Karishma Laghari. He had become fascinated by her and her youthful innocence, though initially she had rejected his advances. Colonel Henry James Harris was not a man to be disappointed so he simply took whatever he wanted.

He regularly raped Karishma and other young girls violently and perversely until one day she had fallen pregnant with his child. To avoid any embarrassment to himself, his regiment and his family, he had strangled the girl and murdered her entire family before setting their shanty home on fire. The story had sickened Harry Scriven and had been much of the motivation behind the planning of the entire robbery.

"Yow gunna' tell her or am I?" Scriven nodded backwards towards the Colonel's daughter.

"If I give you the keys to my private quarters, I trust there will be no further mention of that name?" The Colonel spoke in a whisper so as his daughter could not hear.

"It is not for me to judge you... Yow will meet your maker in good time... Only then will you pay for your crimes..." Scriven looked at the floor... Unable to further look this disgusting human being in the eye.

The Colonel fumbled in his pocket and pulled out a heavy key that he reluctantly passed into Scriven's hand. "I will see you again... You mark my words! In hell!" The Colonel spoke deeply into Scriven's soul and for a moment he froze and said nothing as he considered the eternal meaning of the words. He looked up and once again looked directly into the older man's wicked eyes. "Maybe..."

Scriven then turned slowly around and held up the heavy key in his right hand so that Chad Cooper could see it. The young thief eagerly took it and scuttled outside to the rear of the building to see if it worked.

In the meantime, Hickman's gun remained firmly fixed on the Colonel's daughter's bosom as her father stood at the mercy of Harry Scriven. Scriven thought intently about the poor girl Karishma and her family and about what the Colonel had said to him. *Would he too burn in hell? Would he dangle on the end of a rope whilst this murderous old child molesting rapist lived the life of luxury in this old house? Was he as bad as that?*

The large kitchen now basked in the cold light of the morning sun and Chad Cooper reappeared in the doorway. "It's open!" He proudly announced with a mixture of triumphant glee and relief.

The three robbers then proceeded to use rope from the van to tie The Colonel and his daughter so that they could not escape and alert anyone until well after they had gone.

Before they left the kitchen to load the van, Scriven took one last look at the Colonel's daughter and felt a pang of guilt. *She did not deserve to be caught up in all of this.* She spat at him and screamed abuse... Suddenly he did not feel as bad.

Scriven, Hickman and Cooper hurried to the open rear building and could not believe their eyes. "Happy fucking birthday boys!" Dick Hickman announced as all three gasped in wonder at the hordes of sparkling, shiny gold. Rings, lanterns, obscure ornaments, the likes of which they had never seen before amazed them as they hurried to load every last bit onto the dusty old Austin truck.

"Fuckin hell lads! We'm fuckin rich!" Harry Scriven could not quite hide his delight. Finally, he would be able to hold his head up, pay for his house and feel like a man again.

When it was complete, they piled back into the cab and roared off triumphantly, laughing, joking and celebrating. They had done it!

Chapter 15

T he month of March 1955 passed by with little event. Over the Atlantic Ocean in America, history was made when Claudette Colvin, a fifteen-year-old African American girl refused to give up her seat on a bus to a white woman in Montgomery, Alabama.

Back in the Black Country life went on as it always did. Harry Scriven, Dick Hickman and Chad Cooper had celebrated into the night at various pubs around Cradley Heath after their successful heist, though Harry Scriven had insisted that the gold remained hidden at a secret location for at least a month so as not to raise any suspicion. This was probably not necessary as it was unlikely that Colonel Harris would go to the Police, but Scriven did not want to take any chances.

On Tuesday the 5th of April, Winston Churchill announced his retirement from his second term as Prime Minister due to ill health. He was Eighty years old. The day after, Wednesday April 6th, Billy Mucklow sat inside a swish Birmingham night club, The Grand Casino Ballroom on Corporation Street with his now good friend Isiah Boswell.

Boswell had become rather fond of the young gang boss from the Black Country. He was a war hero, as 'hard' as they came and a man of 'significant character and substance.' Mucklow reminded him a lot of himself in his younger days and he was the sort of man he would rather have as a friend as opposed to an enemy.

The two men sat at the back of the club dressed in immaculately smart tuxedos smoking fine Cuban cigars and sipping chilled French Champagne. Two huge gypsies from Boswell's organisation stood guard and ensured that Mucklow and Boswell were not disturbed.

"How are things going over in Longbridge?" Boswell sat back in his leather seat and reminded Mucklow of the lucrative business he had arranged.

"It's gooin well mate, thanks again for setting that up… How's Northfield Ron?"

"He's in a fucking wheelchair…" Boswell felt a mild annoyance but decided not to linger on it. He was at a stage in his life where he tried his best to avoid trouble. The one-time Peaky Blinder had had heart trouble, was incredibly wealthy and had reached a point where he did not want to risk going to jail or have to deal with the aggravation of gangland violence. He surrounded himself with beautiful prostitutes and enjoyed visiting the races and sitting ringside at boxing matches. He smiled as he noticed Mucklow 'eyeing' an attractive young call girl. "She's a bit tasty isn't she?" Boswell whispered in Mucklow's ear.

Mucklow laughed and nodded. Boswell stood up and walked over to one of the 'gorillas' who was standing guard. He tapped him on the shoulder and told him to fetch the girl for Mucklow. The big man did as he was told and she casually strolled over and sat down at the table next to Billy Mucklow. She gave him a huge beaming smile and Mucklow instantly felt pity for her. She was in her early twenties with narrow almost Oriental brown eyes and long black hair. Her skin was tanned and olive coloured and she reminded Mucklow of the French and Italian girls he had met whilst visiting the Mediterranean shortly after the war. *Why should such a stunning creature be 'entertaining' gangsters in a night club on the orders of Isiah Boswell!* He smiled back and poured her a glass of Champagne.

"I heard about your dealings over in the Jewellery quarter." Boswell blew smoke and hid his amusement.

Mucklow placed a hand on the pretty prostitute's exposed knee and looked at Boswell with confusion. "Ar dow know what yum on about mate?"

"I have my fingers in a lot of pies over that way Bill. Do you know Ernie 'The Fence' Rubinstein?"

The name meant nothing to Mucklow. He shook his head and moved his hand further up the dark-haired girl's thigh.

"He knows your boys… Harry Scriven and Dick Hickman. Apparently, they have been trying to 'flog' a load of 'moody' gold around Hockley. Ernie came to see me last week. He wants me to do something about it." Boswell shrugged and spoke in his best Ernie 'The Fence' Rubinstein impersonation. "We cannot have these fucking schmucks flooding the market with this shit… It isn't fucking Kosher!"

Mucklow looked at Boswell and frowned in confusion. The old man knew something he didn't and it frustrated him.

Boswell took a long drag of his expensive cigar. He trusted Mucklow enough to believe what he was saying. "I suggest you have a little chat with your lads and find out what is going on."

Mucklow respected Boswell and looked up to the older man. But he (Boswell) had an annoying habit of coming across as being patronising and Mucklow always felt mildly irritated in the presence of his 'advice and suggestions'. If Mucklow wanted guidance from anyone, he had his own father to confide in. Though he was often too proud to do so.

Two days later, Harry Scriven sat in his favourite Cradley Heath café looking at the world from over the rim of his teacup.

He had spent the morning calling in on local businesses and was now taking a quick break. He liked to get things done relatively early on a Friday so that he could pick up Fish and Chips from Old Hill and then enjoy them back at home with Irene before meeting up with Billy and the lads at the pub.

Next up was The Regis club and Scriven always approached this venue with caution. It had previously occurred to him that the Hackett brothers had taken their kneecappings on Christmas Eve with little reaction and he did not trust them. It was a two-man job and he had been in the habit of meeting Barry O'Leary in The Wagon and Horses on Redhill Lane at twelve on a Friday so that they could enjoy a swift half, collect from the landlord and then go together to the Regis which was just up the road.

He drained his teacup and stepped out into the lukewarm April sun. It wasn't a warm day but it had been a long cold winter and the early promise of spring was somewhat energising and Scriven enjoyed the delicate rays of sun on his face and hairless head.

He breathed in deeply and the air felt good. It had been over a month since the robbery and they were now ready to start trying to shift the gold. He had already made enquiries around the Jewellery quarter in Birmingham and even though the businesses around there were playing the 'waiting game' he was confident that himself, Hickman and Cooper would soon sell their stash and reap the rewards of last month's heist.

He got into the V8 Pilot and drove the short distance from the high street to The Wagon and Horses.

Barry O'Leary was waiting. He stood leant up against the front of the pub smoking a cigarette. "Billy wants to see yer Scriv" he announced as Scriven got out of his car and walked towards the entrance.

"Ok kidda, ar'll goo raahnd and see him after we sid Bert Hackett."

O'Leary tossed his used cigarette butt to the floor and trod on it. "Billy said he wants to see yer straight away and he's asked me ter bring yer in."

Scriven stepped closer to O'Leary and let out a surprised laugh. *What the fuck was going on? Who did Barry O'Leary think he was giving him orders!* He took another step even closer and pushed his face into O'Leary's. "Yow tellin me what ter dew son?"

"No Scriv, ar'm a just dewin what Billy said. He needs yer straight away... sorry." O'Leary looked at the floor.

"Ok... Get in..."

The two men got into Scriven's car and drove through Old Hill towards the Haden Cross.

The pub was relatively empty at this time of day. O'Leary stayed in the main bar and ordered a pint of bitter and a packet of pork scratchings.

Scriven walked straight through to Mucklow's room and the first thing he saw was an anxious looking Dick Hickman stood in his usual spot near the fireplace. He was sporting a bruised and swollen eye and he raised his eyebrows in an almost relieved greeting as Scriven entered the room.

Mucklow was stood with his back to them looking out of the large bay window. Dick Hickman was always so confident and sure of himself but on this occasion he was quite the opposite. At the back of his mind, Harry Scriven suspected that this probably had something to do with the robbery.

Mucklow turned around, his face was expressionless… He stood staring at Scriven for all of two minutes before finally speaking.

"What the fuck has bin gooin on Harry?" He clenched his fists and struggled to hold back the anger in his voice.

"Ar was gunna ask yow the same question!" Scriven closed the door and took a step closer to Mucklow.

"Don't play yampy buggers with me!" Mucklow kicked a nearby bar stool and it flew onto the floor landing next to Scriven. "I went over to the Jewellery quarter yesterday..." He paused and watched Scriven intently. "Had a chat with a fella called Ernie the Fence." Mucklow posed the name as a question. "Name mean anything to yer Harry?"

Scriven looked at the floor and said nothing.

"He knows yow pair… Said yer bin gooin round Hockley trying to shift a load of fake gold… It's almost fucking funny!" Mucklow spat the word "funny" with annoyance.

"He's a sneaky fucker. He sez its worth fuck all cus he dow want us flooding the market cus he cor afford to buy the stuff!" Scriven shoved a cigarette in his mouth and searched his pocket for a lighter.

"How much of the stuff av yer fuckin' got?" Mucklow snatched the cigarette from Scriven's mouth and threw it at his head. It bounced off his face and landed on the floor. Scriven smiled and gave his cousin a cold hard stare.

"Dow worry, yower mate here has filled me in on everything." Mucklow sarcastically gestured to Hickman who was still standing by the fireplace. "Running round' Himley with shooters! Threatening wenches and roughing up ode fellas?" Mucklow shook his head in disbelief. "Fuck, if the law knew what yow were up ter, they'd close down my entire operation!"

"The ode mon was a right bastard. He deserved everything he got." Scriven tried to explain his rationale but Mucklow cut him short.

"Ar dow give a fuck if he was Adolf fuckin' Hitler! We do not need that kind of attention from the law… Who the fuck do yer think yow am? Yow an' Dick fuckin' Turpin over here!"

Dick Hickman laughed out loud at the 'Dick Turpin' comment and Mucklow saw red, he picked up an empty beer glass and flung it at full pelt towards Hickman's head. The boxer ducked and the glass shattered into a thousand pieces on the wall. "Yow ay so fuckin' smart though am yer! That gold is worth fuck all!"

"Why? Cus Ernie the fuckin' Fence sez so?" Scriven raised his voice and took a step closer to Mucklow.

"No… Me and Dick took some of that gold raahnd ter Henn's Jewellers in Cradley Heath… They'm friends of the family and ar trust em completely."

Harry Scriven knew the Henn family. They were local jewellers who also owned The Cradley Heath Motor Company in Cradley Heath high street where he had worked as a young motor mechanic before the war. Mucklow lowered his voice to a frustrated growl. "They also said it was worth fuck all!"

"Maybe it was just the gold that yer took? Maybe the real gold is mixed up amongst the fakes?"

"No Harry." Hickman entered the conversation. "We drove the chap from Henn's raahnd to see the gold we got stashed… It's all worthless mate… Best gid it ter the rag un boone mon."

Scriven felt a deep disappointment and embarrassment. He felt as if his entire world was sinking around him. It had all been for nothing… The planning, the risks, the needless aggression towards the Colonel's daughter.

"Ar did a bit more digging about this Colonel Harris with some ode army pals… Turns out everybody knew about this fuckin' gold. It's a bit a bit of a joke apparently." Mucklow half smiled. Scriven sat down and held his head in his hands.

"Apparently, he spent a lot of money getting this stuff back from India only to find out that it was worthless tat. Why do yer think he still had it? If it was worth sumet he would have fuckin' sold it by now!" Mucklow took a deep breath, his expression showing a mixture of anger and pity. He flashed the slightest of an amused smile. "Dow goo into armed robbery aer kid!"

Scriven looked up at Mucklow and was relieved to see that he was no longer quite as furious… Though nothing seemed to matter anymore. "Sorry Bill." He said, sheepishly pulling out another cigarette and lighting it. *He had hit a new low… Could this utter humiliation get any worse?*

Harry Scriven's world descended into total darkness. *He was dictated too everyday by his younger cousin and he lived in a house paid for by his woman… All of the wicked violent things he had done in his life counted for nothing.*

He had so desperately wanted to do something for himself, be something other than just another one of Billy Mucklow's goons. He felt as if his whole life he had been 'taking handouts' from his cousin and this had been his big opportunity to prove that he could do something for himself and gain respect from Bill.

Mucklow retreated back to the window and leant casually against the frame. "Who was the other guy?" He asked, knowing full well that it had been Chad Cooper, but the last thing he wanted was to upset his cousin even further by making him punish Cooper again so he pretended not to know.

"Nobody… Just some fella from the boxing club. I dragged him into it… Best leave him out of it." Despite his annoyance, Scriven did not

161

want to create further consequences for Chad Cooper. Of course, he would be having a word with him, but he did not have the heart to break his hands again or worse! Dick Hickman frowned knowingly but chose to say nothing.

Mucklow stood in silence for about five minutes before turning back to face the men. "Dick, goo an' get us some beers… We could all use a drink…"

Hickman went towards the door before Mucklow spoke again. "Just hear this now, yow pair ever try anything like this again behind mar back and there will be serious fuckin' consequences!" He raised his right hand and pointed at Hickman and Scriven. "An ar mean fuckin' consequences, do yer understand?" Hickman nodded and Scriven just stared at the floor.

"No beer fer me Dick…" Scriven shook his head sadly and stood up to walk towards the door. Mucklow tried to intervene but he looked the other way as he exited the room, unable to look his cousin in the eye.

Scriven went out to his car and sat there for what seemed like an eternity. *What now?* He thought to himself. *Go home to Irene?* He had been telling her throughout March that he would soon be coming into vast amounts of money and that he would finally be able to pay for his share of their house. He had even promised to drive her down to Cornwall to see the sea and his old RAF haunts.

He chain smoked and stared morbidly at a piece of rope he had taken from the boot of the car and placed on the passenger seat. As he stared Suzy Miller's words echoed through his head- "Yow'll hang Harry Scriven."

His feelings of guilt, self-loathing and humiliation returned to haunt him… *The rope would end it all, hang mon's noose!* He laughed at the irony as tears flooded down his face, the bitter salt burning the corners of his eyes.

His plan was to drive to a spot just outside Stourport by the river Severn. In the summer, as kids, Scriven and Billy used to cycle to their special place and sit for hours fishing and drinking bottles of stolen beer in the shade of the big old oak tree. Scriven smiled through his tears at the memory. It had been a happy place and how he wished that both he and Billy could return to simpler, purer times… He thought of his mother, he thought of Irene and he thought of Billy… He pushed the key into the ignition and went to pull the starter.

"What yow a' dewin?" It was Billy Mucklow. He had popped out to use the lavatory and noticed that Scriven's car was still sat in the car park. He had wondered across and opened the door. Scriven was startled. "Ar'm gooin home Bill."

"Why yer sat aaht here then?" Mucklow noticed the course rope on the passenger seat and a look of horror and concern filled his face.

"What the fuck is that?"

"Just some ode rope Bill." Scriven could not look at his cousin.

Mucklow was shocked at Scriven's intentions. "Dow worry abaaht this Colonel Harris thing Harry… It's all sorted now kidda. No harm done. Mucklow put a reassuring hand on Scriven's shoulder.

Scriven sighed deeply and concentrated on the steering wheel.

"Yer know what yow need dow yer?" Mucklow patted his cousin on the back.

Scriven looked up. "What?"

"A fuckin' holiday!"

"What daahn Stourport?" Scriven had already made plans to go there…

"Dow be saft, a real holiday… Spain!"

"Spain?" Scriven had never been abroad before and to him the idea was ludicrous.

"Ar… Spain… Boswell was telling me abaaht this place called Andalucía. He stays in a Villa over there, got a swimming pool and everything!"

To Harry Scriven, Villa was a football team and a swimming pool was the outdoor baths up at Haden Hill next to the big house!

He thought about how Irene would love to go to Spain. Mucklow banged his hand down on the steering wheel. "Best of all Harry, its fuckin' hot! Not like Stourport or Weston fuckin' Super Mare!" He smiled meaningfully at his cousin and closed his eyes at the prospect. "Me, yow and the wenches, we'm a gooin..."

Scriven shook his head. "Bill, ar cor keep teckin handouts from yer like this."

"It ay an handout aer kid... There's a bit of business ar wanna look into over there so it will be like work really... Besides, ar need somebody to watch me back whilst ar'm dewin business. Ar dow think ar could put up with two weeks cooped up with Dick an his bimbo Missis! So yow'll atter' come!"

Scriven was intrigued. *What was this business in Spain?* He smiled warmly and agreed to go.

"Now, come back in and have a fuckin' beer..." Mucklow held open the door and the two men strolled back towards the pub.

Chapter 16

The Spanish Civil War broke out in the summer of 1936. For three years the Nationalist forces led by General Francisco Franco fought the communist leaning Republican side.

The War was viciously fought and there were many despicable atrocities committed by both sides. Over half a million people were killed, many of whom were civilians who were murdered for their political or religious beliefs. When Billy Mucklow and Harry Scriven visited the country it had been 16 years since the end of the War.

Unlike his cousin, Harry Scriven had never left Britain before and on Saturday the 4th of June 1955 he touched down at Malaga airport after an expensive and luxurious flight from the UK.

Alongside him was his lady friend Irene Miller, Billy Mucklow and his wife Mary and their two young children. The scorching heat and humidity had greeted them as they left the plane and Scriven instantly loved it.

They had then ventured on an uncomfortably sweaty taxi ride through the city of Malaga and out to the outskirts of the coastal town of Torremolinos. It was here that Isiah Boswell owned a very large private Villa that was permanently occupied by his youngest son Patrick.

Patrick Boswell's name had been chosen by his Irish mother Niamh and he had been very much dotted on by his parents. His elder brothers had all joined their father as gangsters in the family business, but this was not what Boswell senior wanted for his youngest son. He had been sent to live in Spain at the age of twenty-one to look after the family's holiday home and as a way of keeping out of the Boswell's criminal activities.

He had settled into the area perfectly and was very much a part of the mid nineteen fifties social scene that was beginning to develop in Torremolinos. It was made up mostly of hip wealthy British expatriates and was even beginning to attract glamorous visitors from further away in exotic places such as Hollywood.

During the first half of the nineteenth century the town had been rebuilt and by 1849 there were fourteen mills and seven hundred and five inhabitants. When the mills closed in the nineteen twenties, Torremolinos became a small fishing village, however, by the mid nineteen fifties things were starting to change drastically as more and more foreign tourists were starting to make their way to the area.

Patrick Boswell was nothing like his father. Boswell senior had been raised in the back streets of Aston during the latter part of the previous century and had made his way through the cutthroat razor gangs and risen to the top in the nineteen twenties. Boswell junior was suave and sophisticated, smoked fine cigarettes, drank Pina Coladas and would spend his days posing up and down the Mediterranean in his brilliant white Mercedes Benz sports car. He lived in his father's luxurious Spanish property with two young Spanish maids and his agonizingly beautiful Spanish fiancé Antonia. It was here that Billy Mucklow had arranged to stay for two weeks enjoying his friend and business partners' hospitality.

After a couple of days adjusting to the Andalusian pace of life, Harry Scriven found himself relaxing in the mid-day sun on the vast terrace that extended across the entire length of the Boswell's villa.

The sun was relentless and Scriven basked in its glorious heat, its rays reinvigorating him and making him feel happy to be alive for the first time in months. He wore a pair of fawn cotton chinos and a light blue shirt that was unbuttoned and casual. As he lay in the sun a bottle of perfectly chilled Estrella Damn lager stood next to him. He had never really drunk lager before as it had not been readily available in Britain, but like the rest of Spain, he liked it, its crisp, dry flavour perfectly refreshing in the burning heat of the Andalusian sun.

The Mucklows and Irene had complained that it was too hot and had suffered with their stomachs since arriving, but not Harry Scriven, it was hot, it was beautiful and he thought that he would rather not return to the drab, grey and depressing streets of his homeland.

As he lay baking in the sun, he had a perfect view of the Mediterranean that was separated from the Villa by fields of Olives and a far corner of the town that was visible from the terrace. Immediately in front of the terrace was a large elaborate pool that was currently occupied by Patrick Boswell's stunning fiancé Antonia.

Scriven could not help but watch her as she floated and gracefully propelled herself through the cool water. She was easily the absolute most beautiful woman he had ever set eyes upon. She had long dark hair, piercing brown eyes and glowingly radiant tanned skin that adorned her perfectly slender body. Her exquisite Latin perfection intoxicated him as did the beer that was stronger than what he was used to and each day since his arrival he had timed his presence on the terrace to coincide with her daily swim.

Each day she had smiled at him as she made her way back to the Villa after her swim, her wet semi naked body dazzling him in the sun. She knew exactly what she was doing, she did not find these balding, overweight, Englishmen attractive but she had a respect for Scriven and Mucklow's down to earth no-nonsense attitudes. She also hoped that one of them could help her.

Harry Scriven had made it perfectly obvious that he was quite smitten with her and she would use this to her advantage. Her fiancé Patrick was a selfish, self-obsessed man and he had no real interest in her other than her purpose of being an attractive doll on his arm. To him, she was just another accessory of cool like his Ray Ban sunglasses and his Mercedes sports car.

The Sun shone through the palm trees and cast a golden shimmer across the pool as it rippled from the movement of Antonia lifting herself out of the water. She smiled and slowly made her way over to Scriven, exaggerating the movements of her naked hips and pushing her bikini clad breasts firmly to the front. The sun cooked floor burned her feet as she walked but she kept her composure and retained a perfectly graceful movement.

"Ola Senor Scriven." She sat herself down on a chair opposite him and melted him with her smile. She could not have been more than twenty-four years old but Scriven felt like a school boy in her presence.

"It's an incredibly lovely country you have here." Scriven spoke slightly nervously. He tried his best to sound respectable and refrained from his native accent.

Antonia sighed and looked out to sea. "Yes… It is very beautiful country… But appearances can be very deceptive."

Scriven lit another cigarette and offered her one. She graciously accepted and took a cigarette from the case. She lent forwards and he lit her up.

"I like you Senor Scriven. I only know you for few days but there is no bull shit with you… You are what the English and Americans call Gangster right? You are Criminal?"

Scriven took a drag of his cigarette and wondered if she meant the question as a compliment or insult. Her English was not perfect and he was a little unsure of her meaning. He nodded slowly.

"You are here to build Casinos and Hotels yes? Like the Mafia in Las Vegas?"

Scriven shrugged and blew out smoke. He really had no idea of Billy Mucklow's plans. *He did as he was told.* "You have a problem with Englishmen coming to your country?"

Antonia smiled again. "I am engaged to an Englishman; he is very wealthy… Franco seems very happy to allow English money into our country… He wishes to join United Nations and gain respectability to cover up for fact that he is Fascist Dictator."

Scriven was no expert on Spanish politics… He listened intently and nodded his head from time to time in an effort to look as if he knew what she was talking about.

"You English were not so eager to come here in the thirties when Franco and his friends the Nazis were massacring innocent people!"

Scriven smiled and felt a little uneasy at her passionate intensity. He was used to women who talked about pretty dresses and housework!

"Franco may think that he is some kind of God, an almighty ruler for Spain, but I tell you this Senor Scriven, he is asesinando bastardo!" Her eyes flickered with passionate hatred and Scriven was drawn to her like a moth to the flame, her fiery intense eyes so seductive in the heat of the mid-day sun. She was dragging him in and she had him right where she wanted him.

"I must confess Senor Scriven... I have favour to ask you... I know I not know you long, but I would like you to help me?" She crossed her long legs slowly and sat back in her chair. Scriven continued to smoke his cigarette, barely able to conceal his pure amazement.

"You and Senor Mucklow, you have car yes?"

Scriven nodded, they had acquired the use of a black Seat 1400. The first car built by Seat in Barcelona in 1953. It was a rebranded Fiat 1400 which had also been the Italian maker's first integrated chassis model.

"I want you to take me somewhere... I cannot drive." She looked at him, this time her eyes were softer, almost pleading. "It is quite far from here. Over fifty kilometres. It is forbidden place."

Scriven wondered what on earth he was getting himself into, but Mucklow had told him to use the car whenever he wanted. They were not due to travel to any business engagements until the second week of the holiday. *It would be nice to see more of this amazing place and it would be an opportunity to spend more time in the company of this beautiful creature.*

"Where do you want to go?" He asked as he took a refreshing sip of his lager.

"It is forbidden place... You must not mention it to anybody. I will tell you more when we get there."

Scriven was intrigued.

The next morning at 6:30 AM, Scriven met Antonia secretly on the terrace. He had told Irene that he had business to attend to and Patrick Boswell was so far out of his mind on Moroccan Hash that he had no idea or concern for the whereabouts of his fiancé. Boswell and Mucklow had really seemed to 'hit it off' and were up all-night smoking joints and consuming vast amounts of Champagne.

The sun was slowly rising and Scriven kept his eyes peeled for the fascinating lizards that crawled across the walls and caught his interest.

"I wondered if you would come." She whispered in the stillness of the morning air. She was wearing a short summer dress and her face and hair was as captivating as ever. She reminded Scriven of the actress Elizabeth Taylor, but she was even more beautiful.

"I'm looking forward to seeing more of Spain." Scriven smiled and gestured towards the rear of the Villa where the cars were parked. He was still trying hard to subdue his thick Black Country twang in the presence of Antonia.

"You must think I am incredibly foolish Senor Scriven." A vulnerable innocence was in her eyes as she led the way towards the cars. "Going off, alone with a strange man I have only just met... I have had to take a lot of risks in my life... I am desperate."

The car journey was long and as the sun rose higher in the sky the intensity of the heat within the car grew drastically. Antonia fanned herself with a traditional Spanish fan and Scriven relished the faster open stretches of road as the movement of the car would transfer fresh air into the Seat through the open windows. For a man who was used to a three litre Ford Pilot, the Seat 1400 was less than impressive.

They headed north east from Torremolinos along the coast road to the City of Malaga where they continued to head alongside the Mediterranean towards Nerja passing through Torre del mar, Velez Malaga and Torrox until they reached the outskirts of Nerja.

Here they turned left into the Sierra Mountains towards Frigiliana. The road suddenly began to ascend drastically and Scriven was forced to select a lower gear to allow the car to climb up the steep incline through the sharp bends in the road.

The scenery was like nothing he had ever seen before and the roads were like nothing he had ever driven on before. They were rough and dusty and the slightest mistake or lack of concentration would propel them over the sheer cliffs to a certain death.

They eventually reached the village of Frigiliana and decided to stop for a rest. The small village with its rustic whitewashed buildings reminded Scriven of a scene from a Western movie. It was of such a contrast to his homeland and the terraced streets and smoggy factories of the Black Country seemed a million miles away.

He paused to enjoy the dramatic mountain scenery and was amazed by the lack of greenery. In England, at this time of year, the countryside would be a wash with green trees and shrubbery. But here, the ground was scorched and dominated by grey rock interspersed with the green of the odd tree.

It was a beautiful little village; the pace of life was much slower and there were far less cars. Scriven thought that things had probably not changed much in the last one hundred years as Mountain donkeys continued to work the cobbled streets. It reminded him a little of when he was a child in the early nineteen twenties and he would see 'oss n' carts' around the streets of the Black Country.

The sun continued to beat down intently and Scriven's throat was parched and dry. They found a small bar and Scriven felt like James Stewart in a Western movie as he walked into the local saloon and ordered a beer. The locals all stopped and stared at this foreigner, *what was he doing here?* Luckily Antonia was there to do the talking and the cold crisp Estrella felt like heaven as it hit the back of his throat and refreshed his mouth.

"We are almost there." Antonia spoke in a hushed whisper.

"Where am we going?"

"I cannot tell you until we get there… You must never tell a soul where we have been… We would be shot for going there!"

A small tear appeared in the corner of her right eye and Scriven decided not to ask any further questions. He drank his beer quickly and resisted the temptation to take another. The roads were awful and little used by cars. The slightest of mistakes would prove fatal and Scriven wanted to keep his head clear so that he could safely negotiate the sweeping, meandering Mountain tracks.

Scriven and Antonia got back into the Seat and continued their ascent deeper into the Sierra De Tejeda Mountains. Scriven dared not to admire the scenery as the road appeared to get narrower every fifty feet the car travelled. They drove on and on and Scriven began to wonder why she had told him that they were almost there, his concentration unwavering, sweat poured from his brow and dripped onto the steering wheel.

Antonia looked around as if she was trying to remember where to go. "You will need to turn right in a minute Senor Scriven."

Scriven looked to his left for a second and felt instantly nauseous at their altitude and the sight of the ground hundreds if not thousands of feet below, all that separated the tyres of the car from the sheer drop was literally inches of track.

"Stop… Turn right here." Antonia suddenly pointed to what looked like barely a path reaching off to the right and climbing higher into the Mountains. Scriven was having difficulty hearing, his stomach was bilious and his ears were full and throbbing with the altitude of their position.

He could not believe that he was being asked to drive on yet further up into the Mountains on yet an even narrower road! He did not want to show fear in front of Antonia so he dutifully turned the wheel and drove on as instructed. By now he was travelling on auto-pilot and the road seemed to stretch on for ever, growing yet narrower. He longed to stop the car and get out and walk, but something kept him travelling on despite the fact that he knew that somehow he would have to get back down from here!

He turned and looked at Antonia. She was now sobbing and tears streamed down her pretty face. In that instant, he simply did not know what to say. Then, in front of them, about two kilometres down the Mountain track he could see what appeared to be a small village.

"Where is that?" He asked, nodding towards the distant village.

"That is my home…" She spoke through salty tears. "That is El Acebuchal."

Scriven said nothing. He was glad that they were finally near their destination and he was glad that he would be able to get another beer in the village.

The car pulled up at an opening at the side of the village next to a small chapel. Scriven and Antonia got out and Scriven noticed that the trees looked noticeably greener up here. Mosquitos circled around his head and he slapped his right hand against his neck to try and squash one.

He looked around and noticed an eerie silence. He glanced at his watch, it was not quite time for siesta, *why was it so quiet?* He said nothing and followed Antonia along a cobbled path that led into a narrow street of small, whitewashed dwellings with slightly slanted roofs that stood unevenly alongside the cobbles of the path. To the right, trees were unkempt and had overgrown onto the path and submerged parts of the buildings. The whole village appeared deserted and Scriven wondered if another living soul was present.

Antonia led the way and as Scriven wondered if he would find a beer anytime soon, she came to a small house with uneven steps that led up to the front door.

 She climbed up and pushed the door open. Inside was the shell of a room that had once been her home. Gone were any traces of human occupancy and Scriven shivered at the somewhat disturbing eerie silence of the place. He did not believe in ghosts, but if he did, he would be sure that this place was haunted.

Antonia immediately threw herself into the wall and began to sob uncontrollably. Scriven approached her and placed a hand on her shoulder. She turned and embraced him, clinging to him as a distraught child would to their father or mother. He still had no understanding of why they were there and why she was so troubled.

She pulled away from him and hung her head next to the glass-less window and looked out at the rugged scenery of the Sierras de Tejeda.

"This was my home... I was born in this room."

Scriven wondered if it would be disrespectful to light a cigarette. He offered Antonia one and was relieved when she accepted. He lit her up and then took one out for himself. They stood in silence for what seemed like an eerie eternity, not another soul for miles around and then she began to speak.

"I remember it well... Seems like yesterday... February 1937, I was five years old." Her voice quivered and she dragged hard on the cigarette to compose herself. "Some men came here, soldiers, Fascists... They worked for Franco... They said my father was a communist. This was not even true..." She put the cigarette back in her mouth as tears continued to flow down the sides of her cheeks and she recalled memories that had haunted her since childhood. "They took my father and my two older brothers... They were just eleven and twelve years old. They were taken from this building and executed... Buried in unmarked graves, I do not even know where they are buried..."

Scriven looked at the floor, unable to find words of comfort.

"I remember my mother sobbing, I did not understand? Where was my father? My brothers Luis and Miguel?"

The mountain range stood unmolested and unchanged since she was a child. The sight of it was both comforting and upsetting at the same time. "Then, in 1948, Fascists returned to the village. They accused us of supporting rebel communists and ordered us all to leave our homes. Nobody was to return here, it is forbidden place. They said that if we returned, we would be shot... I went to live in Malaga with my mother, she died not long after and I was forced to fend for myself." She took one last look around and as she approached the door. "I have not been here since." She slung the used cigarette butt out of the window and looked appreciatively at Scriven. "Thank you for bringing me here Senor

174

Scriven… I feared I would not see this place again… It breaks my heart… It breaks my heart."

As they walked back to the car through the deserted streets Scriven wondered how such a beautiful place could have such a violent past. He looked up at the tops of the mountains and felt uneasy. They were so high up and he knew he would have to drive back the way he had come, but there was an unsettling, haunted atmosphere that clung to the very fabric of the village and he was more than ready to leave.

The drive back to Torremolinos was sombre and quiet. The descent down through the mountains was just as stressful and as terrifying as the ascent and Scriven was relieved to pass back through Frigiliana and return to the flat and even coastal roads.

On return to the Villa, she kissed his cheek in a show of appreciation and explained that there was no way her fiancé would ever have taken her there. She got out of the car as if nothing had happened. She dried her eyes and fixed her make-up, preparing herself for her wealthy fiancé. Scriven watched her from the comfort of the driver's seat and then watched her figure as she strolled back casually towards the Villa.

Today had been a dramatic, emotional and bittersweet day that was of a stark contrast to any other experience of his 36 years… No beatings, no protection payments and no Billy Mucklow! His love for Spain was growing deeper and he thought right then that he probably never wanted to leave.

Chapter 17

Scriven saw very little of Antonia over the next few days. He spent his time with Irene, taking her out to see some of the vicinity and hoping that she would generate some of the same enthusiasm for the country that he had.

"Yer can teck the girl aaht of Tipton, but yer cor teck Tipton aaht the girl!" she would proudly announce whenever he tried to enrich her with some of the local culture.

Billy Mucklow seemed to be embracing his surroundings though. He loved the sea, the beaches and the long lazy afternoons sat watching the coastline whilst enjoying a bottle of chilled Cava and a selection of fine cigars. He had also started to enjoy the climate and was making the most of the sun.

Exactly a week and a day after their arrival in Spain it was time to get down to business. Mucklow had a meeting in Torremolinos and in typical Billy Mucklow style he sat sprawled out on the back seat of the Seat 1400.

He wore an expensive off-white suit, a pair of Ray-Ban wayfarer sunglasses and was smoking a large Cuban cigar. Harry Scriven wore similar attire and checked himself in the rear-view mirror as he drove. He smiled.

"Where we gewin then?" He asked as he worked the gearbox of the underpowered Seat. "Yer may have told yer Missis that we'm a gooin ter see a man abaaht a dog, but that ay gunna wash with me!"

Mucklow laughed. He had not seen his cousin in such a good mood in months if not years. "Yer like Spain dow yer Harry?" He winked and grinned. "Where'd yow ger off ter the other day? With Paddy Boswell's bird?"

Scriven said nothing and kept his eyes firmly on the road ahead of him.

"Be careful Scriv... The Boswells are valuable business associates and the last thing we need is yow fucking things up by bangin' Paddy's wench!" Mucklow blew smoke into the cabin and looked at Scriven enviously. "Ar dow know how yer do it Harry... First Irene's daughter Suzy and now this tidy Spanish sort? If pretty young wenches am gooin for middle aged bald bastards then ar want mar share!"

Scriven laughed knowing that Mucklow already had his fair share of 'bits on the side!' "It ay like that Bill."

Mucklow raised his eyebrows unconvinced. "She's a lovely bit of stuff Harry, just be fuckin' careful kidda."

The car pulled up alongside the Torremolinos sea front and Mucklow tapped his cousin on the shoulder. "Come on Harry, yer can tell me... Ar bay gunna tell Irene!"

"Honestly mate, it wore nuthin' like that." Scriven may have wished many times that there was more to his relationship with Antonia, but unfortunately for him, this was really not the case.

The two men waited in the car until a fat young man in glasses tapped on the window. "This is the chap!" Mucklow announced and both he and Scriven got out of the car.

"Mr Mucklow?" The fat man extended his right hand and Mucklow shook it firmly.

"Mr Ellis?"

"Yes sound mate, call me Davey." The fat man spoke with a thick Liverpudlian accent. He was well dressed though his accent and mannerisms celebrated his tough working-class roots.

"This is my associate Harry Scriven." Mucklow touched Ellis on the side of the arm and gestured towards his cousin. Ellis extended his right hand and Scriven shook it. Behind the Scouser stood two burly minders who said nothing.

Davey Ellis was a self-made man of twenty-seven years of age. He had made his money as an entrepreneur in the back streets of Liverpool, dealing in petrol rations and anything else he could get his hands on. His latest venture was the setting up of a boutique travel agency business in which he was undergoing pioneering work to send the British upper and middle classes on holidays abroad.

"Look at this place Mr Mucklow, it's a fucken' gold mine!" Ellis took out a huge Havana cigar and offered one to Mucklow and Scriven. Mucklow was already smoking one but Scriven accepted gratefully. One of the minders lit it for him and Ellis started to walk slowly across the seafront, the two men from the Black Country followed.

"Ever bin to fucken Blackpewl Mr Mucklow?" Ellis continued to walk slowly. He rushed for nobody. "Or Southport?"

"I can't say that I have Mr Ellis."

"Please call me Davey... It's a fucken shite hole full of drunkard Scousers and Mancs!"

Mucklow and Scriven laughed, they had met many Northerners during their military days.

"Yer see Mr Mucklow, this place here has got real class..." He sucked on his cigar. "An best of all, it's fucken hot and it never fucken rains!" Ellis stopped walking and looked out across the beach. "This is the place to be lads. Ava Gardner was here last week, with Frank fucken Sinatra! Do yer think Old Blue Eyes ed' go ter fucken Blackpewl?"

Mucklow and Scriven laughed again. Davey Ellis was a likeable character and Mucklow was particularly impressed at the mention of his favourite entertainer Frank Sinatra!

"Der ya know what were gunna call this place lads?" Ellis opened his arms as he spoke and Mucklow and Scriven shook their heads. "The Costa Del Sol!" Ellis smiled smugly. "It means, The Coast of Sun! And just fucken' look at it! It is the coast of fucken sun! People are gunna flock here."

Mucklow took a drag of his cigar and tossed the smoke back into the air. "So what der yer want from us?"

Ellis smiled at the moment he had been waiting for. "Look over there pal." He pointed to a building site that stood at the far end of the seafront… "When it's finished its gunna be the Hotel Pez Espada! It will be the finest fucken' hotel in Europe if not the world!"

Mucklow and Scriven looked on with interest.

"Der yer know what a hotel out here is Mr Mucklow?"

Mucklow shook his head.

"It's fucken money! An the more hotels built here is more people that pay me to bring them here… Things are very different here Mr Mucklow… It ain't like fucken' England! People like us can be somebody over here, cus we don't need permission from the establishment, the old skewl fucken' tie!" Ellis straightened his back and gestured towards himself. "Look at me, a kid from Norris Green! The government here don't give a fuck who you are or what fucken' school you went to."

Billy Mucklow had actually been to a grammar school. He was an Old Halesownian and had also been an officer in the British Army, but at this time he thought it best to keep this quiet!

Ellis turned to face Mucklow and spoke directly to him. "Der yer wanna spend the rest of yer life running fucken' protection rackets in dodgy old men's pubs? Fuck that! Come out here and build a fucken' hotel and casino! The fucken Mafia built Vegas, we can build The Costa Del fucken Sol!" Ellis eyes widened in excitement, he placed a hand on Mucklow's shoulder and raised his cigar into the air.

Mucklow took another drag of his cigar, he stepped forwards and looked out over the beach. Harry Scriven was already sold. He had developed a love for Spain and longed to escape the violent gangland he had become a part of back home.

Mucklow looked at Ellis, his eyes cold and expressionless. "So then Davey boy… How much?"

"Ok… So the Spanish government are eager to get overseas investments in, they got this thing called Credito Hotelero… It basically means they will finance sixty fucken' percent of yer hotel construction costs and you pay em back over the next twenty years with practically zero interest! Spanish builders werk fer peanuts but they are lazy fuckers with their fucken' siestas an all that. I reckon that if ya invest two

179

hundred thousand British pounds yer could build yourselves a nice small to mid-sized hotel. You'd be sold out and making a fortune on the casino too… In ten years' time this whole fucken seafront will be covered in high rise hotels… Yer just gotta strike now whilst the opportunity is there!"

Mucklow winced inwardly at the mention of two hundred thousand pounds… It was an absolute fortune and he reckoned that he could probably raise approximately half of that figure if that! He didn't let this show, he puffed thoughtfully on his cigar and gave nothing away. "Well, I'm sure it beats knee capping fuckers in the Regis Club in Ode Hill!" Mucklow laughed and the other men joined in. "But answer me this Davey, the UK government limits the amount of cash we can teck aaht of the country… They dow like us spending our cash abroad. The limit we can take abroad is one hundred quid mate!"

"Don't worry about that Mr Mucklow… It's all about paying off the right people, no problem at all."

Mucklow suddenly stopped walking and frowned in a deliberately suspicious manner. "So why ay yow building hotels here?"

"I fucken' am mate… But we need more and more, bars, hotels and casinos."

Mucklow nodded and turned and looked at Scriven. He was smiling and Mucklow knew that his cousin would be overwhelmingly in favour of moving to Spain. *But how to finance it?*

Davey Ellis looked down at his watch and held his hand out for Mucklow and Scriven to shake. "Anyway lads, its bin nice talking to yers but I gorra meet some Cockney fuckers in ten minutes… There's a lot of fucken' interest mate and like I said, yer gorra take the opportunity now before some other fucker gets in!" He shook the two men's hands and retreated off towards his Mercedes. "See yer later lads." He abruptly stopped and turned around. "If yer do decide to get involved, have a chat with Paddy Boswell and his old man… They are investing too and I know they are good mates of yours so best talk to them…" With that he held his right hand up to bid them farewell and continued off towards the car.

"That was a pretty quick meeting!" Scriven was hoping they could go for a beer now.

"Ar… It was brief…" Mucklow was deep in thought. He looked out across the scorching beach that was made up of a mixture of sand, shingle and baking hot pebbles that had lay cooking in the Andalusian sun for years. He took off his jacket and threw it over his shoulder. "Der yer fancy a paddle?"

The two men rolled up their expensive trousers and hobbled down towards the seashore, moaning and cursing as they went due to the heat of the rocks on the beach. They reached the seashore and Scriven closed his eyes as he enjoyed the feel of the cooling Mediterranean on his feet and ankles.

"Fuckin' hell mate… Ar fuckin' love it here." Before he could utter another word, Mucklow charged him from behind sending him flying and fully suited into the water.

"You bastard!" Scriven barked as he flung himself at his cousin to try and pull him in, but Mucklow had already dived in headfirst and the two men erupted in laughter. The water was a cooling relief from the sun and passers-by looked on in amusement as the two fully clothed Englishmen relaxed in the water.

"What der yer think of this deal then Harry?" Mucklow stood up and walked back to the edge of the seashore. He lay down and the waves rippled around him as he enjoyed the sun on his face.

"Yer know Bill, back home, ar was in a bad place…" Scriven waded closer to his cousin and sat down next to him. "When we were kids ar used to love the scraps, us against them an all that, but now we'm older, ar'v just had enough… Ar'm 36 years ode, ar live in an house paid for by another mon's wife and ar'm fuckin' sick of looking over me fuckin' shoulder all the time…" He picked up a pebble and slung it out to sea. "Wondering if it's the law or a rival gang coming to teck us daahn…

We cor keep a livin like that Bill… Some of the things we have done just ay right. We keep a gooin the way we am, we'm a gunna hang Bill…"

Mucklow said nothing, he knew deep down that Harry Scriven was right but did not want to acknowledge it. He had been trained to fight, to kill and since the war ended it was almost as if he was unable to let go of that instinct. Here was the perfect opportunity to leave it all behind them and move into the 'serious money league.' Rubbing shoulders with movie stars and the international jet set, here in this stunning coast of the sun! If not for himself, but for his family and his cousin he so wished that he could afford to make the move.

"Yer know Bill…" Scriven spoke again. "Since we bin here, ar sleep at night… Ar dow wake up in a cold sweat seeing that mon!"

Mucklow knew that Scriven was referring to Brian Tanner. He (Mucklow) had killed many men, but death was not something Harry Scriven was used to and he knew that the questionable murder of Brian Tanner played heavily on his cousin's mind. "Ar'm glad you like Spain Harry." Mucklow stood up turned to walk back towards the car, the sun beginning to dry his wet clothes as he walked.

Scriven got up and clambered after him. "So what yer gunna do then?" Scriven remained hopeful. "Am we movin ter Spain?"

Mucklow sighed. "Ar fuckin' wish we could mate… We just ay got that kind of money."

Scriven looked at the floor in disappointment, in that second his dreams and hopes had been shattered. *Hang man's noose it is then!* He thought to himself… He no longer had any intention of driving to the old oak tree near Stourport, in fact he felt ashamed of these previous thoughts, but sooner or later he was convinced that their criminal lifestyle would catch up with them. *Oh well*, he thought, *they were in Spain and they still had the best part of a week to go, best make the most of it!*

The two men returned to the Villa and spent the rest of the day drinking heavily into the night. They both felt bitterly disappointed, so a good hard drinking session seemed appropriate. Patrick Boswell joined them on the terrace and the party was starting to get a little rowdy.

182

One of the young maids who worked at the Villa brought out more Champagne and Boswell slapped her backside. "That's it love, keep it coming you worthless Spanish whore!" Both Boswell and Mucklow burst out laughing, the young girl spoke no English and was oblivious to the insult. "These fuckin' Spanish mate, they work for peanuts and you can call em whatever you want!" Boswell was amused with himself and was grateful of the English company so that he could show off.

Scriven, although drunk and enjoying the banter, was not impressed at the treatment of the girl. His time spent with Antonia had endeared him to the country and its people and he found the behaviour of this loud bigoted Englishman embarrassing and offensive. He eagerly accepted his Champagne refill and puffed on a large Havana. He turned away from Boswell and Mucklow to face the Mediterranean and looked up at the stunningly clear night sky. The stars twinkled and shone and in his intoxicated state he smiled and enjoyed the glow that comes with the effects of alcohol. *Eat drink and be merry*, he thought to himself, *for tomorrow we die…*

"Hey Harry, do yer wanna try some special fakes!" Mucklow giggled and winked at Boswell who had the 'special' Moroccan cigarettes in a wooden box.

Scriven laughed "Ar, gew on then… Why not." Boswell reached into the box and pulled one out. "Let me finish this first!" Scriven nodded to his cigar and continued to enjoy the night sky.

"So then Paddy, yum due to get married soon?" Mucklow patted Boswell on the back in reference to Antonia. "Lovely girl mate."

Boswell laughed "Spanish whore… You know when I found her she was walking the streets in Nerja. She was a poor orphan girl, her whole family was dead!" Boswell laughed again and both Mucklow and Scriven struggled to understand what was humorous. "She is beautiful though, a girl like that on your arm earns you respect! I don't build attachments to anyone personally. They are all whores to me… Do you want a go with her Bill? She's a good little whore in the bedroom!"

Mucklow's face suddenly changed.

183

"I'll play a hand of poker with you Bill. If you win you can use her anyway you want, if I win you can give me that gold Rolex on your arm!" Boswell was deadly serious and found the situation amusing.

On hearing this, a burning rage arose within Harry Scriven but he held onto his temper and said nothing.

Mucklow frowned in disgust "I think your out of order there Paddy. She is a very charming woman and you should give her more respect than that."

Boswell shrugged and took a large gulp of his Champagne. "Here, speak of the devil." He sat up and held out his right arm to stroke his fiancés thigh as she emerged on the terrace. "Hey Antonia, why don't you get down on your knees for the lads!" Boswell erupted in laughter but both Scriven and Mucklow looked at each other in disgust.

Antonia acted as if she had not heard him, lit a cigarette and walked to the edge of the terrace to enjoy the moonlit sky.

Boswell was very drunk, he stood up and walked towards her. "Come here you slut, I want you to do as you are fucking told you whore!" He went to grab her and Scriven suddenly stood up.

"Leave her alone!" He ordered through gritted teeth.

"It is ok Senor Scriven… I am used to this." Antonia spoke, her face embarrassed and slightly afraid.

"Come on lads, maybe it's time we all call it a night ay?" Mucklow tried to diffuse the situation. He finished his drink and gathered his cigars and lighter from the table.

Boswell laughed and took a step closer to Scriven. "Did you say something Peasant?" His eyes narrowed and his humorous tone changed completely.

Scriven smiled and then 'dropped' Boswell with a single right-hand hook. The younger man fell to the floor and lay dazed and semi-conscious. Scriven stood over him and held his foot on his windpipe.

"Treat her like that again and ar'll slit yower fuckin' throat!"

Boswell gasped for air and eventually nodded as he started to turn a shade of purple.

184

The remaining five nights of the stay were a sombre affair. Mucklow, Scriven and their party chose to dine out at local restaurants rather than spend the time in the company of the youngest Boswell.

Initially, Billy Mucklow had worried that this situation would cause problems with Isiah Boswell, however, he knew that Boswell senior would be less than impressed with his son's behaviour so he figured that all would be well if nothing more was mentioned of the night.

On the final day, Scriven waited for Irene on the terrace. He cast one last look over the stunning view as he smoked a cigarette and tried not to dwell too much on the fact that they were going home. He turned back to face the Villa and was grateful to see Antonia again as she emerged from within.

"Thank you for everything Senor Scriven." Her eyes were almost teary and he hoped that he would not embarrass himself and display similar emotion. He took the cigarette from his mouth and looked deep into her eyes.

"You should not put up with shit from that bastard Antonia." He held out his hand and wiped a tear from her eye.

"You can offer me something better Senor Scriven?" She looked at him with a deep longing in her eyes. He held her hand to his face and then kissed it.

"Just give me some time Antonia… I will come back and you can come and live with me here in Spain."

She smiled and kissed him full on the lips… "I hope I see you again Senor Scriven." And with that she turned and left.

Chapter 18

Time had pretty much stood still at The Haden Cross throughout the two weeks Billy Mucklow and Harry Scriven had been in Spain. Mucklow had half expected things to have 'kicked off' again with the Hackett brothers whilst he had been away, but he was relieved to return and find out that life had gone by as normal with no major issues.

Dick Hickman had ran a tight ship in Mucklow's absence and if anything he had taken advantage of the situation and stepped up the aggression. This had created more fear amongst the protection-money paying businesses. In Hickman's mind, Billy Mucklow had been *going saft* and was *taking too much notice of Harry Scriven*. His two weeks in charge was the perfect opportunity for him to remind people that they had to pay, plus he enjoyed the violence…

Mucklow and Scriven walked into the pub and everyone noticed their rich sun tans.

"Where yow pair bin?" Hickman laughed at the sight of his returning comrades.

"In fuckin paradise kid." Mucklow had enjoyed his break but was genuinely pleased to return to 'his' pub. Harry Scriven did not seem quite as eager! "Ger us a pint of propa beer and get one in for these lads… And one fer yerself me wench." Mucklow ordered drinks and winked at the barmaid whilst Scriven noted that Spanish women were definitely prettier!

"Shall we gew through to the office Bill?" Hickman gestured to the side bar.

"Nah Dick, we ay bin abaaht fer a bit, be nice to show our faces." Mucklow took his beer from the barmaid and paid her. "Why, is the summet yer gorra tell me Dick?"

"Nah Bill, everything as bin saahnd." Hickman hesitated slightly and took a sideways glance at Barry O'Leary who was also stood at the bar.

Mucklow raised his eyebrows and glared at him. "What's fuckin happened?"

"Nothing Bill, we just had a few problems with that pimp ar was tellin yer abaaht before yer left."

"Amy Francis?"

"Ar" Hickman took a drink of his beer. "The bastard glassed her in The Castle down Ode Hill… The pub pays us protection an we cor av no fucker glassin' birds in one of our boozers!"

Mucklow nodded. "So what did yer do to him?"

O'Leary laughed and Hickman shot him an angry look.

"What did yer fuckin do Dick?" Mucklow raised his voice and then looked at O'Leary. "What did yer fuckin do?"

"We gid him a lampin', then we dangled him over the quarry up Rowley." O'Leary grinned and looked at the other men.

Mucklow nodded his head and looked relieved. "Fair enough lads."

"Then Dick asked him if he ever fucked his whores." O'Leary spoke again and tried to suppress a giggle. "He asked him if he needed a dick for his line of work then we smashed his bollocks between two fuckin' house bricks!" The men winced at the thought of the pain, O'Leary burst out laughing and Dick Hickman spat his beer across the bar as he erupted in amusement at his own actions. Scriven smiled and wished that he had thought to do a similar thing to Paddy Boswell.

Mucklow tried hard to hide his amusement and joined in with the laughter. "Richard Hickman you are one sick fuckin' bastard!" He patted his friend on the back. "Not too subtle, but ar love it!"

"Yer should'a sin his fuckin' balls man, they were fuckin' purple! Completely smashed with this yella stuff weepin' aaht on em!" Hickman pulled a face of disgust. "It was fuckin sick, nearly put me off me tay!"

The men laughed again and Mucklow finally spoke. "Serves him right fer being a whore mongering scumbag!" He placed a wad of cash on the bar and told the barmaid to get the whole pub a drink.

The friends enjoyed a few more drinks over the course of the evening and they continued to laugh loudly and make crude, boisterous jokes.

The bell for last orders rang and both Scriven and Mucklow felt exhausted from the long flight. "Right, ar'm a gewin home lads." Mucklow drained his glass and took his hat from off the coat pegs. "Anythin else yer need to tell me abaaht before ar gew?"

Hickman searched his mind then suddenly paused. "Ar, that fuckin' idiot Chad Cooper as bin round a few times. Sez he needs ter see yow and Harry... Fuck knows what he wants the time wastin' clot!" He ordered a large whisky and invited the other lads to join him. Mucklow refused but Scriven and O'Leary accepted eagerly.

"Ar'll gew and see him tomora." Scriven raised his eyebrows apologetically, well aware that he had introduced Chad Cooper to the gang.

"Sez he wants to see both of yer?" Hickman paid for the drinks and looked at both Harry Scriven and Bill Mucklow. "He's lucky ar dow knock his bloody block off!"

Mucklow looked at Scriven with an irritated look of 'do I really have to do this?' and Scriven shrugged in confusion.

Mucklow placed his trilby hat upon his head. "Right. Ar'll see yer tomora then." He walked towards the front door and gestured to his friends. "Night lads."

Twelve hours later Chad Cooper was sat in his living room drinking a cup of tea. He watched his daughter play and wondered how he would pay this month's rent. His wife had been nagging him to get a 'real' job, but he just could not face it. He wasn't strong enough for manual labour and he had no qualifications for an engineering career. *The only thing he knew how to do was steal and he was bloody good at it!* But he had had enough of 'small-time blags', ripping off houses and offices. The Police had been clamping down on their observations of him and any job needed to be really 'worthwhile' for him to risk going to jail.

There was a loud knock at the door and Cooper wondered if it was the law. "Ar'll ger it bab" he called through to his wife and he made his way through the front room to the door.

"Hello Chad." It was Harry Scriven and behind him stood an agitated looking Billy Mucklow who very obviously did not want to be there.

"Mr Scriven, oh, and er, Mr Mucklow! Please do come in." Cooper was nervous. The previous robbery, which he had brought to the table, had proven to be fruitless and Chad was still waiting for the repercussions of his most recent 'Fuck up!' Having Billy Mucklow in his home was both exciting and terrifying all at once.

Scriven and Mucklow followed Cooper into the living room and the young thief sent his daughter out to her mother in the kitchen. He shut the door and turned to face the two imposing thugs.

"We heard yer bin looking fer us?" Scriven spoke. He took out a cigarette and offered one to Cooper.

"Yes Mr Scriven." Cooper took the cigarette and lent forwards so that Scriven could light it. "Ar know that things day exactly gew to plan with the last robbery, an ar know that yow were very angry over it Mr Mucklow." He glanced nervously at Bill Mucklow and was hardly reassured by his expression. He took a deep breath and spoke again. "But ar got something big this time."

Scriven and Mucklow looked at each other in disbelief and started to laugh. They stood up and turned as if to leave.

"Look fellas, ar know ar fucked up but ar got summet really big in the pipeline…" Cooper stood up and waved his arms about in a desperate attempt to stop Scriven and Mucklow from leaving. "Dow teck mar word fer it, this has come from Ernie 'The Fence.'

Mucklow suddenly stopped and turned to look at Cooper.

"Cuz on Bill, he's wasted enough of mar time." Scriven looked at Cooper and shook his head. "Sorry Chad. Yum lucky we dow break yer legs kid."

"Hang on a minute Harry." Mucklow raised a finger to his cousin and took a step closer to Cooper. "What did Ernie 'The Fence' say?"

Cooper felt nervous, he lent closer to Mucklow and whispered. "There's this warehouse daahn Oxford way. A load of Cockney Jewellers store stuff in there… Serious shit, hundreds of thaasands of paands worth."

Mucklow was beginning to look interested. "Gew on." He nodded.

"Ernie's brother works daahn theyur." Cooper raised his eyebrows and let out a short smug laugh. "He's the fuckin' security guard!"

"So why do yow expect us ter believe yer after yer fucked up last time?" Mucklow narrowed his eyes. "Twice!"

Cooper took off his glasses and wiped nervous sweat from his eyes.

"Yum lucky ar day cut yer fuckin' fingers off son… Yer can thank Harry here fer that." Mucklow nodded towards Scriven.

Cooper nodded thankfully at Scriven. "Look fellas, dow teck mar word fer it… Let's gew and see Ernie the Fence?"

Ernie 'The Fence' Rubinstein had a small shop in a dingy little corner of The Jewellery Quarter in Hockley, Birmingham. A young girl stood behind the counter and two well-built men wearing black Crombies and Kippah caps stood on the door welcoming customers and keeping a watchful eye on potential thieves. They appeared to recognise both Harry Scriven and Chad Cooper but they regarded Billy Mucklow with a hint of suspicion. Mucklow was a fair few miles from his 'home turf' and his name did not command the same fear and respect in these parts.

Chad Cooper approached the counter as Mucklow continued to 'stare down' the two Jewish tough guys. "Hello there, is Mr Rubinstein around please?"

"Ooh wants ta know?" The girl had a strong Birmingham accent.

Cooper thought for a second. "Tell him its Chad Cooper and his friends Harry Scriven and Bill Mucklow."

The girl disappeared through a door that stood behind the counter and then about two minutes later Ernie 'The Fence' appeared.

"Edna, Edna, fetch these boys some gin..." Ernie 'The Fence' Rubinstein was a middle-aged man whose accent was mostly Brummie but also had a hint of Cockney. He was of about 45 years of age, was of average height and regarded everyone with dark, suspicious Eastern eyes that protruded above the rims of his cheap horn rim glasses.

"Gin's fer fuckin' girls! Ar'll av a whisky." Mucklow was not impressed with Ernie's drinks suggestion.

"Edna, please bring whisky for Mr Mucklow." Rubinstein smiled warmly at the visitors and Mucklow did not trust him an inch. "What can I do for you gentlemen?"

"Ar'v bin tellin Mr Mucklow and Mr Scriven abaaht that bit of business yow mentioned." Cooper spoke quietly so as not to alert the rest of the shop to their business.

"Arr yes" Rubinstein spoke even quieter. He hurriedly pulled up a latch on the counter and ushered the three men towards the door that led to the back room. They followed him into the dusty, cluttered room and sat down at a small wooden desk where Edna placed a tray of drinks. There were just two seats and Mucklow sat facing Rubinstein as Scriven and Cooper stood up.

"I heard about what happened at Himley... That is too bad." Rubinstein shook his head apologetically. "But I think you were let down by poor information." Rubinstein and Mucklow both looked at Chad Cooper in unison. Mucklow returned his intense gaze to Ernie 'The Fence' Rubinstein.

'The Fence' lent in closer and spoke in an almost whisper. "My brother, David, works at a large jewel and gold stock house in Oxfordshire… All of the main guys in London use it as a sort of safe haven from Inland Revenue… I have seen it with my own eyes, hundreds of thousands if not millions of pounds worth…"

Mucklow took a long drink of his whisky and shrugged, "What yer tellin me for mate?"

"After your boys did that heist over Himley, it got me thinking… Your boys did a good job, it was unfortunate that what they took was worthless…" Rubinstein smiled "My brother is a trusted security guard at the warehouse near Oxford, they pay him well, they have to… But if you were to send a small, er, team down there, I'm sure my brother could be of assistance…" Rubinstein allowed Mucklow a moment to consider what he had said. "Of course, you would have to hurt him quite significantly, but he is prepared to make this sacrifice for the greater good… He will meet you at a pub in Oxford to discuss the details, but you will have to be discrete." Rubinstein lent back in his chair and made an open-handed gesture as if posing a question.

Mucklow thought deeply and stroked the rim of his whisky glass. "So, what's in it for yow and yer brother?"

"Forty per cent between the two of us plus I can help you to sell on whatever you steal. It's a big warehouse so you will need my brother's knowledge to locate the valuable stuff as you will not be able to take it all! Certain pieces are worth more than the rest combined. You will be able to walk out of there with just one briefcase each but you will need to be quick before security reinforcements arrive… Basically, without me and my brother, you are fucked…" Rubinstein smiled smugly and waited for Mucklow's response.

"Fuck off." Mucklow drained his whisky and stood up to leave.

"Sit down, sit down." Rubinstein stood up and waved his armed around pleadingly. Edna was nowhere to be seen so he reached behind him to a small drinks cabinet and poured Mucklow another whisky.

"Yer see Ernie, if yow'm too fuckin greedy, what's ter stop me from doing the fucking job and then refusing to give yow an yer brother a fucking penny?" Mucklow eventually settled back down in the chair and took the drink.

Rubinstein smiled. "Mr Mucklow, I know of at least ten men in Birmingham who could do this job, but there is a reason why I am moving outside of my usual circles… The people we are stealing from are major players in London and would slit your grandmother's throat just for us having this conversation, and believe me, they could do it…" Rubinstein breathed patiently. "Now, if you were to hold off on mine and my brother's share, it would be very easy for us to tip off the Jewish gangs in London about who had stolen from them! This is a delicate job and requires the utmost discretion." Ernie 'The Fence' Rubinstein was beginning to show a hint of annoyance.

Bill Mucklow considered his options and eventually spoke. He placed the whisky glass on the table and shot Rubinstein a threatening look. "Who's ter say ar woe slit yer fuckin' throat meself?"

Rubinstein looked visibly concerned.

"Twenty percent." Mucklow spoke again.

Rubinstein shook his head. "Thirty."

Mucklow smiled and extended his right hand, "deal." The two men shook hands and the tension in the room began to ease.

Two weeks later and Mucklow, Scriven, Chad Cooper and Dick Hickman squeezed into one of the tiny little Austin A30s Mucklow was 'acquiring' from Longbridge. Bill Mucklow had insisted that they did not use their own cars in case they were spotted on their reconnaissance mission to meet Rubinstein's brother and to look at the target area. It was an incredibly risky job and getting it wrong would involve evoking the wrath of the entire Jewish Mafia and that was not a force Billy Mucklow and his small-time gang could even begin to reckon with.

Harry Scriven had been at the wheel and Dick Hickman had moaned all of the way down about the slowness of the car and the cramped conditions in the back with Chad Cooper.

They took a look at the warehouse from a far and met with Ernie The Fence's brother who gave them detailed instructions on exactly what to steal and where to find it. A date was set and a toast was drunk. "To wealth and riches!"

Billy Mucklow then turned quietly to his cousin Harry Scriven and whispered "To Spain!" Scriven smiled, turned around and thought of Antonia, El Acebuchal and the beautiful country he longed to return to.

Chapter 19

The car to be used in the robbery was stolen near the town of Bewdley on Tuesday the ninth of August 1955. Harry Scriven was to be responsible for driving duties and he had specified that he wanted something that was large, so as to house the gang and the loot, fast, so as to help them make a swift exit and comfortable, so that they could arrive relaxed and ready to carry out the job. The car that was 'delivered' to him was a 1954 Rover 90 P4 with a 2.6 litre inline six-cylinder engine. It had met Scriven's approval and he swiftly paid the thief and personally oversaw a quick re-spray and changing of the number plates so as not to attract any attention during the journey down to the Oxfordshire warehouse.

One week later and the car was thundering down the A34 carrying Harry Scriven, Billy Mucklow, Dick Hickman and Chad Cooper towards the target area.

Harry Scriven was relatively calm as he sat at the wheel and chain smoked. The previous robbery had presented his conscience with a dilemma of ethics, but on this occasion they were 'ripping off' faceless gangsters with the aim of raising enough cash to fund his and his cousin's escape to Spain. Chad Cooper sat alongside him in the front of the car and remained silent. He was a professional thief, but violence was not his thing. He did not know who to fear the most, Billy Mucklow if the job went wrong again or the Jewish Mobsters who were guarding the warehouse. Dick Hickman was his usual self, but his slight nerves meant that he was louder and cockier than ever before. He sat in the back smoking, drinking and cracking loud tasteless jokes. Billy Mucklow sat alongside him and checked his weapons. He had not felt fear for many years. Nothing could compare to his experiences during The Second

World War and these had taught him to be calm, calculated and ruthless. The British Army had trained him to kill. He did not share Harry Scriven's objections to alcohol before a mission and he generously passed around a hip flask of whisky that he encouraged everyone to drink. His reasoning was that people thought too much when they were sober and that the alcohol was a good way of easing any fears and inhibitions.

David Rubinstein on the other hand was not feeling quite as calm. He had not slept all night and now he stood on guard outside the remote warehouse, rifle in hand and feeling ill with nerves. *What would Mucklow do to him? What if the London gangs found out about what he had done? What if Mucklow had no intention of paying him and he was to be buried in an unmarked grave?* Suddenly he began to have second thoughts about the entire operation, but it was too late to go back now…

He smoked a cigarette, clung to his gun and checked his watch regularly, careful not to arouse suspicion from his colleagues. It was a beautiful hot summer's day and the sweat poured down his neck and onto his shirt. His suit jacket was folded carefully on the floor and a pair of braces held up his trousers as he peered up the long straight driveway that led to the warehouse. On either side of the track were rich, green Cedar trees that provided some shade from the intense sun that beat down on his face making it hard for him to maintain his gaze.

Where the fuck are they? He thought to himself and then he heard the not-so-distant rumble of the smooth straight six Rover. It rounded the corner at the top of the drive and approached, not too quickly it got closer and performed a three point turn before reversing up closer to the warehouse entrance. All four doors flung open and the four robbers emerged in the mid-day sun, each one dressed in an immaculate blue suit with handkerchiefs tied around their faces like bandits from the Wild West. They wore trilbies on their heads and each one was armed. Scriven and Cooper carried ex British army Webley Revolvers, Dick Hickman had his sworn off shotgun whilst Bill Mucklow sported a Lee Enfield

No.4 MK1 military rifle and a large hunter's knife that was strapped inside his jacket.

Before Rubinstein could speak a word to the raiders, a shot from a gun wrapped across his fingers causing him to drop his weapon and fall to ground in agony. Mucklow had arranged for an anonymous ex-army sharpshooter to act as a sniper and conceal himself in the fence that surrounded the perimeter of the Warehouse.

Mucklow immediately kicked Rubinstein's gun away and pulled him up by the hair. "It's just a fuckin' scratch" he whispered in his ear and then held the knife to his throat. "Walk!" he roared, the rifle hanging from his shoulder, his left-hand grasping Rubinstein's head tightly from behind as the jeweller's brother walked forwards slowly, Bill Mucklow concealing himself behind. He gestured with his head for the others to follow him and Scriven, Hickman and Cooper moved towards the large wooden doors that led to the warehouse.

Rubinstein had informed the gang previously that he would ensure the doors were not bolted and he prayed to god that one of the other guards had not come past and bolted them whilst he was outside. Scriven and Hickman kicked the two doors in unison and to Rubinstein's relief they flew open straight away.

"Right you lot. Listen up!" Mucklow bellowed into the warehouse as he prepared to make his entrance. He was eager to conceal his Black Country accent so as not to give away any clues to his identity. "I'm coming in and if any one of you mother fuckers takes a shot at me I'm gunna slit this bastard's throat open all over the fuckin floor!" He concealed himself behind his hostage who acted as a human shield as he ran through the warehouse to a section of wooden crates that stood on pallets providing a makeshift cover.

The three accomplices followed and ran to join him behind cover. Several bullets fired from a balcony that led to the main vault and bullets whizzed past the raiders ears as they dived for cover.

"We don't give a fack abaart him, cut him!" A cockney voice sounded from the direction of the balcony and Mucklow could see that two gunmen stood with semi-automatic rifles.

"Fuck it, yow'll atter kill him or they will know he's a plant and he will give us up!" Hickman spoke to Mucklow in a concealed whisper but Rubinstein heard everything.

He looked at Mucklow and shook with fear, *he should never have gotten into this and now he was going to pay the ultimate price.* Sweat poured from every inch of his body and he nervously shook his head, silently pleading with his captor not to kill him.

Mucklow looked at him and thought deeply for a few seconds as bullets whizzed above their heads. "Keep him here, nobody move until I say... Do not fucking kill him! That's an order!" Mucklow whispered the instructions as he threw himself onto the floor and began to commando crawl across the warehouse to another position to the left of the balcony. As he moved, Dick Hickman held his gun to Rubinstein's temple and Scriven and Cooper held their pistols up above their heads and fired random shots towards the balcony in order to divert the defender's attention and draw their fire away from Mucklow.

Chad Cooper had never fired a gun before and he held his breath in panic as he let off the shots and felt the force of the retaliation round batter against the wooden crates they sheltered behind.

Dick Hickman had always regretted being too young to have been involved in the Second World War by literally months. He had done his national service right at the end of the war and had seen no active duty. It had always played on his mind and he felt that he had missed out on being part of some kind of 'exclusive club' for men who were genuinely hard and had actually killed people! Here was his big chance for his first taste of 'real' combat and he relished the opportunity. He jumped up, shotgun in hand and let off both barrels in the vague direction of the balcony. "Mother fuckers!" He screamed before diving back beneath cover in a fit of crazed laughter.

"What the fuck am yer doing Dick?" Scriven grunted through as he pulled Hickman to the floor.

"Just avin some fuckin' fun Harry! Fucks sake!" Before Scriven could respond a shot sounded out from across the warehouse from where Bill Mucklow had positioned himself.

The bullet smashed into the right shoulder of the second gunman on the balcony and he immediately fell to the ground. Mucklow did not want to kill anyone, and he had purposefully aimed so as to hit the man here as opposed to other more vital regions.

The other gunman immediately dropped to give his friend assistance and this was the opportunity Mucklow had been waiting for.

"Go, go!" he yelled to his comrades as he rushed the balcony and mounted the cast iron stairs before dropping to his knee, aiming his rifle and flooring the other gunman with another shoulder shot. He had purposefully chosen to shoot the men in the right shoulder as he had noted that they were both right-handed and he wanted to make sure that they could no longer use their weapons.

He clambered up the remainder of the stairs and kicked the two semi-automatic rifles off the balcony. *Just fuckin' walk in with a briefcase and then walk aart again! What the fuck!* He thought to himself, remembering how at the time he had doubted Rubinstein's words on how easy the job would be. *There was no going back now!*

The other three raiders and their 'hostage' joined Mucklow on the balcony and he ordered Hickman to keep a watch over the two injured gunmen.

"Right you two, plug your wounds with your jackets and keep as still as possible… Do not move and you will live." Mucklow almost sympathised with the two injured guards who were in excruciating pain.

He turned to Hickman and spoke loudly so that the guards could hear. "If they move… Shoot em."
Hickman threw Rubinstein to the floor alongside them and lowered his shotgun threateningly.

Scriven and Cooper opened up two of the four briefcases they had brought in from the car and pulled out two blow torches with extra canisters. They were well briefed and they quickly set to work on the sealed metal door that led to the vault where the valuable stuff was kept. It took longer than anticipated to cut through and Hickman was beginning to wonder if they should just help themselves to the countless gold that was stored in the general warehouse, but then he remembered that Rubinstein had told them that the stuff in the vault was worth more than the rest of the warehouse put together.

Bill Mucklow gave the injured men whisky and did his best to 'patch them up' as in his opinion they did not deserve to be killed and if anyone did die the whole robbery would quickly become a hanging offence! Though Ernie 'The Fence' had previously assured him that the Police would never be involved as the Jewish Mob would not want officials poking around, but then again, Ernie had also told him that they could "walk in, fill their briefcases and walk out!" Instead, they got a shoot out! Bill Mucklow did not trust Ernie 'The Fence.'

As Cooper and Scriven got closer to cutting their way into the vault, Mucklow coolly took the butt of his rifle and bludgeoned the two guards over the head, knocking them unconscious. This way he could talk with Rubinstein and take him through to the vault without giving away his cover. With the two guards out cold, he approached The Fence's brother and shook his hand, being careful to choose the hand that had not been shot by his sniper.

"Good work man… Yer hand will be fine… Just a scratch."

"Err, thanks." Rubinstein hesitated and still looked nervous though he was immensely relieved. For a while he had expected nothing but death, but then what did he expect? Dick Hickman shot him a cheeky wink and suddenly he remembered how rich he was about to become.

"Help us load up the cases, you know what ter take." Mucklow gestured towards the newly opened vault as Scriven and Cooper discarded their blow lamps and wiped the sweat from their eyes. "But then ar'm a gunna av ter knock yer out mate… So yum like them pair."

Mucklow nodded towards the unconscious guards who lay upon the floor of the black balcony.

Rubinstein nodded reluctantly. He certainly did not want to get knocked out, but he knew that it was necessary.

The five men gasped in wonder at the fine pieces in the vault and they were swiftly loaded into their cases, unable to pause and fully appreciate them. Seconds lost looking were seconds that could be spent filling the cases and their deep suit jackets with what seemed like infinite riches.

The raiders knew that a call would have been made for reinforcements and they also knew that the reinforcements would be coming from nearby Oxford or maybe even as far as London, but either way it was vital that they were in and out as fast as physically possible.

With their pockets and cases crammed to the maximum, David Rubinstein realised that it was now his turn to take the rifle butt to the head. He held his hand out for Bill Mucklow to shake and then closed his eyes as he waited for the impact that sent him plummeting to the ground alongside his fellow bleeding guards.

The raiders then ran down the iron stairs and across the warehouse towards the Rover P4 when they heard the low growl of a four litre straight six engine pull up outside. A black 1951 Humber Super Snipe skidded to a halt and five armed mobsters jumped out with their guns prepared and ready for war. At the first sight of the reinforcements, the raiders instantly ducked back behind the main doors in the knowledge that they had been spotted by the newly arrived gangsters. Bullets ricocheted off nearby walls and one almost hit Harry Scriven in the leg! The raiders responded with counter fire but they were out gunned and pinned in.

"Shit, we'm gunna die!" Chad Cooper began to panic, the other men said nothing. Dick Hickman was loving the whole situation and Bill Mucklow was cool, calm and professional. He knew that his sniper was still positioned strategically in the perimeter of the fence in a concealed location and had been briefed about a possible eventuality such as this.

One of the mobsters suddenly dropped to the ground as a bullet from the sniper's rifle passed through his leg. The others immediately turned and searched frantically for the hidden gunman. This was just the opportunity the raiders were waiting for and on Mucklow's command they made a dash for the Rover and collapsed for cover at the side of the car as the mobsters turned around and let off a peppering of bullets into the side of the vehicle. The sniper spoke again and another mobster took a bullet in the leg. The mobsters responded by letting off further shots into the side of the Rover.

"Shit! Get in the fucking car!" Scriven suddenly realised that if the car took too much damage it would be un-driveable and they would not be able to escape! The four raiders opened the doors and flung themselves in as shrapnel ripped through the inside of the vehicle. Chad Cooper took a nasty cut to his leg and Scriven felt the sharp pain of impact in his left shoulder as he sat and frantically tried to get the car going. He rammed the keys in the ignition and pulled out the starter, firing the in line six into life. He slammed in the accelerator pedal, let go of the clutch and the car wheel span dramatically as the Rover began its descent down the drive and back towards the country lanes that led away from the warehouse. Mucklow and Hickman hung out of the rear windows and continued to fire wild random shots at the mobsters who scrambled to get back into the Humber as Mucklow's sniper continued to try and pick them off one by one.

The Rover was marginally faster than the substantially bigger Humber and Scriven ignored the stinging pain in his shoulder as he kept his right foot firmly planted on the accelerator pedal in an attempt to escape the men in pursuit. He looked at the fuel gauge and was relieved to see that he had more than enough petrol to get home, but the last thing he wanted to do was head north and give away potential clues to their location and identities. Instead, he headed west towards the Cotswolds and continued to accelerate hard in order to put some distance between the two cars. His concern now was that if they were to pass a Police patrol car in a stolen bullet ridden vehicle they would be caught red handed with an assortment of weapons and cases full of stolen jewels!

He wondered how much fuel was in the Super Snipe on his tail as they reached the town of Burford and he started to think about whether he should head south towards Bristol or North towards the Midlands.

"What do yer wanna do Bill?" Scriven turned his head slightly to speak to Mucklow who was sipping whisky on the rear seat. "We can head towards Bristol and try and hide or we can gew towards home, but we dow want them fuckers finding aaht where we come from?"

Mucklow looked out of the rear window and could see that the Humber Super Snipe was still visible behind them. "Just keep yer foot daahn Harry. Try and fuckin' loose em."

"Why don't we stop an av a fuckin' shoot aaht! Shoot them fuckers!" Hickman offered his suggestion.

"Don't be fuckin' stupid Dick, if we kill anyone, they will fuckin' hang us!" Mucklow shook his head and took another swallow of his whisky.

The cars continued to speed on and luckily for Mucklow and his men, Harry Scriven was able to put enough distance between the two cars on a long straight between Burford and Cheltenham for them to escape. The Rover had thundered on whilst the Super Snipe had to pull off the A40 in order to refuel.

The sun still shone brightly in the sky and the occupants of the Rover P4 relaxed and smoked as they cruised on home through Cheltenham, towards Gloucester and then up the A38 towards home.

Chapter 20

The loud ringing of the telephone awakened Harry Scriven from his alcohol induced, nightmarish sleep. He had passed out in his clothes whilst sat in his armchair at home and an empty bottle of whisky lay upon his naval. He had left the Rose and Crown pub at closing time and consumed the entire bottle of Scotch on his return home.

He opened his eyes and spent a few seconds pondering how bad his hangover would be, he raised his head slightly and realised that it was truly thumping and unbearable. He felt disappointed with himself and then remembered what it was that had woken him up.

"Hello" he mumbled as he placed the phone to his dry lips.

"Harry its Bill."

Scriven recognised the familiar voice of his cousin.

"Yow saand fucked mate?"

"Ar, was up the Rose n Crown last night." Scriven agreed and waited for the purpose of the call.

"I need to see yer immediately Harry... It's important... Ar'v sent a car fer yer. It's one of Bossie's boys, chap called Casewell. He'll be raand in about half an hour."

Before Scriven could reply the line went dead.

It had been two weeks since the raid and Scriven had not seen anything of the other raiders as it had been agreed that they would lay low for a while and let Billy Mucklow arrange the sale of the stones through Ernie 'The Fence.'

Bill had been over to Hockley to try and find the jeweller but 'The Fence' had gone missing and everyone was starting to get a little nervous. Harry Scriven had taken to drinking in the Rose and Crown on Halesowen Road which was slightly closer to his house on Beauty Bank than The Haden Cross. Irene had been spending most of her time at her parents' house in Tipton tending to her aging mother and Suzy had long since left home to live with the Ted whom Scriven had cut up outside the Haden Cross. As a result, Scriven had been spending most of his nights drinking alone inside the Rose and Crown and with his friend Johnnie Walker Red.

He threw cold water over his throbbing face and looked at his tired, red eyes. *What was going on? Had they bitten off more than they could chew? Would he ever return to Spain and see Antonia again?*

He walked through to the bedroom and changed into a beautiful black three-piece suit with golden cufflinks, white shirt and a deep red tie. He would not need an overcoat as it was August, so he splashed on a little cologne and reached for a box that lay hidden under the bed. Gone were the days when he walked around with an unloaded weapon... He found the box and pulled out his trusted pistol. It was all very strange that Mucklow had sent a stranger to pick him up and he felt suspicious. He walked over to the large bay window and looked out for a car.

A grey 1955 Ford Zephyr pulled up outside and a tall man dressed in a brown suit got out. He walked to the door and knocked patiently. Scriven shoved the gun into his inside pocket, took a deep breath and went down the stairs to open the door.

"Hello Mr Scriven. My name is Ted Casewell. Mr Mucklow asked me to pick you up." Casewell was about twenty-five years old. His hair was combed into a smart side parting and he had a confident aura about him.

Scriven peered into the car and noticed that Chad Cooper was sat on the back seat. He smiled at Casewell, locked his front door and got into the back of the car alongside Cooper.

"What's gooin on Mr Scriven?" Cooper seemed nervous. Scriven shrugged and lit a cigarette. "Ar dow know kid. Let's just see what Bill sez."

They spoke very little throughout the journey and after about forty-five minutes of travelling they arrived at the small village of Wychbold near Droitwich in Worcestershire. At the side of the village on the A38 stood a large Art Deco style pub called The Crown. The pub had been a popular stop over destination during the 1930s for travellers out of Birmingham and during the Second World War it had been used as a headquarters for the local Home Guard. It was about twenty miles southwest of Birmingham and on this sunny late August day the Ford Zephyr pulled up outside and the occupants got out.

"Please follow me gentleman." Casewell led the way to the front door and through to a large private room at the back of the pub. The walls were lavishly decorated with mirrors and Art Deco artwork and a huge ostentatious chandelier hung above a long ornate table at which Isiah Boswell sat at the head. He was smoking a large cigar and had a look of annoyance and seriousness. To his right were Bill Mucklow and Dick Hickman who both looked slightly sheepish. Scriven noted that he had never seen his cousin look this way before.

"Sit down." Boswell ordered and the two large, ever present bodyguards behind him almost looked amused.

"What the fucks gooin on?" Scriven sat down and lit another cigarette as Chad Cooper pulled up a chair alongside him.

"You fucking tell him!" Boswell sneered at Mucklow.

"We fucked up boys." Mucklow stood up, shrugged his shoulders and walked past Boswell to stand so that he could address everyone. He casually unbuttoned his suit jacket and looked at his friends. "Ernie 'the Fence' is dead… So is his brother." Mucklow lit a cigarette and took a drag. "The fella we blagged them jewels off is some kind of gangland King. The number one boss in the capital… Calls himself the King of London."

Harry Scriven exhaled smoke and let out a short sigh as Chad Cooper who was sat next to him started to shake with fear. Beads of sweat appeared on his forehead and dripped down over his spectacles and onto his cheap suit. Dick Hickman sat with a smirk on his face and said nothing.

"His name is Jack Spot… You may have heard of him?" Mucklow looked at his comrades as he posed the question. Both Scriven and

Hickman nodded but Cooper said nothing, his wide terrified eyes fixated on the floor. "Anyway, before they were killed, Ernie and his brother were fucking tortured and they tode ode Spotty everything... About us, who we are and everything... Apparently he has sent his top chaps up ter find us."

"You fucking idiots!" Boswell banged his fist on the table in anger and Mucklow stared at him in mild irritancy.

"Who gives a fuck?" Hickman suddenly blurted out in an over-confident and arrogant tone as he sat back in his chair. "Tell them saft southern wankers we am ready for em!"

Boswell erupted into a rage, he pulled a pistol from his pocket, rose to his feet and slapped Hickman across the face with such intensity that he almost fell out of the chair. "You think you can fight the entire Jewish Mafia? You and yer band of merry men here? You fucking idiot..." Boswell's voice switched to sarcasm. "There are fucking hundreds of men on their pay roll and they are all hard and nasty and would slit your throat for a five-bob note! These guys ain't from Cradley fucking Heath or Dudley or even Birmingham, these boys are London's top thugs! There are a lot more of them than there are of you mate!"

Hickman composed himself and wiped the blood from his lip. "But cor yow help us Mr Boswell? Yow got a few chaps working for yer ay ya?"

Boswell laughed in amusement. "First of all, these boys are in a completely different league to me and secondly, why would I get myself and my family involved in this? It's not my fucking problem you stupid fucking peasant!"

"We are grateful to Mr Boswell and his organisation for informing us of this situation... This is none of their doing and it is important that he distances himself from us from now on." Mucklow spoke and extended his arm to shake his friend's hand and Isiah Boswell shook it firmly.

"Yer on your own now kid..." Boswell had genuine sadness and disappointment in his eyes. He had really liked Billy Mucklow and had seen him as a kind of protégé. "Take my advice Bill... Leave the jewels where Spotty can find them and fuck off, never come back and prey that he never finds you." He took one last look around the table at the gathered men and shook his head. "I will leave my man Casewell outside to drive Mr Scriven and the kid home... After that, we are done." Boswell put on his trilby and the two bodyguards held open the double doors behind him that led back into the main part of the pub. "Gentlemen." He said one final time. He doffed his hat and turned to leave.

Once the doors had shut and Boswell had left Hickman turned to Mucklow and spoke again. "Ar cor believe yow let him speak to me like that Bill?" Hickman's voice quivered slightly. Billy Mucklow was his hero, his absolute idol, the one person he looked up to more than anyone. *How could he have stood by and let him be treated like that?* The severity of the situation suddenly hit him, they were not invincible and there were things out there that were more powerful than the almighty Billy Mucklow... Dickie Hickman's world was all but shattered.

Mucklow retained his confidence and not a hint of fear appeared on his face, but Harry Scriven could tell his cousin was worried. "What did yer expect me ter dew Dick? We already have the 'Crime King' of fuckin' London after us! Der yer wanna start a war with fuckin' Brum too?" Mucklow could have gotten angry with Hickman, but he didn't see the point.

Chad Cooper had now turned completely white and he suddenly ran outside onto a terrace where he vomited violently into a flower bush.

The other men sat in relative silence until Cooper returned, still white and shaking and with remnants of vomit on his worn oversized suit. Scriven gave him a friendly wink and gestured for him to sit down.

"Ar bay giving anything back... Fuck that!" Mucklow spoke in a defiant whisper so that Casewell could not here from in the main bar. "I have some ode army contacts in New York, mob guys, Italians... Ar'm gunna catch a boat and teck as much of the stuff with me as ar can. Ar spoke to um on the phone already and they said if the stones am genuine, they will pay me a fucking fortune!" Mucklow half smiled, but he did not

208

look confident. "Dick, ar want yow ter come with me as mar bodyguard... Yow can help me to carry the stones."

Scriven immediately looked at his cousin with hurt in his eyes... *Why had he chosen Hickman over him?* Mucklow noticed Scriven's reaction, but he chose not to acknowledge it. He knew that this trip was highly dangerous as it would be significantly easier and substantially cheaper for the New York Italians to assassinate him and Hickman and simply take the stones for free. There was also a relatively high chance of being apprehended by the authorities with the amount of stolen jewels they were planning to smuggle. Harry Scriven was more than a cousin to him, he was a brother and if he had to offend him in order to save his life and sacrifice his own then so be it.

"Ar got tickets to leave immediately. Mar wife and kids have gone to a safe location so ar reckon its time for us ter get gooin." Mucklow looked at Hickman and signalled that it was time to leave. "Ar want yow to goo away fer awhile Harry." Mucklow almost felt choked, he turned and spoke to Cooper. "Yow ay a gangster Chad, they woe know who yow am... Just be a bit extra vigilant."

"So that's it then..." Scriven looked disappointed. "Yum fuckin' off with the jewels and leaving us?"

"No Harry... Ar will see yer in exactly two months' time... Come to The Cross at twelve o'clock sharp... If ar'm there, yow pair will get yer share... If we ay there, assume the worst..." Mucklow finished his cigarette and stubbed it into an ashtray. "Right then Dick... We better goo." He stood up and approached Scriven with tears in his eyes. He did not expect to see him again. He held open his arms to embrace his cousin and closed his eyes.

Scriven looked at him and shook his head, still smarting from not being selected for the job. He felt betrayed. "Bye Bill." Scriven said coldly and with that he turned his back and walked towards the door. He did not understand or had not quite realised the risks that Mucklow was taking for everyone.

In that moment Bill Mucklow felt more heart broken than he had ever done before. He did not expect to return, but at least he had to try. *There was simply no alternative.* He stood and watched his closest relative as he disappeared through the door and a lump appeared in his throat as all of their childhood memories passed through his mind in that instant. *He had to do what he had to do.*

Scriven and Cooper got back into the Ford Zephyr and Casewell drove them home. Throughout the journey there was a very sombre atmosphere. Scriven was still getting over the disappointment of not going with Mucklow and it suddenly occurred to him that he may never see his cousin again. He instantly regretted that they had not parted on good terms. Cooper still looked ill and he struggled to cope with the intense dread and panic that filled him.

"Ar bay a gangster Mr Scriven... What will happen to mar family? Av ar put em in danger?" Cooper broke into tears and began to sob. Scriven didn't quite know what to say, but he certainly did not want to 'give anything away' in ear shot of Casewell who was driving. There was something about Boswell's young driver that Harry Scriven did not trust.

"We ay got noweyur else ter goo Mr Scriven, what shall ar do?" Cooper pleaded.

Scriven made sure that Casewell dropped Cooper off first at his house in Cradley Heath and took the opportunity to speak to the young thief at his front door where Casewell could not hear.

"You will be fine Chad... Chin up... Look after that young family of yowers and ar will pick yer up in two months before we meet Bill and Dick up the Cross." Scriven handed Cooper a wad of cash. "Listen, ar bay gunna be around fer a while... Ar bay tellin a soul where ar'm a gooin, even Bill dow know. But if yow av any problems, if anyone threatens you, contact me at this address." Scriven took out a pencil and wrote down the number and address of a guest house in Cornwall he would be staying at. "Now dow you breathe a word to anyone abaaht where I am…" Scriven wondered whether he was doing the right thing trusting the thief with his location.

"Mr Scriven, yow av mar word." Cooper smiled with genuine gratitude and Scriven shook his hand warmly. "Teck care Chad." With that he gave Cooper a friendly pat on the back and returned to the Zephyr.

"Back to your house Mr Scriven?" Casewell asked as Scriven got back into the car. Scriven looked at his watch and realised that Irene would now be home.

"No mate, teck me somewhere else." Scriven gave Casewell directions to a small warehouse in Halesowen where Mucklow stored the Austin's he 'acquired' from Longbridge before their sale. He did not want to face Irene at this time and he did not want to endanger her by being in her vicinity.

He slipped into the warehouse and helped himself to one of the little Austin A30s Mucklow had stashed there. He took 'enough' cash from the safe in the warehouse office, checked his gun and set off in the little car.   He had spent much of The Second World War in Cornwall and he had contacts there. It seemed to be the ideal place to 'hideout' whilst Mucklow headed off to America to try and sort things out.

Chapter 21

Dark clouds hung in the sky and the late summer rain pounded down hard on the roof of the 1954 Vauxhall Cresta E. At the wheel sat one of Jack Spot's top Enforcers, Alan Goldman, a tall well-built man with mean eyes and immaculately presented shiny black hair. Next to him was his superior, Tony Greenbaum.

Greenbaum was about eight years older than Goldman and was one of Spot's main right-hand men or as he liked to be known, an 'Under boss.' He was shorter than Goldman but was powerfully built and had a particularly loud 'shouty' Cockney voice.

Goldman and Greenbaum had been sent to the Midlands for the specific purpose of tracking down the Jewish Mafia's most valuable jewels and to bring those responsible for the theft to justice- 'gangland style.' They were not local and did not know their way around the area so they enlisted in the help of an outsider to assist them in their enquiries.

The man they hired had been in Ireland for over twelve months but had returned home when he heard through the grapevine that Harry Scriven and the Mucklow family were in trouble. Jimmy Danks was more than grateful for this opportunity to carry out his own personal revenge and was eager to help Spot and his band of London gangsters in any way that he could. He was still smarting from the humiliating beating the Mucklows had dealt him and his gang in The Fountain pub and was harbouring a particular hatred towards Harry Scriven after Scriven had stopped him from having his twisted evil fun with Suzy Miller.

Ted Casewell had also been eager to help the villains from out of town and after driving Chad Cooper and Harry Scriven to the Crown at Wychbold a few weeks earlier, he was quick to sell his knowledge of their home addresses to Goldman and Greenbaum for less than ten pounds.   Their first port of call had been to Harry Scriven's house on Beauty Bank Road Haden Hill, but both Scriven and Irene were long gone. Scriven had telephoned Irene from Cornwall and had warned her to stay at her parents' house until he returned.

Jimmy Danks had also searched for Irene and Suzy at The Fountain in Tipton, but the pub had been long sold and nobody there knew of the whereabouts of the former land lady and her daughter.

After the initial search for Harry Scriven had proved fruitless, Goldman and Greenbaum decided they should pay Chad Cooper a visit. *He was by no means the leader of the Mucklow organisation but at least he may be able to give them a clue as to where they could find the others.*

The dark red Cresta pulled up outside Cooper's house in Cokeland place Cradley Heath and Jimmy Danks sat in the back entertaining his own sickening fantasies that festered within his debauched mind. He hoped in his twisted head that Cooper had a wife or girlfriend that he could use. His mind wondered back to how he had held Suzy Miller on her knees in front of him and how he had longed to have gone further with her, much further.

Goldman and Greenbaum hurried through the rain to the front door and Danks followed.

"You can do the talking Mr Danks. We don't have a fackin clue what language you people speak." Greenbaum half smiled as he commented on the Black Country dialect. Danks grunted and nodded. He liked being in control and he hoped that Cooper was not going to be overly compliant. Much to his approval, Chad Cooper's young wife answered the door and the dark cogs inside Danks' head began to turn. He did not much care that she was unattractive. She looked vulnerable and would do nicely.

The three men instantly barged past Cooper's wife, hurried through the front room and into the back where Cooper was sat playing with his young daughter. Danks saw the little girl and his eyes lit up.

"What's gooin on?" Cooper protested but Goldman grabbed his arm and forced him face down onto the table, twisting his face so that he could see what was about to happen.

Danks grabbed the small girl and placed her on his knee as she started to cry. Cooper's wife screamed but Greenbaum grabbed her and told her to "Shut the fuck up." Danks stroked the sobbing child's hair and a dab of spittle dropped from his lascivious mouth.

"Ar like little girls Mr Cooper... Especially skinny little things like this."

Cooper raged and tried to break free, but Goldman was much too strong. "Leave her alone" He screamed desperately.

"Where's Harry Scrivin?" Danks lowered his hands to the child's throat so that all could see and began to apply a little pressure.

"Ar dow know, honest!" Cooper lied to protect his friend.
Danks lowered his hands further and her mother screamed out. Danks gave a wicked smile of pure evil and placed the girl back on the floor. He stood up and walked slowly towards Cooper's wife.

"Maybe Mommy wants a turn?" Danks turned and looked at Cooper who was pinned and helpless on the table. In that moment Cooper saw deep into Danks' soul, the inner blackness that was within resonated in his wild eyes and Cooper realised that his worst nightmares had all come at once.

Danks stroked the woman's cheek and traced his finger slowly down her neck and onto her breasts. He grabbed her by the neck and forcefully pinned her to the wall as he ripped off her top and exposed her to the eyes in the room. The little girl screamed at the treatment of her mother and Cooper struggled again in vain.

"Where is Bill fuckin' Mucklow?" Danks screamed as he struck Cooper's wife hard across the face and knocked her to the ground.

"Ar dow fuckin' know!" Cooper struggled again.

"Oh dear..." Danks sneered and unbuttoned his flies as he approached the poor young woman who lay semi naked and helpless on the floor.

"Ar dow fuckin' know ar swear!" Cooper's scream was agonized as he watched the pervert approach his wife.

Goldman and Greenbaum looked on with distaste. Admittedly they were not good men and had both done very bad things, but Danks was something else! Their morals could not cope with what was happening before them and before Danks could go any further Greenbaum suddenly spoke. "Stop!" He held out his right arm and stopped Danks from getting any closer to the woman who lay sobbing on the floor. "If this man has anything to tell us he will tell us away from these two... Alan, take him to the car."

Much to Danks' disappointment, Goldman dragged Cooper out to the car and his wife and daughter screamed and agonized as their beloved husband and father was led away. This felt very different to the time when Harry Scriven had taken him the previous year. Deep down, Cooper's wife knew that she would never see her husband again and she was completely and utterly heartbroken.

Danks, Goldman and Greenbaum drove Cooper over to a lock up garage in Tipton that Danks had previously used as part of his scrap metal business. Once inside they stripped him to his underwear and tied him to a chair before sitting down to enjoy a cigarette and a cup of tea.

Cooper knew what was coming. Part of him felt relieved that his wife and daughter were no longer present, but another part of him felt truly terrified as he pondered the horrors that were about to unfold. He had soiled himself and urinated several times through the fear, but still Danks, Greenbaum and Goldman continued to sit, smoke and drink tea.

"So then Charlie boy." Danks suddenly stood up and picked up a rusty old toolbox. He slowly opened it and ensured that Cooper could see all of the sharp forbidding instruments inside. Greenbaum pulled out a flask of whisky, took a sip and passed it to Goldman as the two mobsters continued to casually smoke and watch Jimmy Danks go about his work.

Danks pulled out an Oxy blow lamp and held it up so that the two gangsters could see.

Greenbaum laughed. "How fitting. I believe you boys used one of those to break into our vault?"

Goldman smiled at his bosses' joke and the pair looked on as Danks lit the lamp and lowered it to Cooper's exposed ankles.

Cooper yelped in pain and then nearly passed out as the hairs upon his skin began to singe and then the full force of the heat hit him. He vomited violently with the pain and his spectacles flew off as the cold-hearted men around him erupted in laughter at his sorry plight.

"Where are Billy Mucklow and Harry Scriven?" Greenbaum demanded as Danks eased off on the lamp.

"Ar dow fuckin' know!" Cooper screamed defiantly.

Greenbaum nodded and Danks lowered the lamp again, this time holding it there for a few seconds as the flame burnt through to the bone and the stench of cooking flesh filled the air.

"I'm gunna ask you again." Greenbaum took a drag of his cigarette before stamping it out on the floor. "Where are Billy Mucklow and Harry fucking Scriven?"

Tears fell from Cooper's eyes. He couldn't even remember where Scriven was even if he had wanted to tell them. He just wanted the pain to end.

Greenbaum nodded again and Danks reapplied the torturous heat. This time, a part of his skin caught alight and the men could see straight through to the exposed bone.

"This is your last fucking chance Son." Greenbaum took a drink of whisky and Cooper looked at him in so much agony that he was unable to even talk.

Greenbaum nodded and Danks enjoyed applying the torch yet again, but Cooper was too far gone to even feel the pain now as Danks held the torch to his ankles for a sustained period. Burnt skin and cooked flesh dropped to the floor and Greenbaum and Goldman felt revolted at the smell.

"The kid knows fuck all." Greenbaum shrugged as he passed the whisky flask to Goldman. He looked at Danks and coolly announced "Kill him."

Danks took out a small length of rope and carried around to the back of the chair on which Cooper was tied. He flexed it gleefully and then unceremoniously applied it to the young father's neck before garrotting him violently until the final moment when he threw down the rope and used his own bare hands, thoroughly enjoying the feeling of literally ringing the life from another human being. Jimmy Danks closed his eyes in total ecstasy as Cooper struggled for his last gasps of life.

As he died, memories of his young family filled his head and he recalled in detail a birthday party where he and his wife had lovingly looked on as their daughter blew out the three candles on her birthday cake. They had struggled to afford such festivities, but he had moved heaven and earth to ensure that his precious child had been happy. The little girl blew out the candles and in his final second Chad Cooper half smiled in the knowledge that in his death his beloved wife and daughter were now safe from those that had stolen his future life with them.

Chapter 22

Harry Scriven had left his old friends in Cornwall late on the Tuesday afternoon. He was due to meet up with his associates again at twelve o'clock the next day at The Haden Cross and it was a particularly long journey. He had spent the last two months at a guest house near Newquay that belonged to an old RAF comrade by the name of Johnny Thornton.

Thornton was originally from Hampshire but had settled in Cornwall after marrying a Cornish girl he had met during his national service with Harry Scriven.

The couple had enjoyed having Scriven stay with them and although he had been tight lipped and somewhat mysterious, they particularly liked the amount of money he had spent in their bar.

The journey back up the A30 and A38 was long and laborious for the little Austin's 803cc engine though Scriven had managed to miss the traffic at Exeter as he hit the town late on the evening. He stopped to catch a few hours sleep between Taunton and Bridgwater and then set off again early the next morning.

Throughout the last two months spent in Cornwall he had had lots of time to think things through, about his life, Irene, Antonia and especially the welfare of his cousin Bill. *Would Mucklow and Hickman make it back from New York? Would they have the riches he and Mucklow needed to build a new life in Spain?*

He also thought of Chad Cooper. The young thief had gotten into things that were well above his head and Scriven hoped and prayed that Cooper and his family would be safe. It was his intention to drive to Cooper's house first and pick him up en-route to The Haden Cross for the all-important meeting.

The little Austin arrived in Cokeland Place Cradley Heath earlier than expected and Scriven stretched his body and neck in relief as he climbed out of the tiny car after the long journey. He reached for his suit jacket, adjusted his tie and put on his trilby before opening up his cigarette case and lighting up a 'faike.'

As he approached the door to the little terraced house, Scriven noticed the 'flicker' of the curtains from the neighbour's house and he felt 'eyes' upon him. He knocked the front door and waited… There was no answer, so he knocked again… Still no answer. *Strange.* He thought to himself and then he began to worry slightly so he knocked again harder.

As he waited, he thought he heard movement in the front room and then suddenly the door flung open. It was Cooper's wife.

"What der yow want?" She muttered. Her eyes were red and sleepless and she looked as if she had been crying.

"Where's Chad? Ar'm here ter teck him to a meeting." Scriven looked confused.

The little girl appeared in the doorway and clung desperately to her mother's leg. She was no longer the happy little pleasant child she had been before. Her eyes were haunted and she had soiled herself at the arrival of a 'stranger' on the doorstep.

Cooper's wife looked Scriven directly in the eyes and slapped him with all her strength straight across the face. "He's dead… DEAD!" She screamed hysterically.

"What? How? What happened?" Scriven's heart raced frantically and the guilt of not being there for the young family hit him hard.

Cooper's wife composed herself slightly. "Three men come here, lookin fer yow Mr Scriven!" She broke down and tears began to flow. "He could av gid yow up! But he day, he didn't give yer up Mr Scriven and now he's dead!"

Scriven stared helplessly at the floor as Cooper's wife beat his chest and slapped him hysterically… When the effort became too much, she collapsed in a heap on the doorstep, the little girl still clinging to her.

After a few minutes of searching for the right words to say, Scriven opened up his wallet and attempted to give the woman some money.

"Ar dow want yer stinking money Scriven! It was yow that got mar Chad in ter this an now he's dead! Just fuck off!"

Scriven felt uneasy with swearing around children. "Who did it?"

"Three blokes come to the house… One of um sounded local." She looked away through the shame of what had happened. "He tried ter interfere with me and mar little girl… Look at her!" The poor woman raised her voice and pointed to her agitated child. "She woe ever leave mar side and she keeps askin when Daddy's coming home?"

At the mention of the attackers threatening the woman and child, Scriven could feel his blood starting to boil with anger. There was nothing more he could do here. He took one last look at the destroyed remnants of a family and headed back towards the car. There were no words, no actions that he could do to make the situation any better and he felt miserable.

He looked at his watch and realised that there was still a good amount of time until he was due to meet Mucklow at The Haden Cross and then it suddenly occurred to him that if Spot's men had got to Chad Cooper, they could well have found Irene! He threw himself into the Austin and set off for his house in Beauty Bank Road as quickly as the under powered vehicle would carry him.

The V8 pilot still stood on the driveway and Scriven pulled up halfway down the street from his house. It was highly likely that one of Spot's men was waiting inside for him, so he checked his gun and concealed it inside his suit jacket before walking back up the street towards the house. He ducked into an alleyway and hurried along to the back of his neighbour's garden where he climbed through a gap in the fence and then over the bush so that he was planted on the ground within his own garden.   If anyone was lurking inside his house, they would be expecting him to come through the front door, so he crept stealthily through the garden until he reached the rear door that led to the kitchen.

He turned the door handle and to his horror it drifted open and Scriven could see where an intruder had used a crowbar to break in! He figured whoever had done it had chosen to come through the back as it was more inconspicuous than breaking in through the front. He pulled out his revolver, checked it again and held it firmly in his hand as he pulled open the door and crept silently into the kitchen. He could almost hear his own heart pounding and at any second he expected a bullet to fly out of nowhere and slam him to the floor.

He crept slowly from room to room and the whole experience reminded him of when he, Cooper and Hickman had crept into the Colonel's house in Himley. *A lot had changed since then* Scriven thought to himself as he realised that each room downstairs was totally untouched and exactly as he had left it two months previously. He went back into hallway and slowly began to climb the stairs.

He checked each room and then hovered on the landing outside the bedroom he had shared with Irene. Not a thing out of the ordinary had been found inside any of the other rooms and Scriven braced himself for the prospect of finding Irene dead on the bed.

He took a deep breath and then kicked open the door… Nothing? He looked in every corner, the room was empty apart from the large bed that stood in the middle of the rear wall and the other bedroom furniture that adorned the room.

Above the bed was a photograph of himself and Irene that had been taken by Billy Mucklow in happier times. He smiled at the memory and then went back out of the room and hurried down the staircase to the telephone that stood on a small table in the hallway.

He took out a little black notebook and dialled the number of Irene's parents' house. Not many people were privileged enough to own their own telephones but Scriven had paid for and insisted Irene's parents had one installed as he would be able to contact her there in the event of an emergency such as this.

"Hello," Irene answered the call and Scriven felt immense relief.

"Hello Bab, it's me."

Irene was immediately overwhelmed with relief and concern and flooded Scriven with questions. "Harry! Where have yer bin? Whas a gewin on?"

"Ar'm glad yum ok bab." Scriven struggled to hide the relief and emotion in his voice. "Just stay there fer a little longer bab." He replaced the handle on the phone casing as she frantically called out his name... That was the last time he ever spoke to her.

When Scriven arrived at The Haden Cross his watch read five minutes to twelve. He parked the Austin and glanced around the car park to search for Bill Mucklow's Riley but there was no sign of it. *Not to worry.* He thought to himself, *he was still a little early yet.*

Inside, the pub seemed to have a sombre atmosphere that Scriven was not used to. There was no music playing and he could tell that eyes were upon him throughout the bar. Nobody spoke a word, but everyone knew who he was and everyone, or so he thought, knew that he and Billy were in big trouble with London gangsters. He became obsessed with checking the doors to see who was coming in and felt nervous that at any minute one of Spot's men could enter in search of him! He checked inside his jacket and felt the reassuring cold steel of his gun before approaching the bar to order a pint of mild and a large whisky.

"Not sin yer abaaht fer a while Harry?" The barman was nosey and Scriven said nothing. "I heard yow and Mr Mucklow had a bit a trouble gewin on?" The barman handed Scriven the drinks and took payment as Scriven shot him a threatening look that deterred him from asking any further questions.

The old clock on the wall read twelve fifteen and Scriven's heart began to slowly sink. He didn't really care about the money, what really worried him was the welfare of his cousin. He downed the whisky and ordered another.

As children they had always looked after each other. Wherever Bill went, he went too and what had really hurt was that Mucklow had headed off to New York without him. When he had sat in the car park of that very pub, contemplating the unthinkable, it had been Bill that had saved him. Bill that had taken him to Spain and given him a new purpose and appetite for existence. He downed the second whisky and could feel moisture starting to emerge in his eyes as the alcohol began to loosen up his emotions.

By the time the clock read ten to one and two whiskies later, Scriven felt an intense need to get out of the pub before his emotions got the better of him. It was not like Bill to be late for anything. *What would he tell Bill's family? His wife? His father? His mother? And why was he not with Bill?*

Just as Scriven had given up all hope, the door suddenly flung open and in walked two impeccably well-dressed men who bore striking resemblances to each other. Scriven blinked assuming that the alcohol was causing him to see 'double' before realising that the two men were in fact identical twins.

They were young men in their early twenties, but they had such swagger and an aura of authority around them that Scriven began to fear that they worked for Jack Spot. He lit a cigarette and eyed them across the bar.

The first twin wore a smart black suit with a matching black tie and gold coloured tie pin. He had neat dark hair and confident brown eyes that had an air of violence about them. The second twin looked much the same however he wore a pair of black spectacles that accentuated a crazed psychotic appearance to his eyes.

"We are looking for a Mr Harry Scriven." The first twin spoke and Scriven immediately detected a thick London accent. His heart pounded and he put his hand inside his jacket to touch his gun… *He was not going to go down without a fight!*

Before the barman could answer Scriven spoke. "Who wants ter know?"

"My name is Reg and this my brother Ron." The first twin spoke again and the second twin gave Scriven a chilling smile. "Is there somewhere we can speak in Private Mr Scriven?" The twin's manners were immaculate.

Scriven gestured to the side bar where he had spent many happy hours with Billy Mucklow and the three men went inside. Once the door was fully closed, Scriven pulled out his gun and pointed it at the twins.

"Mr Scriven… That will not be necessary." Reg was in no way worried or intimidated by the weapon and spoke in a confident reassuring tone. His brother stared at the gun with eyes like thunder and began to speak.

"Mr Scriven… We bring a message from your associate Mr Mucklow." Ron spoke with a slightly effeminate voice that Scriven was not expecting. "We are not here to kill you…"

Scriven lowered the gun slightly. "You will forgive me if arr'm a little cautious gentlemen." He sat in a chair opposite the twins and held the gun to the floor, ready to raise it again at any time he felt necessary. Sweat poured from his brow and he felt as though death was near as he struggled to coordinate his thoughts.

"Nice place you got here Harry." Reg lied and made small talk as he looked around the room.

Scriven was not in the mood for small talk, he kicked the table in front of him and spoke nervously through gritted teeth. "Who the fuck are you?"

"We own a snooker hall in Mile End East London… We also do a bit of work for a geezer called Billy Hill."

Scriven had heard of the man and nodded.

"You see Mr Scriven." Ronnie spoke again. "Billy Hill has been at war with our mutual acquaintance Jack Spot for a while now… It appears that they both fancy themselves as King of London…" Ron sat back in his chair and crossed his legs confidentially, knowing that one day both he and his brother WOULD be Kings of London. "Would you like to be a King Mr Scriven?" Ron raised his voice and his pupils widened.

"Ar just wanna know where mar fucking cousin is!" Scriven shrugged and raised his voice to match the twin.

"He's in jail mate." Reg spoke and Scriven immediately felt a sense of relief. At least he was alive!

"You see Harry… That diamond blag you and your cousin pulled off hurt Spot really bad… It facking finished him off mate… He was on the brink of selling um and most of um didn't even belong to him anyway!" Reg chuckled with amusement. "So now, he can't pay his boys and geezers from all over London want their facking money! Believe me mate, he is in a facking mess." Reg took drag of a cigarette as he explained.

"So our mate Billy Hill has pretty much taken over… He is the new Mr Big…" Ron stared at Scriven and cracked another evil smile.

"So why is mar cousin Billy Mucklow in fucking jail?" Scriven, still clinging to his gun, was confused by it all.

"It seems you have a guardian angel Mr Scriven…" Ron spoke again as he continued to stare intently at Scriven.

"Mr Mucklow heard about what had happened to your friend Chad Cooper and he started to worry about you Harry… Billy Hill advised him that if he were to go to the law and confess to the Oxford warehouse robbery, they could convince the Police on Spot's payroll that it was just Mucklow, Cooper and the other guy involved. That way you would be safe Harry." Reg explained somewhat smugly.

"Nobody worth a facking ha'penny knows you exist Mr Scriven… Billy Hill is grateful for what you boys have done for him and he will ensure Mr Mucklow's safety whilst in prison. Jack Spot is facking over, you are free to go Mr Scriven…" Ron shrugged and looked at his twin brother. "We better get going back to London."

"So that's it?" Scriven's head was filled with questions. "What has all this got ter do with yow pair? When will Bill get aaht of jail?"

"We are here because we do a bit of business for Billy Hill… We are just passing on a message." Ron stood up and walked towards the

225

door. He did not wish to spend a second more in this place than he deemed absolutely necessary.

Reg stood up to leave too and suddenly stopped... "I nearly forgot. Here is a letter from Mr Mucklow." He handed Scriven the letter and smiled.

Scriven took the letter and watched as the two Londoners headed towards the door. "Wait." He suddenly called and the two cockneys turned to face him. "Who killed Chad Cooper?" Scriven placed the letter in his suit jacket and waited for a reply.

Reg thought for a second or two and then answered the question. "A local chap I believe." He nodded his head and bid Scriven farewell before giving up the name. "A fella called Jimmy Danks."

Chapter 23

T he interior of the little Austin A30 was cramped and claustrophobic. Harry Scriven sat in the driver's seat and tried to get things clear in his mind. The twins had left the pub nearly an hour ago and Scriven had gone back into the bar and enjoyed a few more drinks. He knew that at some point he would have to open the letter from Billy Mucklow but for some reason he was putting it off.

After draining his final whiskey, he had left the pub and walked out to the car. The pub was due to close at two anyway so he could not have had another drink even if he had wanted to. As he sat in the car he stared at the envelope. He recognised his cousin's handwriting on the front and it simply read "Harry." He took a deep breath, opened up the envelope and began to read.

Dear Harry
I am writing this letter from within the custody of the
metropolitan Police. I hope that you are well and in good
health? The reason for my being in jail is that I have had to
give myself up. Upon my return from New York, I was met
by some charming gentlemen. One of these men was
the notorious London Mobster Billy Hill. You may have
heard of him? Also there were two young twins who I believe
work with him. It appears that the Flying Squad or 'Sweeny
Todd' as these Southerners refer to them, were in the
process of fitting Billy Hill up for the Oxfordshire
warehouse robbery that I am sure you will remember.
To cut a long story short, I have confessed to the robbery in
return for protection from Billy Hill and his organization
and the assurance that your name will not be brought

into this and that you and my family are safe from any
further vendetta. You must ask no further questions
of this cousin and leave the country at once as I am still
unaware of to what extent I trust these people. My
lawyers are in touch with my wife so there is nothing
left for you to do. I expect I will make the papers when
this goes to court. Take care my most valued cousin and
I hope that one day we will be reunited
for a drink. Until that day comes take care my brother.

Yours truly

Bill Mucklow.

Scriven noticed that in the final sentence, Mucklow had crossed out the word cousin and replaced it with the word brother. A lump appeared in his throat as he pondered the enormity of Mucklow's sacrifice for his protection. *For the severity of the crime, he could be looking at fifteen to twenty years!* Scriven wiped tears from his eyes and tried to console himself with the knowledge that Mucklow would possibly get a lighter sentence for his confession. He beat his fist against the steering wheel in frustration, *he should have been with his cousin...* He knew that there was something smug about those twins and he knew that there was more to the situation then they had let on.

He thought about what he would have done if he'd have known that they had forced Mucklow to give himself up? But then he realised that in return for Mucklow's action they were guaranteeing his safety in prison and that of the family. He grunted and gritted his teeth, *he didn't need protecting from anybody!* Then he realised that his own thoughts were sounding as naive and foolish as Dick Hickman's. That brought another sudden thought to his mind, *what had happened to Dick? Was he in jail too? Was he alive?* Before he could ponder the plight of Hickman any further, he noticed that Mucklow had included a PS at the bottom of the letter.

PS: Do you remember when we used to play Pirates
as children?   The treasure is in the ship.

Scriven placed the letter on the passenger seat and frowned slightly as he remembered childhood memories of playing Pirates with his cousin. He started the engine and put the car into gear. He knew exactly where he had to go.

The A30 climbed the steep hill and pulled up outside Scriven's childhood home in Talbot Street Colley Gate. He still owned the property but had not set foot in the building for over twelve months. He wondered about what kind of condition it would be in, *had the damp and mould taken over?* It didn't really matter… He had no intentions of going inside. Instead, he walked down the long narrow yard to an overgrown and neglected area at the bottom of the garden. He paused for a minute and remembered how his grandfather had worked hard to maintain the garden when he was a child and wondered what the old man would think of it if he was alive to see it today.

Next to the garden stood an old shed that Scriven's grandfather had built many years ago with his own hands. The shed was abandoned, run down and in ruins, but as children Scriven and Mucklow had spent hours playing inside. It had been a Sheriff's office when they played Cowboys and Indians, it had been a secret hideout. In fact, it had been many different things, though more often than not it had been a Pirate Ship! Pirates was always Billy Mucklow's favourite game. He got to fight people and steal their gold!

Scriven slowly pulled open the door which required some effort as the wood and metal hinges had rotten and the door was now hanging off. As he went inside, he could hear rats scurrying away and a large spider's web became entangled on his face. For a moment he felt amused as he remembered how his cousin Billy had a ridiculous fear of spiders…The man had literally butchered Germans with his bare hands in

1944 and was generally regarded as the toughest man around, but he always was terrified of spiders!

Scriven cast his eyes around the rotting old shed and noticed that a plush leather suitcase lay upon on old work bench that stood beneath a large window to the left of the door.

He approached it slowly and paused before opening it. *What if it was some kind of booby trap? What if Mucklow had been forced to write the letter and this was their way of dealing with him?* He shook his head. *It would have been much simpler for the twins to have just sorted him out when they met face to face… Besides, if it was a booby trap, it was probably nothing more than he deserved.*

He cautiously pushed open the latches and the case was unlocked. Slowly he raised the lid and marvelled in amazement at what lay before him… Money! Countless wads of £20 notes, more money than he had ever seen before in his life. Tens of thousands of pounds! Sat on top of the money were two Cuban Havana cigars, exactly the type he and Mucklow had smoked together in Spain. Scriven could not help but smile with satisfaction. He quickly shut the case and thought about his escape. But before he left, there was one more thing that he needed to do.

Chapter 24

Jimmy Danks sat in the desolate solitude of his run down Tipton home. He had long since been thrown out of the pub for it's afternoon closing and now he sat on a solitary wooden chair in his decaying front room as he watched spiders and various other creatures climb the wall.

The house had no electricity or running water and had fallen into a further state of disrepair during Danks' time spent in Ireland. He lay back on the chair and propped himself against the wall as he drank cheap Scotch directly from the bottle.

Goldman and Greenbaum had been recalled to London weeks ago and it appeared to Danks that the search for Harry Scriven and Billy Mucklow was no longer a priority. This was of no real concern for Danks, he had thoroughly enjoyed the killing of Chad Cooper and every inch of his dark twisted soul longed for another victim.

He had done some nasty disturbing things whilst in Ireland and now that he was home and had no real purpose, he was free to entertain the darkest most warped longings of his mind. He sat and pondered his next victim... *A random stranger?* No, this did not appeal to him as much.

He closed his eyes and searched his memories until a sick evil smile came across his inebriated face. He thought about Cooper's widow and the little girl he had previously held. *A mommy and her little girl would do just nicely.* He felt a stirring in his body as he began to imagine the sick pleasures he would have with them before sending them to meet their husband and father.

As Danks continued to bask in the deprivation of his own imagination he did not hear the sound of a small Austin A30 pull up outside the house. It was five o clock in the afternoon and he was certainly not expecting any visitors.

There was a sudden knock at the door and Danks bolted upright. *Who the fuck could that be?* He thought to himself as he grabbed a carving knife and shoved it into his pocket. He slowly went to the front door and opened it.

"Hello Jim. Ow bin ya?" Harry Scriven stood in the doorway with a gun in his right hand pointing straight at Danks. In his other hand was an old worn leather briefcase. The mid-Autumn sunshine cast a mysterious shadow over his face and the cold hard look in his eyes gave him a menacing appearance.

Jimmy Danks laughed and showed no hint of surprise or nerves. "What yow want?" He sneered as he looked Scriven straight in the eyes.

Scriven walked forwards slowly with the gun in his hand and Danks backed into the front room. Scriven shut the front door behind them and kept the gun firmly planted on Danks.

"What happened ter Chad Cooper?" Scriven stepped a foot closer and could smell the rotten smell of Danks' breath.

Danks looked at Scriven and a sudden twinkle appeared in his eyes and a smug psychotic grin appeared on his face as he too took a step closer to Scriven and he recalled the killing of Cooper.

"Ar wrung his neck like a fucking chicken! An der yer know what Mr Scriven?"

Scriven could feel Danks' foul breath close upon him.

"It was the best thing ar'v ever fuckin done… Ar fuckin loved it… Gid me an ardon…"

A murderous rage arose within Scriven, he took the gun in his right hand and smashed it hard against Danks' face knocking him straight to the ground. He instantly pulled him up by his wiry, greasy hair and smashed his face so hard into the decaying wall that remnants of plaster scattered across the floor.

"You sick mother fucking bastard!" Scriven yelled through gritted teeth, his spoken syllables in rhythmical sync with his actions as he continued to pummel Danks' head into the wall.

When he was quite sure that he had knocked Danks unconscious he laid him on the floor face up with both of his arms outstretched in a crucifixion pose. He opened up the worn leather briefcase and pulled out two rusty four-inch nails and his trusty hammer. Ironically, Scriven thought, it was the same hammer he had used to shatter Chad Cooper's left hand many months previously.

He placed his left foot on Danks' throat, knowing that the sudden pain would awaken him and meticulously arranged the nail so that it was positioned in the centre of Danks' grubby right palm. Once he was satisfied that the nail was in position and was over the flesh and not a bone, he repeatedly brought the hammer down hard on the head of the nail and drove it through Danks' hand until it was nailed securely into the wooden floor.

Danks awoke with the sudden and intense pain and let out a blood curdling scream. Scriven did not want to arouse the neighbours so he quickly shoved his size ten polished black winkle picker into Danks' mouth to silence him as best he could.

He transferred his weight onto Danks' left arm and repeated the process, driving the rusty nail through the evil killer's palm and securing him firmly to the floor. He stood up, lit a cigarette and stepped back into the dark shadows that now filled the grotty little room as nightfall began to descend upon them.

Danks struggled and cursed and spat and then struggled some more before resting his head upon the floor in realisation that he could not get free and that every movement the torturous nails ripped and tore at his skin and forced him into further agony.

Scriven casually smoked a cigarette and watched on with the satisfied knowledge that he had every right to act as judge, juror and executioner.

"Do yer believe in Jesus Jim?" Scriven joked in reference to Danks' ongoing crucifixion.

"Fuck you" Danks spat, his face filled with venom and hate like a demonic and possessed rabid dog.

Scriven finished his cigarette and stubbed it out on the floor. "There bay no crosses where yow'm a gewin Danksy." This time Scriven spoke with no humour, just a cold reminder of exactly where Danks would end up.

Danks laughed perversely through the pain. "Yes Harry." He winced as he moved and the nails tore at his flesh again. "An ar'll be fucking waiting fer you when yow get there Scriven... Yow mark mar fuckin' words..."

Scriven shrugged knowing that Danks was probably right as he casually walked back to the briefcase. He pulled out a rusty old pair of pliers and held them up clearly so that Danks could see.

"Ever visit the dentist Jimmy?"

"Fuck you!" Danks banged the back of his head of the floor and his breathing got heavier as Scriven emerged from the shadows, the pliers in his right hand.

Scriven paused as he got up close to Danks' face and allowed a few moments so that Danks could fully understand what was about to happen to him. He lowered the pliers into his mouth and gripped one of his front teeth.

"Ar bay a dentist Jim, so yow ul atter' forgive me." Scriven yanked the tooth with all his might, twisted and pulled as blood filled Danks' mouth and ran down his chin. He screamed with horror and pain and Scriven quickly reached for an old rag to shove into his mouth. "It dow look like that tooth wants ter come aart Jim." He stood up and went back to the case and pulled out a chisel. He picked up his hammer and brought the instruments back to Danks' face.

Slowly, he placed the chisel into Danks' mouth and at an angle so that it dug up into his gums and the roots of his front teeth. He gave a sudden sharp hit and a piece of jawbone came away along with the stubborn front teeth.

Danks could no longer scream and was semi-conscious as Scriven returned to the case and pulled out an old bottle that was filled with battery acid. He slowly unscrewed the lid before pouring its entire contents onto the exposed flesh of the remnants of Danks' mouth.

The burn and stench of his own rotting flesh awoken Danks and as Scriven returned to the case and lit another cigarette he tried to talk.

"Kill me... kill me." Danks tried to plead his voice was croaky and barely audible.

Scriven wiped blood from his hands and smoked his cigarette as he made out the gist of what Danks was trying to say. "Oh no Jimmy. Not yet... You see, what yow did ter Chad Cooper and his family has fucked up his little girl fer the rest of her fucking life." Scriven put the cigarette to his lips, took a long drag and then continued to speak. "Her suffering will go on fer eternity." He gritted his teeth and raged at the injustice of it all. "How is it right, that yow die quickly whilst she has to suffer fer what yow did?"

Scriven went back to the case and pulled out a blunt stubby screwdriver. He held the cigarette between his lips and then pummelled the sharp end into Danks' right eye with all of his strength. The eyeball disintegrated into mush blinding Danks instantly and the last thing he saw was Scriven raising the instrument again, his face full of vengeance and hate as he brought it crashing down into Danks' other eye.

He got up, wiped the screwdriver clean and placed it back in the case as Danks lay crucified and whimpering on the floor. He wiped blood from his suit as best he could and collected up his things ready to leave.

"Yer see Jim... Ar left yer ears fer a reason... Yow'm a gunna die believe me, but first ar want yow ter lie there and listen." Scriven picked up the case and looked back at Danks, instantly feeling sorry for whoever ended up with the grim task of discovering the body. "It's getting dark now Jim, and when ar've gone, the smell of yower rotting meat will attract rats from miles around. Hundreds of them, from the cut and from under the floorboards of this stinking flea pit in which you live... Yer woe be able ter see them, but you will hear them... You will hear them creeping, hear them scurrying and you will hear then gnawing on your face as you slowly die…" Scriven turned to leave. "Goodbye Jimmy."

With that, Harry Scriven left. Safe in the knowledge that other people were safe from the sick, twisted and evil mind of Jimmy Danks…

Epilogue

1968 was an eventful year. In Britain, Prime Minister Harold Wilson endorsed the failing 'I'm backing Britain' campaign for working an additional half-hour each day without pay and over in America Martin Luther King JR delivered his famous 'I've been to the Mountain top' speech before being assassinated the very next day… West Bromwich Albion won the FA cup after defeating Everton 1-0 after extra time and the Vietnam War began…

In Torremolinos on The Costa Del Sol, Harry Scriven sat on a sun lounger besides a swimming pool in his own rooftop penthouse that overlooked the vast hotel and casino complex he had built up since he first arrived in Spain 13 years previously.

He sipped ice-cold Cava and looked out at the Mediterranean Sea as he had done years ago. In the pool, floating gracefully upon the sun kissed turquoise ripples was Scriven's beautiful wife Antonia. She was a few years younger than her husband, but she utterly adored him. He had taken her to visit the lost village of her childhood many years ago and had then gone on to rescue her from her abusive relationship with Patrick Boswell. For the first time in her adult life she was truly happy.

As he looked out across the beach and out to sea, Scriven tried not to think too much about the past. He glanced at his beautiful wife bikini clad in the water and he smiled. *Life was good.*

"Senor Scriven, there is visitor here to see you." A maid appeared at the top of a grand staircase that led to the hotel below. Behind her stood a completely bald, lean looking man who was of about fifty years of age. Scriven blinked in disbelief and immediately rushed to greet his guest.

"Hallo Harry... Arr bin yer?" Bill Mucklow had occupied himself in prison by keeping fit and boxing. As he stood with his arms open to embrace his cousin for the first time since their separation at The Crown at Wychbold thirteen years ago, he found it difficult to hide the emotion in his Prison hardened face.

Scriven, overweight and sun scorched from his time spent in Spanish luxury hugged his cousin with relief and patted him warmly on the back. "Just look at all this Bill." Scriven stepped back and proudly gestured to the hotel and Penthouse he had assembled in Mucklow's absence. "This is all ours Bill... From the money we got from that warehouse job... It's ours mate." Scriven smiled with the smug satisfaction that he had finally equalled his cousin. "Equal partners." *Mucklow could be proud of him now and look upon him with respect and as an equal, not as a poor relative who deserved his pity, his protection or his handouts. He would no longer have to take orders from anyone.*

Since his return to Spain, Harry Scriven no longer had nightmares and he no longer felt the need to run away or better himself. *He was no longer a member of The Mucklow gang, he was Harry Scriven...*

Bill Mucklow smiled and nodded. "Well done Harry aer kid... Yow did exactly as ar planned yer would." He looked back to the staircase where his wife and teenage children waited and gestured for them to come out.

"Now be a good lad Harry an gew and fetch them cigars!"

238

Also available by Thomas J.R. Dearn.

Once upon a time in the Black Country.
A 1950s Gangster Novel.

Once upon a time in the Black Country Part II.
Ghosts.

Once upon a time in the Black Country Part III.
Money and Morals.

Costa del criminal.
An English villain in Spain.

Once upon a time in the Black Country 1934.
A 1930s Gangster Novel.

Coming soon...

Once upon a time in the Black Country 1951
The saga continues...

Author and musician Thomas J.R. Dearn was born in the Black Country area of the West Midlands and has a strong interest in early to mid-twentieth century history. He studied Music at Wolverhampton university before embarking upon a long and successful career as a schoolteacher. Thomas now lives in Worcestershire with his wife, three children and Rottweiler/German Shepherd cross. He enjoys football and is a supporter of Aston Villa and Halesowen town football clubs. Thomas is also a classic car enthusiast and collector of vintage guitars.

Printed in Great Britain
by Amazon

14228266R00140